AF261366

BLADESEEKER

Convergent Fates

ROY BLACKSTONE

BLADESEEKER: CONVERGENT FATES

ROY BLACKSTONE

Hardcover ISBN: 978-1-7351441-0-8
Paperback ISBN: 978-1-7351441-3-9

Copyright 2020 by Roy Blackstone. All rights reserved. Unless otherwise noted, no part of this book may be reproduced, stored in a retrieval system, transmitted in any form or by any means—electronic, mechanical photocopying, or recording—without express written permission from the author, except for brief quotations or critical reviews.

To Leah. For pushing me to be my best,
even after you were gone.

CONTENTS

PROLOGUE

The thief tripped through the stone archways of the ghastly cathedral, collapsing on the floor.

A faint rumbling resonated through the halls as the man scrambled to his feet, clutching the glowing relic that had brought him here. The holy artefact in his arms was precious, shining its lone light into the darkness beyond.

Another rumbling. He felt the hairs on his neck stand on end. There wasn't much time.

He moved quickly through the cavernous halls of the cathedral, making his way to the far end of a long hallway, his boots clicking with every step. He approached an open window and took in the cool night air.

He looked down from the window toward the grass-covered terrain—far too distant to land safely. His eyes darted to a second-floor balcony that jutted out in the dark, its position allowing for a safer jump. The man took stock of his situation. Simply running from his pursuer would not end well—with its superior size and speed, the thief would surely be caught before long. He would have to get clever.

A third rumbling. This time, closer.

The thief looked at the balcony again. Perhaps if he jumped, he could delay an encounter with the creature, giving him enough time to get back to the exit of the forsaken church with his life.

There was a crash nearby, the sound of splintering wood and cracking ceramic. Time had run out. Taking one last breath to steel his nerves, the thief vaulted over the window, plummeting through the night air. He held the treasure close, its safety more important than his own. His landing was poor. He felt a sickening crack in his left ankle as he landed. Pain surged through his body—but now was not the time to worry about such small details.

Overhead, he heard the giant creature make its way into the room from which he jumped. The thief crept inside, away from the balcony, listening to the rumblings above. The creature slowed in confusion. Over the next few heart-pounding moments, the man kept deadly still, focusing on the thing above him. The rumbling soon faded, becoming distant. The creature had lost its prey.

For now, the thief was safe.

He took a moment to check the artefact in his hand—a golden scabbard with a sword within. It shone brightly in the dark, radiating yellow, like a thousand rays of the sun coalescing in his arms. The scabbard was worth a fortune; the sword within it was priceless. The thief confirmed it was still undamaged—a full examination would have to be delayed. He was still in imminent danger; the creature wouldn't be fooled for long.

The thief collected himself and once again surveyed his surroundings, another spacious room like the one above it. Perhaps in another time, a visitor could fully appreciate all its intricate statues, ornate furnishings, and little details. For the thief, however, they were mere distractions to a man in peril. He needed to find the exit.

He moved in a half-limp half-jog through a dizzying network of rooms, halls, and foyers that made up the cathedral. The creature's rumblings disappeared. He breathed a sigh of relief as he slowed his pace (his ankle was not doing him any favours) and made his way to the entrance of the old cathedral.

After an endless maze of seemingly identical rooms and unlit corridors, the thief arrived at a small hallway. It led to a door that was slightly ajar. The thief smiled. He recognized this door—he was nearly there. He swung the door open and stepped onto a landing.

His boots tap-tapped on the marble floor as he walked across it. He reached the edge of the landing and looked down at the open space of the grand room below, which served as the cathedral's altar—an impressive area that contained rows of giant pews, adorned candles, and wall-mounted portraits. Though it was nearly pitch black, some vision was granted by the glowing blade he held in his hands.

The thief counted his blessings for his lucky escape. He took a step, another shot of pain surging from his ankle and resonating through his body. The man ignored it, close as he was to freedom.

Just a bit more and he would escape.

Then, it came.

A deafening boom directly overhead, chunks of rock and marble coming undone from the ceiling directly above him.

The thief only had a moment to react, but even then, it was too late.

The giant came crashing through the hole in the ceiling, slamming down on the thief's back and crushing the lower half of his body with its weight. The thief's face collided with the ground. The shock kept him alive for moments longer. The next seconds became flashes of images in the thief's fragmented mind. Only a few details were important now.

He could no longer feel his legs, which had been pulverized by the weight of the giant on top of him.

He looked out to the exit, a glint of blue light streaming in from the double doors in the distance, still taunting him with escape.

Overhead, he could hear the air whistle as the giant swiped at him with its hand.

The man had flung the relic forward and out of the giant's path before the swipe had connected with its target. It, at least, was safe.

The last thing he saw was the treasure, the beautiful golden sword, as it tumbled to the shadows below.

BLADESEEKER

CHAPTER 1

THE SPECTER

SEPTIMIAN DYNASTY, YEAR 237
KINGDOM OF NEMEA, CITY OF KAI-JI

There were some places in Taerestris that were spoken of less frequently. Progress had its own price to pay, and so too did supporting the abundant lifestyle and convenience that the Great Nations afforded.

This is the story of one such place. Far away from the comforts of civilized life and devoid of traditional law, the slave city known as Kai-Ji thrived.

SIR TANDEM THE YOUNGER
HISTORIA TAERESTRIA

"Get in line, everyone," the proctor commanded.

The dark-skinned man wore brown leather and a short-sleeved jacket, light enough to withstand the sweltering heat that was ever-present in the slave city. His oversized boots thudded as he walked across a raised platform. A crowd of ten children stood below him. These were known as the *Kai-Jin*, slaves named after the city. The young Kai-Jin obeyed without hesitation, orienting themselves in a neat line before their master.

The group was situated on a dirt road, normally used for transporting goods in and out of the city. The wind was minimal, offering no distraction from the hot sun. In the distance, thousands of other slaves were busy working the fields.

A line of men in uniforms of different colours stood behind the proctor, watching the children with keen eyes.

The proctor surveyed the children, most entering their teenage years, before he spoke again. "Today is The Choosing, the most important day of your miserable lives," he announced.

The slaves before him shifted uncomfortably at that word—choosing.

The proctor continued. "Yes, today is the day when you privileged ones will seek out your own destiny. Know this—that no other Kai-Jin but the meagre ten who stand here today have earned this great honour. Know this—that you uphold the city's heritage and tradition. Know this—that you are to live and die serving the Great Nations. Know this and prepare to claim your futures.

"It is not easy to have arrived here today. Every year, only the ten most fit and valuable members of the new generation are ever given such a prize."

The proctor motioned to his left at a table on the raised platform. A red cloth covered the small table, and a blue scroll lay over it.

"For most Kai-Jin, the scroll determines their fate. I understand you children know little of the ways of magic, but the scroll works to recognize your best qualities and assign you a task suitable to your unique traits. This is the Sortition. But you ten are different. Some of you are stronger. Some of you are more intelligent, or keen in combat. Still, others are gifted with more *subtle* talents. Regardless, the city of Kai-Ji recognizes your value, and for you ten, there will be no Sortition. We will not decide your fate for you, but give you this choice for you to make for yourselves."

The children looked at the proctor intently.

"There are many paths afforded to you on this day. Will you join the rest of the rabble in the fields as farmers? A safe route, though not glamorous. Perhaps you will join the Instructors, and take my place on some distant day. Some of you may even take the option to leave the confines of the city and work in lands beyond. Or, perhaps you will choose another route. The choice is yours." The proctor halted and pointed at the first child in line. "Step forward," he commanded, "the time has come."

The boy wore his hair short, typical of Kai-Jin youths; there was no need for long locks getting in the way of work. Though his face was young, it was covered in various scars, no doubt from the beatings he'd suffered at the hands of his masters. The shirtless boy's skin took on the full brunt of the stifling sun. He wore ragged shorts, his feet in tattered sandals. He stepped forward; his defeated eyes were fixed to the ground as he awaited his next instruction.

"Good. Now, boy, tell me what your choice is. Once you make your decision, there is no going back." The proctor moved in front of him, staring him down.

The boy shifted, feeling the man's piercing gaze. "My choice..." he uttered.

The other children looked on. His speech was unnatural, the result of little practice—for many Kai-Jin, silent obedience often meant safety.

The timid boy decided. "I choose to work in the fields with the others."

The proctor frowned; discontent etched itself across his face. He regained his composure before he responded. "The tranquil life of the farmer. Though disappointing, 1 cannot blame you for such a decision. Rather, I will commend your desire to cling to the safety of such a mediocre life. As a slave, even the lowest among you has the greatest honour of serving the master, whether that is on the fields or elsewhere."

The man in the jacket turned to the remaining nine children and continued the proceedings. "You, then, come."

The proctor motioned to the next child in line, another boy of similar age. His features were hardly discernible from the first, save for the fact that he was markedly taller.

The tall boy straightened himself before speaking. "I wish to serve the Great Nations, sir." He waited to see the proctor's re-action before continuing. His stone-like gaze offered the boy no relief. "I wish to represent Kai-Ji outside the city walls."

The instructor brought his hand to his chin as he took in the statement. Asking to leave Kai-Ji was a unique demand; most slaves preferred the safety and stability of its walls. Once a slave left its borders, they would have no protection, and it was quite the gamble to find a fair lord. There was a chance one could find a better future, but it came at the risk of greater abuse and, often, mortal danger.

"Very well, young one. If it is a future outside of the walls you desire, then so be it." His voice was firm. "You will be taken to the carriages and sent out to a lord immediately. Serve your new master well and uphold the glory of our city."

The boy nodded and returned to his position in line.

One by one, the remaining children stepped forth and made their decision—the only decision they would ever make. As with most years, many of the children settled on relaxed roles within the city, giving themselves just rewards for being the best of the best. The process was quick for such a prestigious day; such was the way of things in the city of Kai-Ji, and it was short work for each child to announce his decision. The proctor eyed the tenth and final child.

"Step forward."

The final child was different. This one was a girl. The boys and even the instructors on the platform had all been watching her during the ceremony. She was, after all, a special case. She had short, dirty hair and various smudges covered her face and skin. She wore simple white covers, more resembling tatters than clothes. Unlike the others, her body looked untouched, as though she hadn't suffered the same beatings as her peers, and her unmarred hands had the appearance of someone who had not worked a day in their life.

Her hazel eyes flashed defiantly at the man before her. She said nothing.

The proctor's brow rose with impatience. "Well, girl? What is it, then? Or are you so simple you did not—?" The man was cut off as the girl responded. Though he had heard her perfectly, the girl's words were surprising enough to make the proctor lose his composure. "What did you say?"

"The scroll."

The man was taken aback at her words, the last words he had expected. The rest of the group made wild looks at her, the instructors in the back whispering among themselves.

Finally, the proctor responded. "I will ask you one more time, girl. What is your choice today?"

"I want the scroll. I have made my choice."

As she repeated her wishes, the man's eyes darkened. "Ignorant child, you are the first girl to ever be given such a gift, and you choose Sortition like the rest of the rabble?"

The girl maintained her silence while the proctor mulled over what to do next.

She kept her eyes on the man before her as she repeated for the third time, "I want the scroll."

The proctor took another moment before he sighed. "I've heard about you. You're the daft girl who they say can work without rest. It's surprising that one as meek as you managed to outwork the rest of the boys. I don't know what trick you're pulling, but despite your strength, your head is still too thick to comprehend your position."

The proctor knew that she did not fully understand what he was saying, but she knew what he meant; it had been said to her in different ways a thousand times. His colleagues were always surprised that this little girl possessed such raw strength, and her endurance far outlasted that of even the slave drivers themselves. For this, she was ridiculed—being different in Kai-Ji was the same as being hated. Here, it was worse to be unique than to be normal.

The proctor sighed again. "Very well. The decision is yours to make, in the end. Take the scroll."

The girl stepped onto the platform and moved to the table. The rolled-up scroll had a regular appearance, save for the ends, which had a gleaming blue hue to them that seemed almost otherworldly.

"Good. As you open the scroll, look into its centre. Your role within Kai-Ji will reveal itself to us in a few moments."

The girl unfurled the elegant scroll, clumsily at first. As she opened it fully and peered into its depths, she noted the centre was blank, the edges covered with strange scribbles and text. Though she could not read, the proctor would be able to discern its contents for her. She heard the man speaking behind her as she focused on the centre of the scroll. As she gazed into it, the proctor's voice grew more and more distant, the images of the dusty road blurring out in her periphery. In moments, the entire world fell away around her.

When she realized the wind and the sun and the proctor's voice were gone, she abruptly looked away from the scroll. She gasped. She was no longer on the platform—she was no longer anywhere she recognized.

She stood in an ornate hallway made of stone, with large gilded paintings adorning the walls. A rumbling shook the ground, dust falling to the floor. She could hear hundreds of men screaming and shouting from far away, accompanied by the unfamiliar clashing of metal. There was a set of wide doors in front of her. The doors swung open on their own as she peered inside.

"Come in," a voice called from within.

She stepped through the archway and toward the voice. It came from an old man sitting in the cavernous room. The room was empty save for the wooden desk he was currently seated at. He scribbled on a piece of parchment, several books on his workstation. She made her way toward the desk and stopped in front of him.

Another rumbling resounded in the distance.

"Ah, my apologies. I was busy finalizing some details," the old man said. He looked at the girl. "You don't speak much, do you?"

She shook her head.

"Do you have a name?"

Another shake of the head.

"Well, that's a shame. Names are so important, you know. Perhaps you should think of one."

The girl's eyes opened wide. She had never considered the idea of naming herself. For Kai-Jin, names placed far too much importance on ones as expendable as slaves.

"Where am I?"

"Straight to the point, eh? Oh, it will be such fun working with you."

The girl's confusion only grew as the man spoke.

"In another place, in another time. Or more accurately, right inside your head." He tapped on his temple.

The roar of some distant creature could be heard erupting through the air in the distance.

"But I am rather curious. Tell me, why are *you* here? You had the choice of deciding your future, and yet you chose the scroll. You chose to come to me."

"How did you know that?"

The man reached out with a weathered hand for a red book and opened it, showing the girl its contents. Across its pages was the scene of The Choosing, the raised platform and the scroll. It included darkened images of all the participants, her own face represented with startling detail.

"I see many things from my little perch within the scroll. I know you're stronger than all the boys, though you try not to show it." He flipped through pages of his red book, each image as eerily accurate as the last—they were all images of the girl, scenes of her life within Kai-Ji.

"I know that you mysteriously heal all of your wounds, which angers your masters. I know how your skills embarrass the boys and how they hate you for it. And I know that within you, you feel there is something more to life than Kai-Ji."

The girl tensed up, clutching the scroll within her hand. Her legs trembled. She had no friends in Kai-Ji, and thus never revealed her feelings—but somehow, this man knew her entirely. For the first time in her life, someone had exposed her completely, and like a mirror, bounced her thoughts back at her.

She wasn't prepared for such this turn of events. The girl's legs felt weak, and she felt her body shaking. If the man knew this much about her already, there was no use in hiding anything.

"I'm alone."

There was a crashing sound near the castle, along with the crunching of glass. The sound of footsteps was getting closer.

"Do not feel alone," the old man reassured her, "I've been looking for someone like you for a very, very long time." He put his hands together as the sound of the footsteps grew like thunderous rain. "A storm is coming, child, and we must prepare for it, together. Will you join me?"

"I—"

Before she could respond, another roar of the creature boomed overhead, and the room was engulfed in flames. The noise of collapsing walls and screaming men assaulted the girl's ears. White-hot fire traced around her. The girl closed her eyes as she tried to withstand it, feeling her ears going deaf and her head splitting from the sensation. Fire coursed through her body before it concentrated on her left hand.

She screamed before she opened her eyes again. The creature was gone. The men were gone. She was back in Kai-Ji, crying in pain as she dropped the scroll in her hands.

Though she did not understand it at the time, her future had been irrevocably set. Later, she would look at her left hand and find the only scar of hers that would not fully heal—the symbol of a sword.

RED SHIELD

SEPTIMIAN DYNASTY, YEAR 241
KINGDOM OF NEMEA, CITY OF SILICO

*To understand Tyr Lancelt, you must first learn of his
origins, of the Nemean boy before he became
the Shooting Star.*

SIR TANDEM THE YOUNGER
TALES, VOLUME I

"That'll be eight argents."

The boy rummaged around in his worn pockets, delaying the inevitable. Slowly, he lifted the coins out and counted them, hoping that somehow, the sum would be different, or that someone would come and save him. He knew his unkempt blond hair and ragged tunic would purchase him no further favour here.

He looked at the baker. "I'm sorry, sir, I only have five."

The baker sighed. "You know my cheapest loaves are four argents each, Tyr. I understand the situation with your mother, but I'm running a business, not a charity. I'll sell you the one."

The boy's face got hot. Around him were others in line, waiting to purchase their daily bread. It was always embarrassing for Tyr to do the family errands, but if not him, then who? He had endured worse embarrassment.

Tyr handed his four argents to the baker and received his single loaf of fresh bread, a far cry from what he needed. "Thank you, sir."

"I'm sorry, little one."

The boy turned and hurried to the exit, eager to get as far away from the bakery as possible. His eyes were rooted to the ground as he exited the building. He stepped through the doorway and felt Silico's cool morning air hit his hot ears. Tyr took a deep breath as he collected himself.

At least I have one, he thought, picturing the single argent in his worn pocket. Alone, it could not afford much, but he had a growing collection of them at his house, hidden underneath his bed. He had been saving leftover coins he'd accumulated over the years. He imagined it as his own personal allowance, just like the rich boys had.

Tyr walked the cobblestone street back home, a bag of bread in hand. Around him was the cosy vista of his hometown, Silico. This was Eolis Street, where families would procure their daily necessities. Tyr ran his daily errands here, though it was usually only for the bakery or fruit vendors. Lining the street were speciality shops with more costly foodstuff. Savouring the tantalizing aromas that came from them as he passed through was the favourite part of Tyr's day.

Seared beef and pork would sizzle and pop in one store, their meaty smells combining with the next store's sugary sweet puddings and cotton candy. Yet another store would feature 'silicones', a special type of frozen treat which was said to have a texture that was lighter than a cloud. A horde of noblemen's children would frequent that particular shop daily. Tyr himself could never join in, the family finances being as they were. The boy was never too concerned about this, however. He had figured that, while the other children spent their allowance on sweets, his savings would be put to far better use.

I'm just not sure what, he would think.

The boy was coming of age, and dreams and fantasies filled his mind, the special sort that only a thirteen-year-old like Tyr could create. Visions of claiming heroic victories, fighting epic battles, and facing dangerous creatures were the scenes his imagination would oft visit. He was an avid reader, which was rare for a boy of his upbringing—and the tales he read would only further fuel his fantasies.

The bells from a nearby church atop a hill rang, signalling the boy's morning routine would soon come to an end. The clamour of the crowd on Eolis Street faded as Tyr rounded a corner and onto an ill-maintained dirt road, the path home. Ahead of him was a quiet neighbourhood, thoughtful constructions of cobble and oak that formed the houses lining the street. Tyr approached his home, a quaint building of which nothing stood out, and arrived at the door. Carefully unlatching it, he stepped inside.

"Oh, yes," said a voice from within, "I think it looks great on you."

Tyr froze in place. He focused intently on the sound of the woman speaking, dreading what he had intruded upon.

"Don't worry. I'm sure Tyr will like it, too."

The boy closed his eyes, his hand shaking as it held the bagged bread. He knew that only the physicians came to the house nowadays, and they weren't supposed to be in yet.

Please, Mother.

"He looks just like you, you know. Like father, like son!"

In one moment, Tyr felt his legs lose strength. The next, his weakness passed. He steeled his mind, grit his teeth and shut the door behind him with a thud.

"Oh! Here he is now," said the voice.

Tyr walked into his house, a neat combination of barren floors and barren walls. There was not much in the boy's home, the family having sold most of its items to survive. One thing was still the same, though. Tyr stepped into the living room of his home, the one unchanged area of the house. It was replete with exquisite carpets, a pair of sofas, hand-crafted drapes, lamps that decorated the oak stands, and a fireplace at the centre of it all. Above the fireplace was a painting, a portrait of a tall man with short, blond hair and a scar on his left cheek. He held a red shield and a silver sword.

"Hello, Mother." Tyr dropped the bread on a stand next to a basket of fruit.

His mother stood in front of the painting, her curly, dark hair and porcelain skin giving her the appearance of a doll. Her youthful face was blemished only by her sunken eyes. She wore a light blue smock that fit her perfectly, only accentuating her good looks. The boy's mother was beautiful, no doubt, and suitors would come to the house now and again, but they quickly turned back once they realized the true nature of her condition.

Maybe for the better, Tyr would think.

"Hello, darling." She beamed at him. She motioned at the painting on the wall. "Ulfric and I were just discussing his new uniform. Don't you think he looks dashing?"

Not again, Mother.

Every few days she would get like this. Tyr's father had passed nearly a decade ago, and all that remained of him were the boy's memories and the mania that had taken hold of his mother. His presence hung over them like a ghost, and his mother would often relapse into her madness. It was especially hard when she mistook Tyr himself for his father. Though the boy was too young to have real recollections of his father, he had memorized by heart the stories his mother recounted about his heroics in wars past.

"Yes, Mother," Tyr said, playing along with her delusion, "he does."

She smiled at him again, that look of half-consciousness eating away at him. "How was your trip to the baker?"

"Good. Here's the bread for tonight."

"Oh, but dear, you only have one. That's not enough for the two of us."

"Don't worry, Mother, I ate mine on the way back."

"That's a relief."

His mother believed anything he said these days, and it was important that things stayed that way. She didn't need to know what had happened at the bakery earlier. Tyr's eyes wavered around the room before eventually settling on the wall opposite the fireplace, a familiar red shield hanging from it. Emblazoned on the shield was a depiction of a wolf, a symbol of the Lancelt family line.

"Mother, don't you think it's time we sell that old shield there? Father won't be needing it."

Tyr's family was once wealthy. Money came from his father's line of work, and it was enough to afford them a good living. The family income had disappeared along with his father's passing, however. As finances were difficult for Tyr and his mother, it only made sense to get rid of the things which weren't useful anymore. Though the two had had this discussion many times, his mother would seemingly forget it every time.

Her brow furrowed. "Oh, please. You know what your father

says about his shield. It's going to be yours when you're ready. It's not for sale."

"Yes, Mother."

Worth a try.

"Now go upstairs to your studies, dear."

"Right away."

Tyr took one last look at the red shield on the wall and made his way upstairs, obeying his mother without a word. Though she was prone to her fits of delusion, her full sense would occasionally return, and she would remember if Tyr had been unruly. A mother always knows, after all.

The moon dipped below a grey horizon, heralding the coming shift to morning. The cool air was crisp, the type that only entertains those early enough to meet it at the fleeting dawn. Silence pervaded the neighbourhood, save for the crunching of the boy's shoes on the dirt path of a sleeping street. Tyr was near the city limits of Silico, out on his usual morning routine. His stomach growled fiercely with hunger, but he did his best to ignore it. It usually went away if he stopped thinking about it.

At the end of the street was the official entrance to Silico, symbolized by the marble gate that rose to match the tops of the nearby steeples. The gate was impressive, featuring engraved artwork, bevelled stone, and colourful flags. Though Silico was by no means as vast as the Nemean capital, it was still one of the larger cities in the nation. Victorious knights would come through the city's gates, and when they did, there was always a lavish welcome, a ritual that had begun centuries ago. Tyr's father had crossed the entrance in this fashion many times, and the boy always tried to emulate him.

Tyr turned around after exiting the city, facing the entrance once more. With his back upright and his chin out, he marched forward, doing his best impression of a regal pose. Bit by bit, his imagination filled in the details of today's fantasy. With the first few steps, he pictured the people of Silico surrounding him and ushering him forward.

With the next, his mind filled in their faces—his mother, his friends, and even a smiling Ulfric. Then he added the noise, the cacophonous cheers of the crowd that hailed him home. He was no longer Tyr the child. He was now Tyr Lancelt, Knight of Silico, returning home from a fierce battle against the Eastern Realms, or a dragon, or what-have-you. His armour clinked with every step. Behind him, the sound of horse hooves marched in rhythm with his gait. He could almost feel the presence of that horse, his noble steed flaring its nostrils as it followed Knight Tyr. He could—

"Hey, you there, can you move over? You're in the way."

The voice was so unexpected the boy's heart skipped a beat. He swivelled around and was met with a brown horse staring him in the face. Atop the horse was a man wearing chain armour and a deep red surcoat. Standard attire for Nemean messengers. In his arms was a stack of parchments.

"S-sorry," the boy stammered as he backed out of the way. His cheeks grew hot with embarrassment.

The man motioned his horse to move forward as he grumbled about the youth these days.

As Tyr's embarrassment faded, creeping curiosity took hold.
Just what is a royal messenger doing here?

Messengers typically only came for more important matters, and it had been some time since any had visited Silico. Something had happened. The daydream that had occupied the boy's mind was now replaced by a new mission. Sneaking behind the man on the horse, Tyr followed him into the city and through the main street. The man occasionally scratched his head as he looked around for the right direction. Tyr took the cover of nearby buildings and followed the messenger all the way to the town square, where the citizens would come to get their daily news.

There was a statue in the centre of the square, a nameless Nemean knight, raising his blade directly upward, as though challenging the skies themselves. The Forum, where citizens would discuss new rumours, and the Scribery, where record-keepers would note Silico's daily operations, were situated in the square, as well as the Newsboard, where reports and announcements were published. It stood next to the building that constituted the town hall.

Tyr snuck behind the corner of a building as he watched the messenger dismount and approach the board. The man procured a mallet and a set of nails from a burlap sack on his side. He placed the parchment in the centre of the board (over several other messages, no less) and fixed the parchment to the wood. He finished with a few tap-taps of his mallet, taking a quick look at his handiwork and remounting his horse.

Tyr waited for the man to pass before making his way to the newsboard. The parchment looked authentic enough from afar, with various designs overlaid on its edges. At the bottom was a red stamp, the seal of the Nemean king himself, King Remus. After several agonizing moments of anticipation, the boy finally reached the parchment, putting his reading skills to use and inspecting the contents within:

ROYAL DECREE
FOR LOCATION AND RETRIEVAL
OF THE LEGENDARY SOULBLADES

IT HAS COME TO THE ATTENTION OF THE KING'S COURT THAT CERTAIN SACRED RELICS KNOWN AS THE "SOULBLADES" HAVE MANIFESTED IN THE REALM. THESE VALUABLE RELICS ARE AS OLD AS THE GREAT NATIONS, FORGED IN THE EARLY DAYS OF NEMEA'S HISTORY.

THE SACRED OBJECTS HAVE THE APPEARANCE OF BLADES AND ARE SAID TO POSSESS DANGEROUS POWERS.

IN LIGHT OF SUCH, THE KING PROCLAIMS: ALL KNIGHTS, NOBLES, AND ABLE-BODIED OF HIS SUBJECTS WILL BEGIN A SEARCH FOR THE WEAPONS POSTHASTE, RUMORED TO APPEAR IN HOLY SITES IN NEMEA AND BEYOND.

A GENEROUS REWARD OF A KNIGHTSHIP, 20,000 PLATUMS, 700 AURUMS, AND 30 ARGENTS WITHOUT LEVY ARE RESERVED FOR THE BRAVE AND NOBLE SUBJECTS WHO RETURN THE SACRED OBJECTS TO THE NEMEAN THRONE.

SIGNED,
HIS HOLINESS, KING REMUS SEPTIMIUS,
RULER OF NEMEA, AND LORD OF HOLY BASTION

The boy was dumbfounded. He read the declaration again. A third time. He looked at the royal messenger, a short distance away, then back at the parchment. His eyes focused near the bottom of the decree.

Twenty thousand platums.

Tyr had never seen the green-coloured platums, but he knew that even a few of them was more than a small fortune. It was enough for himself, his mother, and more importantly, her health care. He thought of the costly physicians and their costly substances, treatments to balance the humors and restore the senses. Before his mind could finish processing it, his eyes jolted to another word.

Knightship.

Becoming a knight was a straightforward process—one either

fought for the crown during wartime or became an apprentice to another knight. The Great Nations, however, had known relative peace in the last decade, meaning new knights could not be minted on the battlefield. Tyr had attempted the second path to knighthood, but his low social status made it difficult to even place himself in front of a knight, much less in their consideration. Though his father was well known in his time, such honours ended with him; Tyr himself was afforded no special privilege. The royal decree before him now afforded a third option.

Tyr chased back after the royal messenger, casting aside his stealthy approach. "Sir!" he yelled, his voice ringing across the empty street. "Sir!"

The man stopped his horse and turned back to face the boy. "You again? What do you want now?"

"Sir," Tyr said, catching up to the man, "might you spare me one of those decrees?"

The messenger debated contesting the child's request, but after a moment apparently thought better of it. "Here you are—"

He hadn't finished his sentence before Tyr ripped the parchment out of his hand and raced back to his house. An idea had dawned on him—a bold idea that, though dangerous, felt like the thing he had been waiting for his entire life. Fate was calling now, and he would be the one to answer.

Before long, Tyr was inside of his home, sneaking up the stairs, being careful not to wake his dear mother. He arrived in his room in a flash. He dropped the parchment on the floor as he flung the covers off his bed, getting low to the ground and pushing his hand underneath the bed. His fingers explored the dark underside before they finally met with a solid object, a wooden handle that he took hold of. Carefully, he pulled the handle toward him, revealing a rickety wooden box—his private coin collection.

It had been some time since he recorded its contents, and so a recount was in order. The box was full of hundreds, thousands, of small silver argents with the occasional golden aurum strewn in between. Light of the rising sun streamed in from the outside window as he worked.

This is enough, he thought. Before him was his entire savings—eleven glittering aurums and one thousand nine hundred and eighty-two argents. An impressive amount for a boy his age. It was his accumulated wealth from years of thrifty saving, doing odd jobs, and even selling some of his prized books. It was by no means much, as altogether it could not even match the value of a single platum—but for Tyr's purposes, it was more than enough.

Closing the wooden box, he carried it gingerly out of his home and to Eolis Street. Several people were now on the roads, beginning their daily routine. Tyr crossed the street and entered the bakery where he had been the day prior.

"Good morning," he said, the metal in the box clanking with each step.

"What's that there—?"

The baker had only a moment to speak before the boy dropped the box directly on the counter with a thud. "Good morning," Tyr said again, "I'd like to purchase some bread." Lifting the cover of the box, he revealed the treasure within.

The baker's eyes widened, doing a double-take.

"This is enough for a few years." Tyr took out a quarter of the coins and placing them next to the box. "Please have someone deliver your bread to my mother during the day. Just ask for Marianne Lancelt."

"Wait a minute. I don't run no delivery. And where did you get this money anyway? Did you steal it?"

"No, sir. But if you don't want to do it, I can just—" Tyr reached his hands out to scoop up the coins.

"Wait a minute." The amount of business the boy was offering was far too tantalizing to give up. "Fine. I'll deliver your bread."

"Just for her, please. I won't need any myself." Tyr grabbed a few loaves beside the baker, placed them in his box, covered it once more, and ran out of the building before the man could stop him.

Good, he thought. *This can work.*

He went all around Eolis Street, haggling similar deals with other shop owners. By the end, he had managed to secure deliveries to his mother's house for bread, water, meat, fruit, and vegetables. He also took a bit of food for himself from each shop. His heart pounded with excitement as he rushed home, sneaking back into his house for a second time.

Once more in his room, he took a worn satchel and placed within it all of the food and supplies he would need. The satchel was bursting to the brim with its contents, and he even managed to save a few coins in a pouch for later. Tyr took the copy of the king's declaration and placed it on his bed.

Mother will understand.

He tip-toed downstairs. As he walked through the living room, he took one look at his father's portrait on the wall. He turned around and stared at the red shield for several moments, his father's only heirloom. His mother's words echoed in his mind: *"It's going to be yours when you're ready."*

The boy took a deep breath. He approached the shield and gingerly lifted it from the wall. It was sturdier than he had expected for such an old item. He ran his fingers along its surface, feeling each groove and ridge like some distant connection with his warrior father. He fastened the belt it was attached to onto his body. It fit him well. He was not sure how long his quest would take, but when he crossed the door of his childhood home, he imagined it being for the last time.

THE WARNING

SEPTIMIAN DYNASTY, YEAR 241
CITY OF SKYFALL

The winged seraphs have lived in isolation for millennia, sequestered to the spires of the floating city of Skyfall.

As legendary kings and buried secrets revealed themselves once more, so too did Skyfall's denizens make their grand return to the world below.

SIR TANDEM THE YOUNGER
TALES, VOLUME I

The gleaming city of Skyfall, a colossal metropolis the size of a mountain, floated high above the plains of Taerestris, towering over its peaks and drifting on a sea of air. It hid above the clouds, suspended by powerful magic.

Its buildings were made of foreign metal—bright purples, reds, and yellows mixing with the resplendent white of marble. Metal discs, religious symbols of the sun, decorated its buildings' rooftops. Roads were immaculately clean. Light from the nearby sun flooded the area in its warm glow.

The magic of levitation was not the only secret Skyfall held—it was also the last bastion of the civilization known as the seraphs. An ancient race that existed on Taerestris since the dawn of history, the seraphs were both physically strong and culturally advanced, having lived in peace for most of their illustrious past. The seraphs put their talents to work, dedicating their lives to the arts—the city itself was one such testament to their capabilities.

At the centre of the sprawling city was an enormous stone statue that rose up above the backdrop. The statue had the likeness of Sithe, the seraph's primary deity. Its head faced the skies, arms outstretched. Six stone wings protruded from the statue's back, the very image of divinity. A dense network of rooms and pathways filled the contents of the hollow statue. Two figures, commanders of the Isthalin, chosen warriors of the High Priestess, sat inside one such room, a wooden board fixed between them.

"Soldier advances, B6."

"Cleric advances, E4."

"Marshal captures Soldier, G7."

"Cleric promotes to Cardinal, B1."

"Stella," the male said. His armour was comprised of red leather and silver metals; his eyes glimmered with a white glow. The male's muscular body and spiky, black hair accentuated his form. His two feathery wings were a milky white, save for the small black markings littering the base of the wings. As with all seraphs, he had a sort of tattoo on his neck near the shoulder, a perfect circle containing dizzying geometric shapes.

"Yes, Mordrin?" she responded.

Like Mordrin, she wore Isthalin colours, though hers were blue, matching the azure glow of her eyes. Her white wings also carried black markings near the base. Long, blond hair flowed down her back.

"You've attempted this strategy once before. Your tenacity is appreciated, but your success is not likely."

Mordrin spoke with the formal diction that was expected of his station. He brought a clawed hand to a wooden figure holding a long spear and moved it to the end of the board. "Soldier promotes to Commissar, A8."

Mordrin looked up at his opponent. The corner of her mouth twitched almost imperceptibly with this latest play. Her next move was nearly instant.

"I don't know what you are referring to," she replied. "This is something new." She picked up a robed seraph with a swift motion and placed it near the centre of the board. "Magician advances, D4."

That's surprising, Mordrin thought, *what sort of trickery is this?*

Stella's latest move had left her Goddess wide open to attack. He eyed the seraph opposite him. She looked on at the board, hiding any further tells. Mordrin knew his apprehension was justified, but Stella had just left her most important piece completely vulnerable. It was madness to abandon the Goddess—and Stella knew it.

"Well?"

The male seraph picked up his promoted piece and attacked. "Grand Marshal captures Goddess, D8."

With this move, I am the victor.

Stella brought her hands to her lap and looked at the board. With the Goddess captured, Mordrin had won the game—her position was unwinnable now. The Goddess was the most powerful piece, and without it, Stella's great disadvantage would surely lead to a loss if she continued.

He let out a sigh. "Why make such a foolish gambit? Your game was flawless until you brought your Magician into play."

The female seraph remained silent for a time. A pair of birds fluttered near the window, the sound entering the room and breaking the silence. She smiled faintly. "I suppose—I suppose I've been thinking about things differently of late."

"Differently? Does something trouble you?"

"No, nothing like that." Stella brought out a hand, taking a piece and placing it on Mordrin's side of the board. "High Priestess promotes to Goddess, H1."

Mordrin's eyes jolted to the board now. He had expected a surrender, but not this. His eyebrows rose as he finally understood. With one move, Stella had recovered her Goddess, cracked open his defence, and pressured his own Goddess from multiple angles.

Nothing short of brilliance.

A bead of sweat rolled down Mordrin's temple as he examined the state of the game now—there was no way out for him. He'd lost the game. It was a trap all along.

Mordrin grit his teeth. The move to use her Goddess as bait was insanely risky; even his own offensive style would never allow for such an opening. *Perhaps such thinking was my downfall.* Mordrin leaned back and exhaled, accepting his defeat. "Sacrificing your Goddess for the victory, eh?"

Stella did not respond.

"I will commit that play to memory. Clever of you. I concede."

Stella nodded gravely. Before they could continue, the two were interrupted by a sound emerging from the entrance of the room. It was another seraph, who, like Stella, sported glowing blue eyes that matched her Isthalin armour. Her small features and short stature gave her a much more youthful appearance when compared to Stella, features that Mordrin so often doted on. She was his little sister, after all.

"Taela," Mordrin said. "What brings you here?"

"Sorry to interrupt," she said, her squeaky voice only highlighting her dainty qualities. "It's the High Priestess. She wants to see both of you in the scrying chamber at once."

The two climbed a large circular staircase. Taela, having delivered her message, had left the commanders to their fate with the High Priestess. Mordrin felt a sense of trepidation as they ascended the staircase and neared their destination.

"What could it be, I wonder?" he mused.

"We cannot hope to know," Stella answered plainly.

"I find it strange. That scrying chamber has only known disuse for many years. Why now?"

Stella hesitated before responding.

Mordrin looked at her intently. *We both know what it is. It's—*

"The Spellseal. It's been getting worse."

"Right."

Mordrin glanced at Stella's neck—the same symbol, just like his. The truth of the Spellseal was well documented; it was the cause of the black markings on their wings, a curse that every seraph was born with.

The curse was benign at first, causing no ill effects to its subject. It was only when the user cast a variety of magic known as Soul Magic that the Spellseal reacted, damaging its host and degenerating the body. Those who had experienced its effects displayed black markings on their wings, and for this, the afflicted had come to be known contemptuously as blackwings. Mordrin's pride would never accept such an insult, however—he always wore the name like a badge of honour, and Mordrin the Blackwing was his commonly-referred-to title.

"The Spellseal is minting new blackwings every day now," Stella said. "seraphs who've never cast a spell in their lives are showing the marks."

"It is the same as my case, then," Mordrin said. Though Mordrin was no magus, he had become a blackwing as a child, along with his sister, Taela. "Do you know what I surmise? It's obvious, isn't it? The ones who live near the bottom of the city degenerate more quickly than the ones elsewhere. They are reacting to the magic that keeps the city afloat. This damnable curse of ours is growing more sensitive by the day."

The two grew silent as they reached the top of the staircase. It was taboo to talk about the Spellseal out in the open, and the ruling class of Skyfall preferred to keep it that way. As Isthalin, Mordrin and Stella had to serve as the guiding example, and it was only during furtive moments that the two could discuss such matters.

Stella pushed open a set of bronze double doors, the entrance of the scrying chamber. Shadows spilled out from within. As the seraphs adjusted to the low visibility, the scene in the room revealed itself.

The circular chamber contained no windows and was lit only by braziers mounted along the walls. Lines of glowing green light ran along the surface of the stone floor, giving it a labyrinthine appearance. Ghostly coloured orbs floated gently just above the floor.

There was a set of stairs that led to a raised podium at the back of the chamber. A set of three braziers lit the podium brightly, and standing on it was… *High Priestess Alystra,* Mordrin thought.

As Mordrin was her greatest warrior, the two were no strangers—still, her stunning beauty and perfect features never ceased to surprise the seraph. The golden glow of her eyes, the chalk-white hair that matched her dress, the six flawless wings that set her apart from all other seraphs—all of these contributed to her special status in Skyfall. Atop her head was a tiara with a sapphire gem in the centre. She was more than a Whitewing—those seraphs whose bodies had not yet begun to deteriorate like Mordrin's and Stella's—to the people of Skyfall, she was divine. The thing that lay on the ground before the Isthalin commanders, however, was enough to draw attention away from even Alystra.

At the centre of the room, in a nightmarish pose, was a dead female seraph. Her wings were fully blackened, and tufts of her feathers littered the area. Her contorted face had a look of horror sketched upon it, and her limbs were disfigured.

"What is—?" started Stella.

"How quickly can you two mobilize?"

Mordrin was taken aback. Such a question was unprecedented. The High Priestess had not once called her warriors into action during her lifetime tenure. The seraphs had lived peacefully on Skyfall for as long as anyone could remember.

"It would not take long," Stella said. "Is that... Scryer Reina?" Stella directed attention back to the dead seraph.

Mordrin stepped forth to get a closer look. *Stella is right. It's her. What madness happened here?*

"She came to me in a hurry," Alystra said. Her voice carried powerfully across the room, befitting her regal appearance. Even during an event such as this, she did not lose her composure. The commanders waited for her to continue.

"It was the Spellseal." Alystra waved her hand above the glowing ground, calling attention to the lines and orbs. "She cast the magic you see before us now, and it had a violent reaction on her body. It killed her."

"Then this is Soul Magic?"

Mordrin put a hand to his chin as he examined the corpse and spoke. "Curious that she would use magic despite the ban. Unless..." The Blackwing pondered the situation.

The two main classes of magic in use on Skyfall before the banning were Arcane Magic, which used energy in the environment to achieve a particular effect; and Soul Magic, a more powerful type that had near-infinite applications, but required a portion of the user's life essence in order to cast. The Spellseal only reacted when a seraph used Soul Magic, but it seemed that was no longer the limit of the curse.

Mordrin was a non-magus who nevertheless had an advanced form of the Spellseal, one which seemingly reacted to mere exposure to Soul Magic. For others, it was worse; his sister Taela, an ex-magus, would suffer violently when casting the Arcane variety. His thoughts wandered to Alystra, a wave of panic washing over him.

"We must get the High Priestess away," Mordrin said. "She must not be exposed."

"No," Alystra said, "I am no blackwing. Not yet."

"But still—"

"Enough," Alystra said. "Before she died, Reina left a message. It concerns Taerestris itself. And has much to do with what lies below."

"Below?" Stella asked.

"Below the clouds," the High Priestess said. "I can no longer hide this secret. You must know."

Mordrin listened intently to Alystra, watching her face as she entered deep thought. She was carefully considering her next words.

"You know that the common folk live on the surface of Taerestris. We have lived on Skyfall and away from them for a very specific reason."

Alystra descended from her podium to meet her commanders near the body of the dead scryer.

"Living among a people who resort to magic as often as they do would surely trigger the Spellseal. I cannot allow that to happen." Alystra motioned at the body lying between the three.

It's true, then, Mordrin thought. *The Spellseal reacts to mere exposure now. How long did you know, High Priestess?* Though he was curious, he thought better than to challenge the divine Alystra.

He opted for a less brazen question.

"Then why mobilize?" he asked. "For what purpose would we return below? We have not had contact with the common folk for thousands of years."

"Look around you, Mordrin," Alystra said. "Reina's final spell—a map of the world."

The two Isthalin re-examined the glowing lines put in place by the now-dead Reina; though it was difficult to decipher, the lines had a logic to them. It was indeed a map that traced out the regions of Taerestris.

"What are these lights?" Stella asked.

"Powerful sources of Soul Magic. Relics," said the High Priestess. "Skyfall is here."

Realization dawned across Mordrin's face. "Then that must mean…?"

"The common folk are using Soul Magic?" Stella asked.

Alystra's face grew grim. "Not only that, but potent Soul Magic as strong as the spell that keeps our city afloat. Strong enough to be visible on this map. Scryer Reina's last message was a warning. She called me into this room in her mad rush, speaking of powerful weapons. The lights here denote their locations."

Mordrin contemplated the High Priestess's words. It was true that the common folk below were known to be practitioners of magic, but as far as the seraphs knew, most of them only practised the Arcane variety. The multitude of blinking lights on the map of the world was unlike anything he had expected. *Common folk using Soul Magic?*

"But why now?" he asked. "What heretical aim could these weapons achieve?"

Mordrin stared at Alystra. The High Priestess was again in deep thought.

She finally spoke. "Our first concern is their retrieval. Once we have them collected, we may discuss such matters."

Stella raised an eyebrow. "But—"

"No," Alystra commanded. "Let us waste no more time on this. I have made up my mind on the subject. Your orders, then. Descend below the clouds. Find the weapons and bring them to me. Make no contact with the common folk. We will lock them away so that this power can never be used against us."

Mordrin nodded at Alystra. He would follow her orders no matter what—that was his duty, after all. But a thought had now occurred to him.

She is hiding something. But what?

DISCOVERY

SEPTIMIAN DYNASTY, YEAR 242
KINGDOM OF NEMEA, WILDERNESS

There are three types of magic that comprise the trinity of spellcasting. The first order of these is Arcane Magic, which manipulates the residual energy of the elements. Next is Soul Magic, which uses one's lifeforce in exchange for power. Finally, there is Dragon Magic, said to be exclusive to the Eternal Dragons of legend.

LORITHAS THE MINDWEAVER
A BASIC GUIDE TO MAGIC

Tyr stepped through the forest clearing onto the weathered stone path before him. He walked alone, unprotected, save for the red shield on his belt. Above him, an overcast sky threatened to rain. Perhaps months ago, his heightened sense of caution might have felt strange—but he was used to it now. To each of his sides were short hedges, leading him onward, the looming silhouette of an abandoned ruin coming into view.

Almost there.

Though he had travelled extensively, his body moved with the same energy and confidence he had since the beginning of his adventure. He relished the fact that whatever he was after would soon be his. *Just a few steps away,* he would think.

A year of exploration had made his body tougher; his mind had also developed. The boy was now fourteen years of age, but his travels had made him wise beyond his years. He felt he was ready for any challenge, his experience on his adventures being a sort of preparation for what lay beyond.

The boy halted as he reached a set of iron double doors.

He figured this to be the place he had been seeking, placing his hands on the doors to investigate. The door's arch was three times as high as he was, with stone walls stretching seemingly endlessly to each side. A familiar poem was engraved on the metal in the centre of the doors:

> *In the land of ancient kings,*
> *Where eternal Dragons lie,*
> *The War of Three upon the wings*
> *Would blot the sun on heaven's sky*
>
> *To split the three, a plan devised*
> *That would protect the world a'round*
> *The skies, the lands, the Great Divide*
> *And hide the swords in hallowed ground.*

If you seek divine defence
Call their names, the ancient rite,
Send the world again to rest.
Blades of power, lend your might.

Tyr recalled the many times he'd heard the poem. When he initially set out on his quest, he had not considered the true nature of the Soulblades; during his year-long journey, he had had much time to ponder them, however. The Soulblades themselves were artefacts said to possess great power, but there was never much proof beyond myths and rumours. The Soulblades came to life only in hushed rooms and bedtime stories—that was, of course, until the Kingsguard declared their holy quest to find them, granting legitimacy to the fables.

There was only one problem—the weapons were impossibly difficult to find. One could seek out the holy sites quite easily, yes, but the blades themselves would rarely make an appearance. Even the great King Remus and his noble Kingsguard had only claimed a handful of the swords once the search had begun.

Looks like someone was here already, Tyr thought, noting the entrance. It was slightly ajar. He gathered his courage and pushed the doors. They creaked and groaned, revealing what lay beyond at last, like a centuries-old gift.

The boy's eyes widened as he beheld the sight before him. It was the largest structure he had ever seen.

Tyr had stumbled upon a giant cathedral, replete with gleaming golden lights streaming through the glass-lined walls at the far side of the building. He took a few paces inside to examine his new surroundings.

The first thing he noticed was the open ceiling. Spanning dozens of floors, trying to find the top gave him a sense of vertigo. The pews on the ground floor towered above Tyr, too; he could barely see the top of the dusty seats. The marble floor beneath him was decorated with artwork of the divine.

Built by giants, he thought.

This place is too large to cover in a day, and if the doors were open, that means someone was here.

Despite this development, the boy remained confident—he knew a blade hadn't been claimed from the old cathedral yet. Such an event would surely reach the local news.

Time to get started.

The adventurer moved up and down the aisles of the prodigious pews, hoping to find some clue that might help lead the way. The task was time-consuming, but necessary. The boy craned his neck as he occasionally examined the high ledges and platforms of the floors above.

One such platform piqued his interest in particular. Above the central congregation table was a landing with innumerable cracks running through its surface. The cracks seemed unnaturally made, but the thing jutting out from the landing was even more starkly distinct.

Is that...?

Hanging over the platform were the bones of human arm. Dried blood covered the pallid white of the bone. The fingers were splayed open, as though trying to open a door. Tyr stiffened as he became hyper-aware of his surroundings—from here, he could not see the skeleton the hand was connected to, but his mind filled in the image with perfect clarity. Someone had died a mere floor above him. He looked around wildly, feeling eyes behind him as he checked to make sure he was alone.

Silence.

The boy breathed in deeply as he gathered his wits. He could not stop here. The ghastly hand was a warning, but he would not run like a frightened child. It was only when he took another timid look at the congregation table directly below the hand that he saw a faintly glowing object. Tyr took hurried steps to it as he covered the cathedral ground.

As he approached the object, he could make out its details

more clearly. It appeared to be a golden scabbard. *Could it really be right here?* Deep in his hurried thoughts, the explorer arrived at the table, the scabbard in arm's reach.

The object was embellished with blue sapphires running from base to tip. It emitted a soft, golden light, radiating warm energy. Wisps of light emanated downward from the scabbard, settling like heavy fog on the floor. The boy raised his head, eyeing the bones that hung directly above him. He looked down at the scabbard again, at last resolving the puzzle of what had happened here. The thrill of the find overwhelmed his fear of the skeleton above him.

Then this must be...

The light felt like it was welcoming him, almost drawing him into it, making him feel like nothing else was as important as the item in front of him.

Tyr had imagined this day for a year, but to finally be in front of his prize was a shock. Soulblades were so rare that it was difficult to know when one had truly encountered such a prize—however, the special qualities of this particular item had erased all doubt. Unless this was an elaborate trick, the object before him was certainly the real thing. Taking a deep breath, Tyr pulled upon the sword from within the sheath.

This is... The boy's mouth hung open in awe.

The sword's pristine beauty matched the scabbard it was placed in. It was long and slender, not at all like the bastard swords that swordsmen in Nemea preferred. The flat blade was wide near the hilt and came to a narrower flat at the end. It was a dazzling metal, almost white, with sapphire runes that matched the scabbard in Tyr's hands.

So, these are the holy relics.

He unsheathed the weapon completely and touched the blade for the first time. The metal was cold, unlike the warmth of the scabbard. The sword vibrated with a low hum the moment he touched the metal. The twinkling sapphire above the hilt of the blade shone brightly, drawing Tyr in. Before he realized it, the cathedral had become a blur, and he felt himself falling. A feeling of dread was the last thing that filled his mind before it went blank.

It seemed like hours before Tyr came to his senses again. His mind was groggy. The ground touching his back felt different from the marble floor of the cathedral. It was a soft feeling—like a bed of warm feathers. The boy's head ached, and it strained him to remember what had occurred. He recalled the cathedral and ghastly bones. As he put together pieces of his memory, he stood and examined his new surroundings.

He was presently in a white room. There were no walls or corners, and the white space continued in all directions with seemingly no end.

Where am I? The bewildered adventurer decided to call out for someone. "Am I dead?"

His voice pierced through the white void, cutting through it unnaturally.

"Would you like to be?" a serene voice replied from behind him.

The response made him jump in the air. He spun around to get a good look. Behind him, sitting in an antique wooden chair was a girl.

The girl looked some years older than Tyr. She sat backwards on her chair, her arms folded over the top of the back support. She swung her bare feet playfully over the ground. She wore a long, white garment complete with golden accents that matched her delicate voice, hiding most of her creamy white skin. Her jet-black hair curved down her back and ended at the top of her hips.

The stranger stared intently at him, her youthful face in focused composure. She was expecting a very serious answer to her very serious question.

"O-of course not!" he stammered, heat rushing to his face.

"Then why are you here?" she pressed him.

How should I know that?

"If you don't know why you're here… you must not know what you just found."

Wait a moment. Are you a mind-reader?

"Another one found me recently, you know. He was an older sort. Not like you. I didn't talk to him, though. He died shortly after."

Died? Is she the cause of those bones I saw?

The boy could not believe that such a thing was possible, but he had already seen many impossible things on this day.

"Where are we?"

"Inside your mind, at the moment." She enunciated every word perfectly as though putting on a performance. "But it seems your mind is blank. I rather like it here." She giggled, then tilted her head to the side. "The fact that you're here means you've come across a very special item."

Instantly, memories of a bright golden sheath and a glittering white sword flooded back. *How could I forget? That weapon shook in my hands, and now I'm here.*

"So, you live inside the sword?"

"Correct. Perhaps you're not as dumb as you look." The girl smiled in a joyful manner.

The boy was baffled at this sudden turn of events. He could only imagine the kind of sorcerer it would take to bind a person within a blade; such magic was unheard of, at least to him. *Is she even real? Why is she inside a sword?* Tyr wondered if he could trust this girl.

As if in reply, the girl furrowed her brow, showing offence. "I've been here for as long as I can remember. But I've been asleep until just recently. Tell me, why have you come for me?"

"Well, I, uh…" *Should I just tell her I'm looking to give the sword to the king?*

"Oh, I see. So, you don't have intentions to keep me company for long?" Her mesmerizing gaze now reflected sadness. She swung her legs slowly, a sombre gloom taking precedence on her face. The sight made Tyr feel pity for her. "Just for a little bit, I suppose. There are some people who are offering a reward for turning the weapon… erm… you, in."

"Just for a bit, then. What's your name?"

"Tyr."

"Tee-er," she practised. The girl repeated his name as she brought one of her hands up and played with her black hair.

Hearing her say his name in such a way made Tyr's face flush red again, and the mysterious girl smiled at his reaction.

"Well, I'm very pleased to meet you, T—" She cut herself off. Her face darkened, and her smile vanished. Anxiety etched itself across her features. "Do you wish to go back now?"

Tyr looked at the girl in the chair. *Why so soon? Is it really that simple? How do you eat, anyway? What about the last person who found you? Are you really a person? Are you alive? I have a lot more questions for you.* Tyr fired off queries in his head, hoping the peculiar girl would answer one of them. *How can I come back here? Is there some magic phrase? If I leave, will you be all alone again?*

The girl's worried look shifted to a happy smile and she answered promptly. "As long as you have me, we will be able to talk to each other whenever we like." The girl seemed excited at this prospect. "We can discuss things later, but you really should go back now."

"All right, send me back," he agreed unenthusiastically.

"See you around, Tyr." The smiling girl said her goodbyes, and her eyes flashed in a similar fashion to the sapphire runes of the sword from earlier.

Almost immediately, Tyr could again feel the dizzying sensation as everything shook around him. His mind was losing focus, and he tried to retain his concentration on the girl in front of him.

"Wait! What is your name?"

The sight of her became blurry, but he could see her place a finger to her lips.

"That's a secret," she said.

Then, everything went blank again.

It was some time before Tyr came to. He opened his eyes to the sight of stained glass and stone walls. He was once again in the cathedral. Though the entire experience had felt like hours, the boy stood upright and took a quick look at the sunlight streaming through the stained glass to confirm his suspicion.

It's only been a few minutes, then.

Tyr got his bearings before he examined the beautiful sword once more. It seemed like a work of art, rather than anything meant for real combat. It reminded him of his father, Ulfric, who had had a similarly artistic blade for formal occasions. *Maybe someday I can be like that?*

He reunited the blade with its sheath once again. The sapphires of the sheath beamed a brilliant blue as the blade locked into place.

It was at this moment when Tyr heard quaking behind him. Overhead, he could make out the cathedral bells ringing. The sound of the walls falling and rocks crumbling away nearby put Tyr on high alert. The ground shook and threw the boy off balance, and a loud rumbling went off from near the entrance. A low roar from a bestial creature accompanied the sound. Whatever was behind him was very large, and very angry.

NEMORIS

SEPTIMIAN DYNASTY, YEAR 242
EASTERN REALMS, NATION OF XERAS

Nemea's Iron Wall was a peculiar woman. Found as an orphan in the Eastern Realms, she became a knight as the adopted daughter of King Remus Septimius. Under his instruction, she would become one of the only females to have ever risen to the rank of Kingsguard.

Her countless victories became the stuff of legend, and she served as an inspiration to young men and women alike throughout her life.

SIR TANDEM THE YOUNGER
TALES, VOLUME I

"You should be familiar with this place, should you not?" The pale-skinned man's raspy voice cut through the wind.

He wore a black leather coat with matching legwear, more suited for an award ceremony than travel. The man walked as though he carried some great burden. His eyes were out of focus, his mind on more important matters. His stony face revealed his age, easily in his early forties. His messy, short black hair matched his rugged beard. He carried no weapons on his person, unlike his partner, Cecilia Scarlet.

"It's been almost two decades, Baou," Cecilia replied. "I hardly remember the local language."

Lady Cecilia Scarlet, the Iron Wall, strode along confidently. Her deep red hair, fitting of her surname, flowed gracefully and met with her metal shoulder guards. Her lithe body was protected by a custom combination of steel, red cloth, and chain. On her belt was a sheath which housed her weapon, granted to her by the Nemean king.

"But I should be asking you what you're doing completely unarmed. I understand why you left your blade, but… the king asked that the two of us travel together. Why do you think that is?"

Baou let loose a grunt. The duo was situated on a long, winding bridge connecting one rocky plateau to another. The winds at their high altitude buffeted the pair on occasion. The wooden bridge swayed easily in that wind, making sure attention was paid to it as a toll for passage.

"There's no need to worry when I have the Iron Wall with me. They say you still haven't lost a battle."

"*They* say a lot of things. You and I both know I'm nowhere near the strongest of the guard. I simply don't fight battles I cannot win."

"Yet, here you are, having risen through the ranks as our king's personal favourite. Perhaps you give yourself less credit than you deserve, Princess Scarlet."

Cecilia's lips curved subtly upward. She knew that Baou was baiting her now. He would often toss out poorly disguised quips as compliments. The two had known each other for years, and their lighthearted verbal sparring made their travels more engaging. She took only a moment to devise a counter-strategy.

"Are you envious, Daylight Assassin? I care little for titles or positions; you should know that by now."

The man did not flinch at this attack; her rebuttal was ineffective. "Yet you wear your signature armour even while travelling. You enjoy recognition, though you may not admit it. One could go as far as to say that you revel in it." The man spoke promptly and efficiently, his diction remaining blunt and matter-of-fact.

"I carry more than this armour when I equip it. I carry the hopes of our nation, his holiness, and the pride of our people. The armour is a symbol to them, something to look up to. I won't deny them that privilege. And I won't make mention of your own attire."

The man gave a simple "Humph," in response.

Cecilia knew that her little speech had won the match. The two fell silent as they focused on the task, making their way to one of the Eastern Realm's villas. The entrance to the villa was close now, at the end of the winding bridge.

The villa of the Magister Francis was in the mesa region, far away from the heart of the capital. The Eastern Realms was a republic well known for its great wealth, mysterious magic, and progressive politics. The nobility of its member states had coin to spare, and it was a common occurrence that a prince or some other nobleman would purchase a villa. This was one such estate, the summer home of Magister Francis. The magister hailed from Xeras, the human hub of the realms and its largest constituent. Francis was the direct aide to Prime Chancellor Renault and one of the *Cellerati*, a hopeful to receive command over the realms in the next election.

The travelling knights crossed the winding bridge and approached the front of the villa. The building was grandiose, befitting the noble bloodline of the magister. It featured a traditional design, contrasting the steeples and spires of Nemea. Atop the doors to the villa were Xeran flags, depicting the symbol of a staff in white over a dark blue background. Unlike in Nemea, residents of Xeras prided themselves on their magical mastery and secular society.

Two soldiers stood guard over the villa entrance. They were clad in the standard blue steel armour of Xeras, each with a pike in hand. They watched the two knights as they approached and readied their pikes when the travellers came near.

One of the guardsmen spoke in a foreign tongue to Sir Baou, who glanced at the guard, then at his compatriot, and uttered, "Cecilia, I'll leave this to you."

Cecilia made a slight nod at Baou before reaching into one of her many belt pockets and producing a note.

"From the Nemean king," the woman declared as she extended the note to the guardsmen.

The two Nemean knights stood with bated breath as one of the men took the note.

The guards conversed with each other as they examined the letter. They spoke briefly, taking odd looks at Cecilia and Baou in turn. Eventually, one of the guards nodded and stepped aside. He rang a bell thrice, and the villa doors swung open.

The duo entered the foyer, wary of whatever lay ahead.

The inside of the villa was inconspicuous, eerily ordinary for a building owned by a wealthy Xeran like Francis. Midday light streamed in through the windows. There were various staircases leading to other floors from the far side of the doors.

"We should wait here for now," Cecilia proposed.

"I'm curious as to the contents of that note," Sir Baou said. While they talked, his eyes scanned the room. With a thud, the door behind them closed, leaving the two alone now. "It doesn't matter. I doubt those guardsmen even read the damn thing. They were only looking for the king's seal." Baou changed the subject. "Security seems light here. On top of that, they let you in with your weapon. Curious."

Baou was always on high alert, questioning the how and why of everything. In this case, his paranoia was justified. Though the Eastern Realms were officially in a truce with Nemea, it didn't stop them from encroaching on Nemean territory and inciting small proxy wars on the edges of their control. The only thing that kept the realms in check was the constant infighting between their member states, a power game that had gone on for centuries.

"Ah, so you have arrived, my Nemean friendsss! I hope the trip was not too taxing!" A voice sounded from a staircase as a figure approached the knights.

The eccentric man spoke with bravado and a Xeran accent. He was dressed in a dark blue robe made of exotic satin, and he wore odd-looking sandals that wrapped around his ankles like a snake torturing its victim.

Cecilia spied rings of different sizes, shape, and colour along each of his fingers, an ostentatious display of wealth.

He clapped his hands together and descended the staircase. "Two Kingsguard in my presence! It would be an understatement to say that I am honoured." He arrived at the bottom of the stairs and approached the older knight. "You must be Sir Baou, the one they call the Daylight Assassin. I am quite intrigued as to how you conduct your businesss."

While Sir Baou was well known as the Daylight Assassin, none but the inner circle of the Kingsguard knew exactly how it was that Baou killed people without leaving a scratch on them. This great mystery led to the usual talk of dark curses at play; some even believed that the enigmatic Sir Baou was nothing more than a fraud.

"With all due respect, Magister Francis, I hope you never have to find out," Baou grimly remarked. The knight's eyes gave little attention to the nobleman addressing him and continued to examine the room as though he were searching for something he had lost.

Francis looked at Baou with thinly veiled contempt, his lip curling up at this perceived threat. He turned his attention away from Baou and onto his companion. "Princess Cecilia! You look as fearsome as you do ravishing." He did a quick bow of his head as she responded.

"Thank you for the compliment, Your Excellency," she replied gracefully. She was well accustomed to being recognized for her beauty and had become adept at handling such compliments.

"Now then," Francis said, raising his finger as if to make a point. He motioned them to follow him. "Shall we take a stroll through my gardensss?"

He strode, knights in tow, to an entrance underneath a staircase—an unobtrusive door, previously hidden from view. With a quick turn of its golden doorknob, the trio stepped inside the gardens.

The gardens within contrasted heavily with the arid region outside the villa. Hedges, flowers, and vines grew in the lush plot of land. The scents were intoxicating, as though the verdant plant life was welcoming the knights. The centre of the area was graced by a tall, white fountain and, from it, stone pathways led outside in the four cardinal directions.

"A sight to behold, yesss?" Francis asked pompously. "It is a rare Arcane enchantment that only we in Xeras are privy to. Our mages breathe life into the plants to create our beautiful gardens. It is quite the luxury, even for a man such as I."

"Are the plants adversely affected by this process?" Baou asked as they neared the centre of the garden.

"As long as the spell holds, the plants are healthy. Our mages simply make them as lively and beautiful as can be. Perhaps I will let you speak with one of them later to discuss more on the matter." He paused. "Ah, but you two are not here to enjoy my gardens, are you?"

The party stopped short of the white fountain as the satin-robed man faced the knights. His look turned serious, a departure from his previously casual expression. He gave them each a stony gaze.

"On to business, then. For what purpose am I honoured with the presence of two Kingsguard at my estate?"

Sir Baou continued scanning the environment as always, ignoring the man's question, giving Cecilia the cue to speak.

"Magister Francis, aide of King Renault and Celleratus of Xeras. We come on Nemea's behalf to request a favour of you."

The foreign man looked at Cecilia, waiting for her to continue.

"My king, his holiness, has declared a search for the Soulblades. He has tasked his knights with the mission of finding the legendary artefacts and returning them to Holy Bastion. The blades are believed to be scattered around the world—"

Before she could continue, Francis finished her proposal.

"And this is where you need our assistance." Francis walked forward again as the two knights followed.

Throughout the gardens, the various plant life seemed to respond as they got close, turning at them, and twisting around on their stalks as if to dance.

"Correct," Cecilia said. "We require a charter from an Eastern Realm authority. The charter would let us seek out the artefacts that remain in the countries under your banner."

"The blades have begun appearing again, as I am sure you are aware," Sir Baou said. "You know as well as we do exactly what that means."

The magister mulled over the request. Whatever he was thinking, it appeared that he did not like this proposal. It was some time before the nobleman spoke again. "These artefactsss... could you tell me more about them? There is very little in the books."

"It was a surprise when they first appeared," Baou said. "A Nemean city was brought to ruin twenty years ago by a localized seismic quake, the work of one such blade. Centuries of human industry was reduced to rubble in seconds. Thousands of families gone in an instant. We recovered Albion, the blade used to cause the quake, but others with similar powers have manifested over the years. We've been seeking out the weapons within Nemea ever since, though our search has so far been relatively fruitless."

"Save for the weapons the Kingsguard wield. Tell me, how is it that these artefacts have come to be? What is the reason?"

"You know the reason," Baou said.

"Please, we'll have none of those fairytales. I believe only what I can see. Let us change the subject. How many are currently in Nemean possession?"

Cecilia said, "We may be the king's personal guard, but it doesn't entitle us to speak of everything that goes on in Nemea. That information is on a need-to-know basis."

The magister gave Cecilia a deadly stare. She could feel the temperature of the room drop.

"These blades you seek. It would seem to me to be a simple task to spot them. Why have you found so few?"

"It's not that easy. Most of them appear in ruined temples or ancient battlegrounds, but *when* they appear is anyone's guess. We have no idea when a sword will show up. One can search a location fruitlessly, leave, and unknown to us, it could show up there a day later."

"And what will Nemea do with these blades once they're in your possession? You understand that we cannot simply give extremely powerful weapons to other nations, even if they are... *tentatively* allied with usss." The man's tone was vicious and cold now, his accent only making the words harsher.

Baou responded. "It's a public risk to have these weapons waiting to be abused by whatever madman gets his hands on them. We can't have another tragedy. That's our first priority."

Francis placed his jewelled hands together. "Not the only priority, I am sure."

"As to whatever other motives the crown may have, we are not aware of them," Cecilia said.

Francis paced around the fountain, the sound of its streaming water filling the air. He turned back to Cecilia and gave a token smile.

"Very well then, my dear. But I know a liar when I see one. Perhaps this will make you two sing." He pointed at Sir Baou and chanted an incantation, familiar words that Cecilia recognized. She realized it now—the villa guardsmen from before had spoken in a tongue that not even she knew, preparing a latent spell that Francis had now activated.

She tried to rush at the man just a few meters ahead, but her feet would not budge. She could not move her legs, a powerful binding rooting her to the spot.

Her heart raced as she awaited the magister's next move. *I can still move my arms. That's all I need.*

"A pity you Nemean brutes don't know the first thing about hospitality." Francis clapped his hands and gave a smile of genuine delight.

Cecilia darted her eyes to Baou, who was as unmoving as a statue. She looked back at Francis.

"It is my mind domination at work, you see." He turned to Baou. "I'll get the truth out of you, my knight. Now come, kneel before me."

Sir Baou's movements were sluggish. He took slow steps to the young man, grunting in opposition all the way. Baou was a magus himself, and only second in skill to Lorithas the Mindweaver, another of the Kingsguard. Despite Baou's skill, however, the enchantment on him was stronger than he could combat. It wasn't long before he was kneeling before the nobleman.

"Excellent. Now tell me, why is Nemea gathering the Soulblades? What are your plansss?"

Sir Baou's eyes fogged over as he explained. "I don't know. The king has tasked us with retrieving them, but he only entrusts that level of information with Vandar the Red and Cecilia Scarlet. He wishes to bring them together for some purpose. The Soulblades we have collected thus far are wielded by the Kingsguard."

"Who created the Soulblades? What are their powersss?" Francis was hungry for knowledge and spoke savagely.

"We do not know how they were created. As to their abilities, we have learned a few things thus far. There is always a persona within each blade, but we believe they are mere representations of the weapons. An expression of the will within the artefacts."

"Tell me more."

"The blades each house some kind of power, usually unique to them. It takes a great amount of effort, skill, and compatibility between the user and weapon to invoke the powers contained within them. One must first learn the name of their Soulblade to use their power, known as invocation."

Baou answered Francis as fully as he could. Despite this, the magister seemed displeased with something. "That must mean you have a Soulblade, correct?"

"Yes."

"Hand me your Soulblade, Sir Baou."

"I don't have it right now. Cecilia and I decided that it was best that I keep my Soulblade away from this place."

This revelation left the magister with an enraged look on his face. "Why? Why did you decide to do that?"

"We knew from the start that you would attempt to neutralize or otherwise subdue us. Lady Cecilia and I planned for this eventuality. We were especially tipped off when you let us into the villa while armed. To prevent you from taking possession of my Soulblade, we didn't bring it here."

As Baou explained, it dawned on the magister that he had played directly into their trap. He turned to Cecilia to cast his mind domination, but it was too late. The woman had already put her hands on her claymore and brandished it. She swung her sword through the air in a wide, horizontal arc and summoned the power within. "Nemoris!"

A shockwave of invisible force expanded out into the gardens from the tip of the blade as she swung. Complex runes appeared and disappeared in the air as the enchantments nearby were all dispelled. The shrubs, vines, and various plants inside the garden wilted at once, their allure and aroma all but vanished. In seconds, the gardens transformed from a lush green paradise to a lifeless brown.

The spell that had taken hold of Sir Baou was broken, and his body shook with renewed vigour. He stood, after regaining his composure.

"We knew the realms would try to deceive us, so we planned for it." Though the mind domination was broken now, Baou took great pleasure in explaining the magister's folly. "Nemoris. It can break all magic and enchantments within a specified radius. Xerans pride themselves on their leverage over the Arcane arts. With a blade like Nemoris, you are powerless."

As Sir Baou finished his statement, a sinister smile found its way onto the magister's face. Cecilia sheathed her Soulblade back into the scabbard as Francis laughed heartily.

"That is some incredible power," he exclaimed, clapping his hands together once more. "Powerful enough that they needed to be seen to be believed." Francis looked at the knights ominously, his voice becoming stern and calculating. "But make no mistake, Nemeans, those blades will be ours."

CROSSROADS

SEPTIMIAN DYNASTY, YEAR 242
KINGDOM OF NEMEA, WILDERNESS

Taerestris is home to a wide variety of species, cultures, and regions. Of particular note is the distinction between Wingedkin such as Harpies, and the ground-dwelling common folk.

While the common folk comprise such species as the Gnome, Human, and Elf, there exist far rarer peoples such as the Dryad and the Colossal—some of which are exceedingly dangerous.

SIR TANDEM THE YOUNGER
HISTORIA TAERESTRIA

What is that thing?

Tyr's mind raced as he deftly dodged a crumbling rock that fell nearby. His eyes shot up and he gasped as he beheld what now faced him.

The walls at the entrance of the cathedral were being broken into a makeshift opening. He could see a pair of giant hands indiscriminately breaking the wall apart. Tyr attempted to get better view of the creature, but before he had the chance, his pursuer dashed through the broken wall.

There was no time for the boy to calculate the situation—the behemoth's movements were lightning fast. The only thing that he registered was the image of a mighty spear several times his size pointed directly at him. Tyr instinctively rolled forward in order to dodge his assailant, making use of his relatively small size.

Behind Tyr, there was a metal clang, a thud, and the sound of the floor cracking. The boy turned to see the damage. Soot and dust filled the air like a heavy cloud. His enemy was hunched over the spot where Tyr had just been. The giant's entire body was shaking off the recoil of its own attack. It remained hunched over for a moment before it stood and turned to face its target.

Tyr stared in amazement at this mighty creature, which would have passed as a human if not for its prodigious size. It stood four times as tall as the boy and was covered in a full set of ancient armour. The spear held in its hands had two vicious prongs meeting at a point on the end.

I've read about these before, Tyr thought. *This must be a Colossal.*

Suddenly, everything clicked. The cathedral must have been built by colossals, an ancient race of giant humanoids that had once inhabited Nemea, but died out thousands of years ago. Of course, that didn't mean that they were gone entirely; a few colossals still remained, guarding their old treasures and tombs. Tyr knew that the old cathedral was dangerous, and few adventurers had ever dared set foot inside—but he did not expect that a live colossal had been protecting its sacred treasures.

The armoured colossal stared at the boy, perhaps in surprise that he had escaped its first attack. Tyr considered running, but judging from its lightning-fast lunge, he reconsidered.

"My name is Tyr," he spoke anxiously. "1 came here to find—"

The colossal interrupted him. It roared and trained the spear on Tyr, preparing to charge at him once more, squatting like a great cat ready to pounce. In the next few seconds, the mighty creature would take another attempt at ending his life. Tyr's next moves would decide whether he lived or died. He mimicked the colossal and gathered his energy, awaiting the charge. Once the next lunge came, there would be no second chances.

The colossal tore at him again, its spear leading the way. Its movements were so fast that the air whistled behind it.

Tyr sidestepped to the right of the spearhead as far as he could, but the colossal, with its monstrous size, still managed to connect. Tyr had miraculously avoided certain death at the point of the spear; in exchange, he was struck directly at the waist by the giant's metal pauldron. The wind in his lungs left him as he felt the power of the charge; the creature missed its lethal blow, but perhaps this would still be enough to kill him.

The armoured giant continued its charge after it had pinned Tyr to its shoulder. It burst through the double doors of the cathedral as it ground to a halt outside. Tyr's body, now at the mercy of physics, was flung like a ragdoll off the colossal's hulking form. He flew some distance until his body collided with the old stone path.

The armoured creature was not done yet. The ancient colossal, having overexerted itself in this second charge, took an exhausted breath before standing once more and lumbering toward its prey.

Tyr faded in and out of consciousness from the great blow his body had just received. His lungs struggled to breathe in, and he felt sick to his core.

Get up! he thought, as he attempted to will his body into motion. Tyr could hear a rumbling around him, no doubt the movements of the armoured titan that was on its way to finish him off.

I'm going to die if I don't do something. With laborious effort, Tyr pushed himself back on his feet and watched the colossal heading toward him. His body ached with pain as he coughed up blood and attempted to regain his breath.

The giant lurched, tired from the second attack it had launched on the boy just moments ago. The dual-headed spear that came ever closer roused the boy's dazed mind—it was clear that the colossal would not end its assault until the task was complete. Tyr wobbled on the spot, shaking his head.

The colossal gained on him. In his current condition, he could not run, nor dodge this next attack. Tyr had come to the horrifying conclusion that his only option now was to fight. Hopelessly, he removed the glimmering sword he had obtained from the cathedral and raised it at the creature, his hands shaking with anxiety. In his other arm was his red shield, ready for the next hit.

Last words. "Come then," he panted, "if you want this so bad, then you have to take it from me."

The giant lowered itself once more and readied its spear. The colossal would make a third attempt at Tyr's life, and the boy knew there would be no way out this time. He kept the sword raised in a final gambit against the enemy. If he could somehow unlock the fabled power within the weapon, perhaps he still had a chance.

What's your name? his mind raced. No response.

The colossal charged, the air cracking again as the spear raced toward the boy.

Tyr closed his eyes and awaited the spear. His mind wandered now, knowing his life would soon be over. He had felt some level of contentment in the fact that he had found his treasure. His mother would miss him to be sure, but—

"Rime!"

Tyr heard the voice to the left; he opened his eyes as a new scene now unfolded before him. His body wasn't skewered, and he was still alive. In fact, the lunge never connected. A red-caped knight had suddenly leapt between Tyr and his attacker, blocking the spear with an enormous diamond shield. The collision was so powerful that the force of the impact reverberated through the area, shaking the trees themselves.

"Get back, kid!" the knight shouted.

Tyr acted quickly on the opportunity and hobbled some distance away to watch from a place of safety. The knight had negated the colossal's blow, his shield having absorbed the hit entirely. The giant roared in frustration as it recovered.

The man brandished a pristine blade in his left hand. The sword was coated with a sort of red metal, and it bore a resemblance to a traditional Nemean bastard sword.

He raised his weapon heroically.

Is that who I think it is? he wondered, taking note of the Nemean crest on the knight's cape.

The knight took a glance at Tyr before resuming combat with the colossal. The creature was still recovering after its third lunge. The knight took full advantage of this fact and went on the offensive before the armoured behemoth could fully respond. Though the shield in his right hand looked impossibly heavy, he carried it as though it were light as a feather.

The colossal took a quick strike at the knight with its spear. The knight was now too close for the long-range weapon to be effective, rushing through the colossal's legs and making two long slashes of the sword near its ankles. Though the creature was well protected, its armour was crafted for fighting much larger foes. There were small areas of unguarded flesh that the knight took full advantage of. Its ankles damaged, the creature toppled off balance and fell backwards.

The knight made haste in dodging the colossal's falling body. A loud thud went off as it hit the ground, with an even louder groan of pain coming from the fallen enemy.

The knight continued his onslaught. He bolted to the armoured creature's head. The man then raised his sword, aimed it at the colossal's face, and thrust it straight into one of its eyes. The felled brute roared in pain, sending a hand at the knight to knock him away.

"Rime!" The knight yelled, raising his shield once more to block the blow; Tyr noticed this time that the shield glowed brilliantly with the call.

Magic shield. Then this must be—!

After failing this last, desperate attack, the colossal lay on the ground, dazed, its legs now neutralized. Its spear remained on the ground, unable to assist its owner. With the colossal's energy expended, it was easy work for the knight to finish it off. The man placed his red blade over the creature's neck and made a clean, decisive cut. As ghastly as it may have looked, Tyr was thankful that this heroic knight was here to save him. One last groan from the titan sighed through the forest, the final expenditure of its energy. The colossal was defeated. Moments passed. As it died, the overcast skies above finally succumbed and light raindrops fell around them.

The knight sheathed his weapon and walked to the boy. Tyr examined the middle-aged man fully. He wore golden armour. A lion's face was emblazoned on his chest plate. His armour covered most of his body, save for his handsome face. A mane of blond hair flowed down onto his shoulders. Epaulettes bearing several insignias and symbols of Nemea glistened in the light. Behind him, the red cape matched the metals of his sword. He carried his huge diamond shield delicately, completing the ensemble.

Tyr stared, awestruck, at the man who'd saved him.

"Are you …?"

"Vandar."

It is *him, then.* Tyr was well aware of Vandar the Red—his favourite knight of the Kingsguard.

Before Tyr could speak, the golden knight went on, "I trust

you're not terribly injured? I saw you blown clean off those doors by that creature as soon as I arrived. My apologies for not intervening sooner. I certainly would have arrived earlier if there were any way to know a blade would manifest itself here and now."

And knowingly take on that creature? The boy's awe for the knight grew.

"Aren't you scared fighting one of those things?" Tyr asked, eager to learn more about the hero before him. The clouds above them darkened the scene, dulling the knight's golden armour.

The knight smiled warmly at him and responded, "The secret of battle is to know your advantages and limits." He stepped away from Tyr and looked at the colossal. "That armoured giant used a spear, notoriously weak weapons in short range. I simply closed the gap."

"Is that the magic shield?" Tyr pushed, asking as much as he could—it was always his dream to meet one of the Kingsguard, after all.

The knight flourished his heavy shield (impossibly quickly, no less) in front of the boy before speaking. "Ah, yes. Do you know of the Soulblades? This is my weapon. The best offence is a good defence, I say. I merely incant the name of my friend here, and she will absorb any hit. This shield is as unbreakable as my faith."

"The king only mentioned swords in his declaration," Tyr looked at the reddish blade in Vandar's hands, who chuckled.

"There's much the king doesn't mention. As for my own blade here, it's just an ordinary weapon, see?" Vandar swung the blade in the air to demonstrate.

Tyr looked on, starry-eyed and speechless. He felt that his awkward questions would only disrupt the heroic composure of the caped knight.

Vandar sheathed the red sword. "I prefer protecting His Highness rather than going on the offensive. Of course, that doesn't mean I'm one to avoid such an option." He motioned at the giant.

The sun was setting now and darkening the scene, the light drizzle pattering away against the stone of the old pathway.

The man gazed at Tyr's newfound treasure and changed the subject. "Seems the big guy wanted that particular blade badly."

Tyr looked at his weapon, now tucked into its scabbard and wondered if Vandar would ask for it.

Reading the situation, Vandar continued. "Oh, no. I don't intend to take it from you. My orders are simply to make sure that those artefacts make their way to His Highness. I believe we may share the same intent in that regard."

"…Yes, I'd like to give it to the king for the bounty that's being rewarded."

Vandar nodded. "Tell me, boy, where are you from?"

"Silico, sir."

Vandar nodded. "Silico is past the capital. That makes it rather easy for us, then. It seems the rain will not relent, so we should be taking our leave. Come, then, if we are to return that treasure to His Majesty, we should get moving. We won't want to be here when the carvers come for that body."

The realization of what the knight had said dawned on the boy. *Travel with you?* The *Vandar?*

The man was already walking away before the boy could say anything else. The knight spoke again without turning back. "Well? Are you coming?"

CHAPTER 7

VISIONS

SEPTIMIAN DYNASTY, YEAR 242
KINGDOM OF NEMEA, CITY OF PORTIS

Famous for their awe-inspiring spectacles and death-defying stunts, no better entertainment could be found than a gladiator match with the Kai-Jin gladiators.

The dangers were great, but the spoils were even greater, for those few gladiators who survived and succeeded in their gruelling profession acquired both repute and influence.

SIR TANDEM THE YOUNGER
HISTORIA TAERESTRIA

The girl collapsed on the stone bench of the holding room. Rays of the setting sun filtered in through small holes in the dark stone walls, granting low visibility. She could hear the marching steps above her from satisfied people who had seen the performance. The girl dropped her shield and spear to the ground, the clatter of metal resounding throughout. She wore a single pauldron on her left shoulder and black leather armour, standard attire for Kai-Jin gladiators. Blood stained her otherwise spotless body—the blood of her comrades.

"Well, well, well, that's five you took down today. A new record," a voice rang out across the room.

The girl instinctively flinched and turned her eyes to her feet. The man strode across the room toward her. Unlike her, he had no armour, but wore a tight-fitting leather tunic. He had a short, grey beard and a red sash across his chest.

The two were currently in Portis, a city located a week of travel away from Kai-Ji. Every year, Portis held a fair, which included gladiator combat featuring Kai-Jin slaves as the combatants.

The girl did not respond. She shifted uncomfortably in her seat, eyes remaining fixed to the ground. The five years of knowing her master, Guff, mattered little; she had never truly grown to tolerate him. The man came in close and grabbed the girl's chin, forcing her to face him.

"Look at me when I'm speaking to you," he said in a honeyed voice. The acrid smell of his breath hit her nostrils.

"You know, you're a keeper. Untouchable in combat, able to give the audience a real show." He spoke with a malicious grin, brushing aside her short black hair. "And so quick to slaughter your own kind."

The girl pulled his hand off her face and stood defiantly, glaring at him. She was used to Guff's cruel words, but she could not help but feel remorse for the men she was forced to kill for sport.

"I don't want to hear it," she said, her voice heavy.

Guff let out a laugh, knowing his words had cut deep.

"Five years ago, the slave masters sent you to me," he said. "And in those five years, I've given you everything. I've taught you how to live. How to fight. I've filled that empty head of yours with the skills you need to serve. Under my instruction, you have become my greatest warrior. But still, you have never learned to show proper respect."

Though his words dripped with venom, she knew he wasn't wrong. Guff had trained her ever since her vision in the scroll so many years ago. It was Guff who had helped her become a rising star in the bloody tournaments he arranged, all in the name of Lord Rahab, the opulent slave lord of Kai-Ji.

In battle, the girl was untouchable; her feelings, however, were another story. It pleased Guff to expose her where she was truly vulnerable. *See*, he would say, *you're not so invincible.*

"You don't deserve my respect," she said.

Guff grunted. "Your backhanded insults are meaningless. You may think you're special, but you're not. You're just like the dead ones you leave in your wake."

"Bastard," the girl said, her voice shaking, "I'll leave you in my wake soon enough."

Guff frowned and slapped the girl in the face. "Don't threaten me!" he said, taking a step back. Suddenly, a smile crossed his face. "You know, part of an entertainer's role is to give the people a name to cheer for," the man said. "Wouldn't you like a name? Even a dog has a name."

"I'll never accept a name from you," she retorted. Her hand closed into a fist.

Guff laughed again, the horrible laughter that haunted the girl in her every waking moment.

"I have an idea," Guff said. "Since you wish to be a nameless dog, why not sleep with them tonight? Maybe you'll learn some respect."

The girl fell silent. She did not contest her new punishment.

She always did so as her chosen atonement for the brutality she was forced into committing. It enraged Guff when she accepted his punishment without a word—this time, he would deprive her of a bed for the night. The girl gathered her weapons and followed her master back to the barracks.

She awoke with a start some hours later. Her empty belly growled in pain as she came to. The smell of her comrade's dried blood filled her nostrils. She sat on a pile of straw in an animal pen with a wooden fence around it. Nearby were several sleeping fanghounds, beasts of choice for the gladiator fights. Unlike her, the hounds were fed and sated. She could hear music and the chatter of people at the nearby fair, giving her a sense of longing. The full moon shone brightly on the scene as she looked toward the entrance of the enclosure.

She stood and walked to the gate, checking the locks. She pushed the gate forward and it swung open with ease, giving off a tiny *clink*.

Guff had left the gate open for her. *Try to run*, she could hear him say, *you've got nowhere to go.*

The girl decided to take Guff up on this imagined provocation and opened the gate. She looked at the barracks nearby to check that the candlelight in the master's quarters was out before leaving silently.

The dirt path that led to the fair was short. As the girl got closer, she could smell the scent of fried food teasing her stomach. Though she still wore her armour, she would not look out of place here compared to the elves, midgets, multicoloured men, and other strange creatures of the fair. It was not the girl's first time being out alone, but it was always a small taste of freedom when she could find these moments. She had thought many times of escaping her master, but there was little hospitality to be found on Taerestris for Kai-Jin slaves, much less for a trained killer. Tonight, however, she could try to be a regular person.

The girl hungrily eyed the food shops as she walked down one of the fair's lanes. To each side were stands featuring curiosities, such as one which held two dwarves suspended in a bubble in midair, or another that had a man so tall he could easily be mistaken for a giant. The smiling and laughing faces of happy partygoers surrounded her, though it only filled her with a silent longing to have some interaction—any interaction—with such happy people.

She explored the travelling fair for some time; having no coin on her person, she could only watch from afar. She looked on from behind a crowd at a magic show as she rested her tired eyes.

"Having fun?" a tiny voice behind her asked.

It broke the girl out of her stupor. She turned around and saw nothing.

"Down here, sweetheart," said the voice.

The girl's eyes drifted down before spotting an old woman dressed in a purple gown, and an elaborate styling of her white hair that gave her the appearance of a bird. She wore various bangles on her arms and a flashing jewel on her forehead.

Her dark, beady eyes were fixed on the girl.

"Come, come," she said as she raised her index finger. She was pointing behind her, at a small purple tent with a sign above it. Though the girl could not read, she could make out some of the sign:

READ—25 ARGENTS

"Sorry," the girl said. "I don't have money."

"Don't worry about that, dear," the woman said. "I know exactly who you are. I am a psychic, after all."

Who I am?

"Yes," she said. "You were the one who fought in the theatre today. I'm so very interested in doing a reading for you."

The girl frowned, taking no pleasure in the fact that she had been recognized for her violence.

The woman beckoned the girl to come inside once more. "Come, come."

The girl hesitated for a moment before following the psychic into the tent. It was a moment before her eyes adjusted to the dark space. A lone candle on top of a circular table provided dim light. The fabric of the tent featured glowing stars and moon shapes. The insides had various flasks, insects in jars, and strange tomes strewn throughout. The old woman sat opposite the girl and motioned for her to take a seat.

"Now, I usually don't do free readings. But the little spirits tell me you have purpose."

The girl sat on the soft chair, suddenly conscious of how dirty she was. She looked at the old lady. The psychic went to a small table next to her and retrieved a pipe before lighting it and taking a puff. She walked back to the main table and sat opposite her again.

"Give me your hands, if you please," she said with her enchanting voice.

The girl removed her single leather gauntlet and pushed her bare hands toward the psychic. The psychic took them in and closed her own hands around the girl's, feeling her skin. She turned her left hand over.

"Ahhh, what is this?" she murmured, eyeing the sword mark on the girl's hand.

"It happened... in an accident."

The woman caressed the edges of her scar delicately, as though inspecting a valuable gem.

"Hmmm ... five years ago?"

"...Yes." The girl fidgeted uncomfortably. Clearly, this psychic was the genuine article.

The woman took another puff on her pipe. "Oh, now this is interesting... Tell me, child, do you believe in destiny?"

The girl took a moment to answer. Such academic questions were certainly out of the norm for a slave with her lot in life to consider—still, she had overheard much similar talk during her travels as a gladiator, and such concepts always interested her. Still, she did not want to speak out of place before the psychic. "I've never thought about it."

The psychic turned the girl's hand over again and traced out the wrinkles. "What do you believe in?"

"Doing what is right," the girl surprised herself by blurting out.

The psychic made a small humming noise as she took another drag of the pipe. "Hmm... yes... The little spirits tell me much about you. So very much. But it's difficult to hear, noisy as things are."

The woman picked up a nearby beaker with a fuming purple liquid inside. She drank its contents before staring into the girl's eyes. The psychic's own eyes then shook and swivelled in their sockets as she took another puff of her pipe. Tufts of smoke coalesced and formed into dancing figures on the tip of the pipe.

Several of the dancing figures drifted to the girl's pauldron, while one went to the old woman and whispered in her ear.

"Ahhh, I see. A man did appear in an old memory, but this memory is not yours."

The figures now whispered words in an ancient language in the girl's ear. As the figures spoke, the girl saw flashes of memories, both old ones she had experienced and new ones that had yet to be.

"He has a plan for you, a cunning plan, one that is centuries old."

The girl leaned in. The psychic had caught her full attention now. She had never told a soul of the man who had marked her, and yet, somehow, this woman was accurately recounting the details. The little dancing figures were now on her hand, tracing the lines along her palm.

"Yes, it's true; you have a strong desire to do what is right.

Perhaps the strongest of us all…" The psychic leaned into the spirit whispering in her ear. "But there is one thing you still lack." Her eyes stopped swivelling as she stared right into the girl's eyes. "A sacred test. Yes, a challenge you must first complete before your true undertaking. Your body is pure, but your mind is filled with darkness. It must be excised."

The figures drifted to the edge of the woman's pipe as the enchantment started to fade.

"The nameless king is travelling. He rides with his court… seeking brave new subjects. But few will aid him now, with his long slumber and taxing demands. For he demands not coin now, but life. Bodies to build, souls to claim, drunk on promises of adventure and glory. Will you help him?" The old woman spoke slowly, teasing out the spirits' last words. "You will find what you seek at the top of the tallest mountain. But first, you must reunite with… him."

As the figures faded into the air, so too did the girl's visions.

"But be careful, for the way is perilous—and soon you will make your final performance. Be sure that it is not the end of you."

STELLA'S GIFT

SEPTIMIAN DYNASTY, YEAR 242
CITY OF SKYFALL, GRAND PLAZA

The difference between Arcane Magic and Soul Magic is twofold. First, the power of the effect, and secondly, the cost.

With Arcane Magic, one merely chants sacred words and their body acts as a focusing lens for energy that resides in the environment.

Soul Magic is far more powerful—to cast it, users must give up a portion of their life energy.

LORITHAS THE MINDWEAVER
A BASIC GUIDE TO MAGIC

Mordrin worked his way through the nighttime crowd, the full moon above providing ample light to the denizens of the floating city. The seraph moved with confidence, singular purpose on his mind tonight, the object of months of preparation. As usual, he wore his Isthalin armour. He held a glaive with a red ribbon in his arms which made a soft *clink* with every step. He had faced several setbacks, but wide eyes and stern looks were the only obstacles to his progress tonight.

Go on, then, he thought, *make way for the Blackwing.*

Cutting through the busy crowd, the seraph crossed the plaza and made his way down an inconspicuous set of stairs. He descended into a sublevel underground. The atmosphere shifted, regular patrols being the only movement in these old halls. Mordrin moved carefully through a convoluted blend of stairs, walks, and tunnels as he continued his descent. Light was scarce here, for the Skyfall Underground was not a place that was meant to be traversed. The lack of upkeep contrasted the pristine condition of the maintained paths and gilded buildings aboveground. For Mordrin, however, here was away from judging eyes; here was home.

He took great care to move silently, stopping every few minutes to let a patrol move past him. This was not a place where one should be found, especially a commander like him. Thankfully, he had experience to draw upon—having lived in the underground in his younger days, it was a simple task to move silently without drawing the roving guards' attention.

It was not long before the seraph arrived at his destination, an entryway to another seemingly ordinary tunnel. He quickly stepped backwards and crouched behind a corner as he heard two guards approaching from within the tunnel. The seraph strained his ears to listen in on the conversation.

"...I'm not sure what the High Priestess is planning, but those are the orders."

"You know, sometimes I feel like she's gone crazy. First Stella gets exiled, now all these battle preparations? Are you thinking what I'm thinking?"

"Yeah, the commanders go missing for months at a time, then they suddenly show up again before Stella disappears. If you ask me, I think those two left Skyfall on some secret mission and something happened."

"You'd be careful mentioning that to the clergy... but... if we're speaking plainly, it does seem odd. All of the recent orders are."

"No matter. We shouldn't concern ourselves with these things. We can let that blackwing girl hold the fort tonight."

Their conversation faded to nothingness as they left the entrance. A bead of sweat trickled down Mordrin's face as his mind wandered to Stella. Their task had been simple—find and retrieve the blades. It was only after Stella had brought one of the treasures back that she voiced her concerns. Her argument made sense—that the blades reappearing meant that they must be used and not hidden. Going so far as to defect, however? It was madness.

Mordrin knew what was coming—and what he would do tonight was necessary. Getting up, the seraph made his way down the long tunnel before finally reaching its end, a mysterious door covered in markings.

Mordrin's sister waited patiently next to it. The seraph gave a small grin as he approached. What they were about to undertake was expressly forbidden by the clergy, but the siblings had a bond much stronger than their duty to the High Priestess. The plan may have been Mordrin's, but his darling sister had made it all possible.

"Taela," he motioned backwards to the guards that had disap-peared down the hall. "Thank you for that."

Taela smiled at Mordrin as her wings relaxed, revealing the small black markings the Spellseal had inflicted on her. Though the two were both blackwings, when they were alone together in these moments, it didn't matter. Skyfall was a limited area, and some families had to live underground, closer to the toxic magic that allowed the city to stay afloat—such was the fate of the two in their younger days.

Despite their lot, they had proven their prowess to High Priestess Alystra and gained entrance into her Isthalin in adulthood. It gave Mordrin a sense of purpose, fulfilling his duties as Isthalin—but his recent suspicion had given him a new mission. Mordrin knew that Alystra was hiding something—he just didn't know what. Tonight, he would find out.

"I'll ask you one last time, dear brother," Taela spoke, a hint of pleading in her voice, "you're sure you want to do this?"

"I am. The church may specialize in feigning blindness to reality, but it is a specialty of my own to gaze upon the ugly truth. And…" He paused. "This is the only way I can protect you."

Taela smiled at him again, reminding him what he was truly fighting for.

"Very well. Let me open the seal." Taela turned to the door, a slab of stone with various gems inlaid on its surface. She raised her hands and muttered incantations, taking pained breaths as the harmful magic worked its way through her body.

Before the ban, Taela was one of the few practitioners of Arcane Magic in Skyfall, a practice that had accelerated the damage the Spellseal caused to her body. For her, the Spellseal was so advanced that even light use of Arcane Magic caused a reaction. It was a risk to keep using that magic, but one she would take if her brother asked.

Mordrin wanted to look away, but he would not forgive himself if he did. An ethereal circle manifested itself underneath the seraph's feet as she continued her work, unlocking the seals which held the door shut. Before long, the gems on the slab were completely lit, and the door moved aside.

"There we are," Taela said, collecting herself. "Side entrance to the Acropolis. The guards tonight know I'm covering their post. We have a little bit of time before the shift change."

Mordrin nodded. "Shall we?"

The two stepped forth through the doorway and into another dim tunnel. Small blue crystals to each side lit the way, a century of old dust filling their lungs. The tunnel led to a room resembling a library. The room's layout was dizzying, with a multitude of exits and entrances that seemed like the organs of some great machine. The Acropolis housed all the magical experiments and items of old before Skyfall had declared a ban on magic. Rows packed with literature on magic, failed experiments in jars, and various other oddities lined the shelves of the Acropolis.

Taela moved to a row and reached for a trinket resting on a shelf.

"Amazing," she said, examining the item. "I never knew there was so much buried underneath here. You could spend years digging through all this knowledge."

Mordrin smiled. His sister had always been an academic, having spent most of her days in the city libraries, poring over tomes.

"Perhaps another time," he said. "Right now, we have more urgent matters."

"Right," Taela said, returning the trinket to its spot. "I have a tip on our object. It should be this way."

Taela led Mordrin forward along one of the rows for several minutes, taking care not to topple into the messy labyrinth. The two hurried along, a sense of urgency to their step. A cryptic aura permeated the haunting air, and one could hear the slightest movement as the two shuffled on.

Eventually, the row ended, and the duo had reached a small doorway that led to a circular room. The old floor was decorated with concentric circles that matched the walls.

"This must be it," Taela said, announcing their arrival.

"And there it is," Mordrin replied.

Suspended in the air at the opposite end of the room was a

set of sword grips, held aloft by the enchantment of the pedestal beneath it. The grips were small, crafted for use by humans.

"Stella's gift," Taela said, "The boons of her service before she betrayed us."

"It will be enough," replied Mordrin. He motioned for Taela to begin her work.

"I'll need a powerful incantation to tease out the spirit," she said. "Please stand back, brother."

Mordrin made way for Taela as she initiated the spell. She stretched out her arms along with her wings as another ethereal circle appeared on the ground where she stood.

"*Spirit, hear me!*" she began. "*I summon thee to my side and invoke thy blade and thy soul.*" Taela's voice resounded across the cavernous room, aided by the magic of the spell. Bright lines of power emanated from her body, reaching the walls. "*If thou will consent to this contract, answer my call and find thy spirit manifest.*"

The suspended sword grips glowed in response.

"*It is my Oath to thee that I shall free thee from limbo in exchange for thy might.*"

Mordrin looked to his sister, once again forcing himself to watch as her body was damaged by the magical energies coursing through her. Her breathing was hurried. Her wings twitched.

"*I call upon you, accept this sacrifice in both blood and body—O Spirit, come forth!*"

The sword grips shook a final time as the incantation ended. The circle beneath Taela faded out. A shadowy figure had now materialized next to the sword grips, slowly taking form, connected to the grips by a thin, intangible thread. Before long, the figure had manifested completely. The figure resembled a knight, fully geared in black armour, styled in the form of a dragon. Its helmet had a red plume flowing from the top, and two glowing red eyes could be seen between the slits of the helmet. It was unarmed.

"This is a surprise," the knight spoke, a hollow quality to his voice. "I must say, I'm rather disappointed. I wasn't expecting seraphs."

Mordrin moved to the figure, red glaive at the ready. "What is your name, Spirit?"

"Impatient, are we? Why have you summoned me?"

"To have a little chat."

The knight gave no response. Mordrin had thought for months about how to best approach the situation. He had settled on diplomacy as a first policy.

"I'll be direct, Spirit. Our people are dying. Something in this world has… tainted us. The seals on our necks begin a change within, weakening the body and killing its host."

Mordrin tilted his head, showing off the tattoo on his neck. The pallid knight remained unmoving.

"The first appearance of the Spellseal was millennia ago, after the great war with the humans. Given the choice between total destruction and slow torture, we made the only choice we could, and escaped here, to Skyfall. We have been trapped on this forsaken floating city ever since. In that time, this damnable curse has only grown stronger. Some of our kind can no longer use Arcane Magic without triggering damage. Simple exposure to Soul Magic also damages the body." Mordrin spread his wings wide, displaying the black markings near their base. "It works slowly. You see the results."

"An unfortunate situation," the knight said. "But that is no concern of mine. The Soulblades were created by the common folk in order to defend Taerestris against its enemies. That includes your seraphs. What interest do I have in your curse?"

Mordrin paced around the room. The phantom knight would not make things so easy.

"Don't lie to me, Spirit. That ancient blasphemy is somehow related to you and your common folk. I've had much time to ponder it. How is it that the Spellseal only appeared after the war? I have my doubts it is a natural disease. The church and the

High Priestess may deny these claims, but *you* will confirm them."

It was a gamble on the seraph's part, but he was betting that the knight knew something about the distant past. It was commonly taught in Skyfall that the Spellseal had unknown origins, but Mordrin reserved his doubts.

If humans can use such powerful Soul Magic, then why are they not affected by the Spellseal? Why is it only us?

The knight narrowed his eyes. He stepped up to the floating grips and placed his hands on them. "You may have uncovered a piece of the truth, demon. But there is much more to this drama than you could ever hope to know."

Blades appeared from the grips the knight held, taking the same qualities of the knight's ethereal energy. He was looking for a fight.

Mordrin's diplomacy would no longer aid him here. He took a moment to look at his sister. She nodded.

Very well.

"First, I will subdue you," Mordrin said, turning to the knight. "Then you will tell me what you know. The High Priestess and her cohorts wish to lock you away due to their fear of the curse. My old compatriot, Stella, chose to side with the human scum. I see things another way." The seraph readied his glaive at the knight. "What is your name?" Mordrin demanded.

"You'll have to defeat me," the knight said.

"Come, then!"

The knight dashed forward to strike at the seraph.

"Sister, get back!" Mordrin shouted. Taela retreated to watch the scene unfold.

As the knight approached, Mordrin quickly sidestepped to the right, away from the danger. Mordrin readied his counter, a quick thrust of the glaive into the knight's backside. His movements were precise, and his timing impeccable. The glaive made a direct hit and pierced through the knight's body. However, it merely phased through the surface of his armour, as though stabbing empty air.

The knight cackled, his hollow laughter ringing through the ancient halls. "Did you really think it would be so easy? Physical weapons cannot harm me. But you…?" The knight pivoted and slashed Mordrin with his phantom blades, cutting deep into his shoulders. The seraph leapt back as he cried out in pain. The knight gave no mercy and was instantly on Mordrin again, lunging at him with a powerful strike. Mordrin leapt upward with a flap of his wings, ascending into the air and dodging the lethal blow.

"I'll clip your wings!" the knight shouted, as several phantasmal swords manifested above his head. With a wave of his hand, he flung the swords at Mordrin, who quickly rotated his glaive to block the oncoming projectiles. One blade managed to make it through his defences and pierced a wing, blood staining the white feathers.

The knight shot off another salvo; the seraph dropped to the ground and avoided the hit. The projectiles made a clamour as they crashed against the wall.

Mordrin knew this would be difficult, but such a battle was unexpected. The knight could form weapons both from the grips he held and seemingly from the ether itself. He had to devise a new plan.

The knight transformed his weapons again now and formed a long glaive similar to Mordrin's.

The two charged at each other, with the knight aiming straight for the seraph's heart. Mordrin made a quick manoeuvre to sidestep the plunge, aided by the propulsion of his wings. He stabbed forward with his glaive, trained directly on the pallid knight's grips, aiming for the one thing he knew could be tangibly damaged.

The force of the strike was brutal. The knight's glaive disappeared, one of the grips instantly destroyed from the hit. This was the turning point. In this moment of shock, Mordrin made another attack, aimed this time at the second grip. Using his lightning speed, Mordrin connected with his target before the knight could react. In a flash, the knight had fully lost his advantage; the battle was over. Blood from Mordrin's wing spilled to the ground, but it mattered little to him now. He had won.

"It's over," Mordrin said. "Tell me your name." The knight dropped to the ground. The destroyed grips, having now lost much of their power, could not maintain the ghastly knight's body, his form quickly evaporating.

"Only death and misfortune await you, demon," he said, "… but I will keep my word. I am…Bolverk."

"Now, tell me," Mordrin pushed, "what is the cause of the Spellseal?"

The knight shuddered as his cold cackle filled the air. "What good will such knowledge do you? You cannot hope to do a thing about it. But, if you must know… it is an enchantment, cast long ago by the old king of Nemea. Put in place as the king's punishment against the seraph race."

The Blackwing was stunned. He thought of all the mad seraphs, the plight of the curse, and the pain caused to his sister due to the Spellseal. His rage mounted. His tone was vicious.

"What sin could possibly merit such an unconscionable act?"

The knight's final words hung in the air as he faded almost completely. "Losing. Is such a fate not deserved by those who lose in war? Believe me, demon, you will lose… again."

The Blackwing tightened his grip on his glaive. Naturally, he had a hatred of the curse, but its origins had mystified him completely. Now he knew the cause. This was the secret Alystra had hidden from him; from everyone. The seraphs had fought a war with the humans and lost. Details of that great war were always kept in confidence, and it was only known that one was fought. Now Mordrin knew why. For the transgression of defeat, they were cursed with the Spellseal. His anger turned into a desire for vengeance.

"Not this time, spirit," Mordrin said, "This time it will be different."

He nodded to Taela, who cast another magical incantation, preserving the soul of the knight as he faded, the shadowy energy turning into a sphere of pale white light.

"Are we ready?"

"Yes. We should hurry and do this before the guards come," his sister said. "They will have surely heard the commotion. But… brother?"

"It's all right. I have to."

The seraph held the sphere before him in his clawed hand, feeling the power of the felled knight emanating from it. Such vicinity to a powerful source of Soul Magic triggered his Spellseal, and he felt a burning sensation through his body. He knew what he had to do—and that he might perish in the act. Without a moment's hesitation, he crushed the sphere, taking in the power of his defeated foe.

In an instant, the seraph dropped to the ground in pain as his body reacted violently to the overwhelming amounts of energy it was now absorbing. His senses were on fire, the twisting feeling of flames engulfing his body.

"Brother!"

As Taela watched from afar, she could see her brother's transformation take place. Mordrin's wings burned away to tatters, the white feathers darkening to near-black. The seraph's glowing eyes took on a red hue, that of the knight's soul he had defeated.

Mordrin screamed with unspeakable pain, the relentless torment of toxic magic clawing at his veins.

Time ceased to exist. All his mind could manage was his torture, and the thought of his sister. His feelings of vengeance helped to maintain his sanity during the pain—the desire to mete out justice on the hand that wrought the terrible deed upon his people. An eternity passed, and the pain began to subside. Simple recognition of the fact had meant that his mind remained intact. He flexed his fingers and breathed in the dank air of his surroundings. As the seraph slowly stood, he felt newfound strength residing within him. He was alive. Somehow, he had done the impossible. He had conquered the very magic that threatened his people.

He heard a noise behind him.

It was his sister.

She was quivering. "Brother... What have you become?"

COMMUNION

SEPTIMIAN DYNASTY, YEAR 242
KINGDOM OF NEMEA, NEMEAN OUTSKIRTS

The Nemean crown was handed down not by blood right, but by merit; it was Nemean law for the king to adopt an orphan child and groom him as the next in line.

When an adopted heir ascended the throne, they officially claim the surname of their father. Such dynasties lasted hundreds of years, such as that of the Septimian Dynasty.

SIR TANDEM THE YOUNGER
HISTORIA TAERESTRIA

"Welcome back," said the sing-song voice. Tyr felt the same sense of drowsiness as the first time he had entered the world within the blade. The boy opened his eyes in anticipation of the view before him.

"Hello."

The girl smiled at him as the two examined one another. She looked the same as the first time Tyr had met her, only now she sat on her antique chair properly. The two were once again in the undefined white space of his mind, nothing to distract them from their conversation.

"I see you have a new friend. He's very nice."

"Sir Vandar is amazing! Do you know him?"

The girl leaned back on her chair. She twirled her onyx-black hair. "I know everything you know," she said delicately. "I'm thankful he has protected you so far."

"He says you won't talk to him."

"He's not interesting to me. Not like you."

Tyr looked away in embarrassment. "So… how do you know what I know?"

"You and I, we are connected now. You can hear me out there, too. In your head, remember?" The girl pointed to her temple.

I suppose that makes sense. Why haven't I heard you, then?

The girl smiled. "That's simple. I'll speak to you when the time is right."

The boy furrowed his brow. Though the two had just met, he was still frustrated that she hadn't answered his call during his fight with the colossal. Regardless, he felt it unwise to bring up such a topic with her now.

"So… what do you do here?"

"Watch you, mainly. Before that, you already know. Waiting for someone to find me. Sleeping." The girl's look became wistful, prompting Tyr to speak again.

"Well, we're going to be together for a little longer. What's your name?" he asked, pressing the delicate question before he could hesitate.

The girl stood from her chair. She folded her arms as she addressed him again. "Tell me," she said. "Do you know the purpose of the Soulblades?"

Tyr contemplated the question. There were the usual myths and legends that circulated about the artefacts, but the boy was starting to believe they were much more than mere stories.

"Their purpose is... *to protect the world a'round*." He recited the famous poem.

"Yes, that's part of it." The onyx-haired girl walked in a circle around Tyr. "There are many others like me, in different shapes and sizes. The one thing we all share in common is our function."

"Function?"

"Precisely. When you know my name, you will know the power of the king. But such power comes at a cost. Do you know what that is?"

Tyr stood bewildered for a time, racking his brain as he recalled his studies. "All magic needs an energy source. The cost of a Soulblade's power is..."

"Your own soul. Your very life energy." She was now behind the boy. She continued. "I wouldn't wish a toll like that on anyone, lest they misuse it. Our powers eat away at the remaining years of life you have left, little by little. Eventually, you die."

The girl's grim statement sent a chill down Tyr's spine.

She paced around and back to her chair. "I won't risk your life just so you can play the hero. I rather enjoy your company."

"But Sir Vandar said I should try to get your name. What should I tell him?"

"Whatever you want." She reseated herself on the chair and folded her legs together. "My only cares lie with you."

The boy's cheeks flushed red again; the girl chuckled.

Who knew Soulblades were so finicky? "But why me?"

The girl laughed again. "Because you're different. You're not like the others. I know that you won't let me down."

Tyr looked at the ground, mulling over their conversation.

Let her down how?

The situation was certainly complicated. Vandar had asked him to discover the name of the weapon, but so far, the girl was not willing to comply. Moreover, he was quickly becoming friends with the spirit in the sword. The idea of turning her in to the king felt like a betrayal, both of her and of himself. He'd always wanted to be a great hero like his father was—and a great hero needed a great weapon, after all. In his heart, he wondered if he could somehow hold onto his treasure. His mind was a jumble of worry, desires, and fears.

"I think I'm ready to go back," he said finally.

"Already?" she pouted.

"Sir Vandar won't want to be kept waiting."

"Very well, then. You may go. Come back soon, Tyr."

He nodded.

"Make sure that you do. Otherwise, I may go up there and bother your thoughts."

The boy felt himself being whisked away again, his vision of the girl blurring out and his consciousness dimming to darkness once more.

"Still alive, eh?" Vandar's now-familiar voice asked.

Tyr looked around groggily, gathering his bearings. He shook himself out of his stupor. The two were located at an inn on the outskirts of the royal capital of Nemea. They had been travelling for several days and had finally arrived near their destination the previous night. The boy shook his head again as he took in his surroundings—a wooden room with basic amenities.

"How long…?"

"Just a few minutes. You get used to it, don't worry. It was the same for me when I started." The knight stood and paced around the room. Like the girl, Vandar seemed to know exactly what was on the boy's mind—unlike her, it was not due to magical insight, but the wisdom of experience. "You're developing quite the relationship with that weapon. Are you certain that's the best idea? You'll need to part with it for your reward."

Tyr's face turned sombre, unable to express his emotions. It was true that he had become fond of the blade that he now held in his hands, but he did not forget the entire reason he had undertaken such a dangerous task. It had been a year of travelling, and he imagined his mother was eagerly awaiting his return.

"Tell me," Vandar asked, "What is your profession?"

"I don't have one. My father was… gone by the time I could learn to work. But Mother did teach me how to mend fabrics and knit."

"A tailor! You probably know this, but I was an orphan as a child. King Remus found me at the ripe age of five and took me in."

Tyr nodded. It was strictly forbidden for a Nemean king to have a blood child; instead, they had to adopt an orphan and groom them as next in line. In King Remus' case, he had adopted two children—the first being Vandar the Red, and the second being Cecilia Scarlet, the Iron Wall. The resemblance between Vandar and Remus was always uncanny, however, and it led to mass speculation among the citizenry of Nemea.

"I started as a smith in my younger days. I hated the damned job, but the king always insisted it was to make me strong—I suppose I have him to thank for my ethic." The knight moved to a window, the city of Nemea in the distance. "When the king demanded I learn to fight, it became an even greater challenge. I hated the idea of harming people, and I was worse with a sword than with a hammer."

Vandar stepped over to a wooden table, his diamond shield, Rime, resting over it. He lifted it easily and inspected its flawless beauty.

"One day, I picked up a shield. It was then that I felt something within me, something calling out. The thought of protecting the ones I love, that was what gave me strength. The philosophers speak of finding one's true calling in life—in my case, I felt it quite literally." Vandar looked to Tyr now, his stern face increasing the tension. "You've found a powerful artefact. One that wishes only for *your* company. I doubt it's a coincidence. Tell me, do you feel that calling? The same calling that I feel every time I raise Rime?"

Tyr considered Sir Vandar's words. He thought of his father's bedtime stories and the great feats he had accomplished in the military. He could feel Ulfric's presence in everything he did. His own calling was rather simple: to be like his father. It was why he was fascinated with his idols, knights of the Kingsguard like Sir Vandar, Sir Baou, and Sir Waine.

"I think I've felt… something like that for a long time. Even before all of this."

It was why he had not tossed aside the gleaming blade and run once he had encountered the colossal. Somehow, Tyr felt that he could live out his dream of being a virtuous knight—and the spirit in the blade was the one who would help him do it. Tyr gripped the handle of the sword tightly, picturing the girl smiling at him.

"I'd like to be like you. I'd like to protect the ones I care about."

Vandar nodded. "If you truly feel that calling, then you'll need to learn how to fight properly, to think and live like a warrior. It may take some convincing His Majesty, but I have no doubt you'll impress him." Vandar lowered his shield and folded his arms. He faced Tyr once more. "It won't be easy, you know. The life of a warrior is nothing regular. It's hard, it's messy, and bad things happen. There may come a time you might have to make a sacrifice for the greater good. Or a time you may have to leave your own family behind for the sake of duty. Think of what your father left behind. It must not have been easy for you. Are you sure you could do the same to a child of your own? To someone who needs you?"

Vandar's face tightened, his features becoming more en-
hanced. His blue eyes looked at the boy with a certain fierceness,
one that Tyr had never seen before. This was the strength of his
conviction. "Tyr, knowing this, are you truly prepared for that? To
walk the path of the warrior?"

The boy's hands shook. He was sure of it now. The man in
front of him was the example. His fierce composure, his endless
bravery, and the power to help those who needed it. He wanted
it all.

"Yes," he said. "Teach me."

SNEAK OUT

SEPTIMIAN DYNASTY, YEAR 242
KINGDOM OF NEMEA, CITY OF KAI-JI

Slavery in Taerestris was a hotly contested subject, both among slave kings looking to maintain their dominion and abolitionists seeking to end the industry.

While in Nemea, slavery was an accepted facet of life, the practice had been all but eradicated in the east due to the industrial revolution taking place within the realm's nation-states.

SIR TANDEM THE YOUNGER
HISTORIA TAERESTRIA

"All right, maggots. There's no time to waste tonight, so pick out your weapons," Guff's voice roared from within the building, prompting his gladiators into action.

The group was in the Kai-Ji armoury, situated directly beneath the fighting theatre known as The Pit. Guff had brought a handful of his warriors to the stadium for a special show. Every year, Kai-Ji hosted a gladiator match in the centre of the city, entertainment for the slave king, Rahab. Visitors flocked from all over Taerestris to the yearly performances; even nobles from the Eastern Realms would attend. The spectacle was not to be missed.

"Remember, you may pick up to two," Guff said.

The underground armoury was vast, with weapons hanging from the ceiling, pieces of armour resting on the walls, and various trinkets in wooden crates. Every few moments, thunderous vibrations made by excited attendants in the arena above shook the walls. Cheers and screams accompanied the spectators' stomping feet, the ceremonies having already begun.

Behind Guff, his lone female gladiator was inspecting the various weapons scattered across the armoury in uninterested fashion. She never took such matters lightly, but she had no idea what she would face that day and had decided to avoid the stress of guessing.

"Sir," a boy asked, "what will the challenge be today?"

Guff looked to the warrior, no older himself than the girl. "Today's challenge is a special one just for you maggots. I won't spoil the surprise, but I can tell you one thing." Guff raised his index finger. "You won't be fighting among yourselves tonight. Whether that is to your advantage or not is for you to decide."

The tension in the room was palpable, but it rose to fever pitch with this revelation. Gladiator matches between trained individuals were one thing; an unknown threat presented more deadly possibilities. In response, one of the recruits picked up the largest shield he could lift. Another went for a long spear from a stand.

The girl kept moving, finding none of the weapons satisfactory. She shifted to a section of the armoury labelled 'MAGICAL ITEMS'. Her colleagues looked at the girl now, bewildered by her actions. It was not that magical items were not useful; rather that none of the gladiators had been properly trained to wield them.

"Eh?" Guff started, taking note, "What are you doing there?" He made his way to the girl.

"I'll take this." She held out a scroll.

Guff looked at the object—it was covered in golden trim with blue ends. The man laughed. "You never cease to amaze me, girl. Your stupidity knows no bounds. That scroll is for the Sortition. Just what do you hope to achieve with such a thing?"

The girl looked defiantly at him. She had made her decision. The scroll was placed in the armoury whenever it wasn't being used for the Sortition ceremony; she had held it many times before, during quiet moments in between training. She always stared into its blank centre, hoping to have another vision and meet the old man she had encountered years ago—sadly, nothing had ever come of it. The girl did not understand how the magic of the scroll worked; only that she desired to meet the man again, the one who had gifted her with the scar on her left hand.

"I'll not have my most valuable asset fighting out there, unarmed. Keep your useless scroll, but at least take this," Guff said, throwing a small dagger at the girl.

It was a rare moment of empathy from Guff, but the girl savoured it, nonetheless. Despite whatever insults he threw at her, she knew that she was the reason Guff's career as a trainer had skyrocketed in fame. She accepted the dagger without hesitation, sheathing it within a pocket on her toolbelt. The scroll was enclosed in a sort of metal cage, allowing the girl to attach it to the other side of her toolbelt.

"Ladies and gentlemen, welcome to The Pit!" a booming voice went off above ground, the opening ceremonies now complete.

Another quake from the cheers of excited spectators reverberated through the walls.

"Time to go," Guff said. He led the gladiators out onto a set of stairs. "Keep your heads on. This year's challenge is quite the surprise."

The group was led up through the set of stairs and above ground to a holding cage. The girl's eyes adjusted from the dark underground to the flickering torchlights that illuminated the night above. The Pit was enormous, and the girl could see thousands of people on wooden stands cheering for the main performance. More torches lined the outskirts of the dusty arena, providing uneven light for the match ahead.

Far away, she could see Lord Rahab seated to the centre of the stands, watching impatiently. He wore a regal robe made of exotic materials. The sight of his uninterested visage made the girl's blood boil, and she closed her fists in rage. She had only seen Lord Rahab a few times in her life, but the thought of him always made her livid. *If not for people like you, maybe things would have been different*, she would think.

"We are pleased to announce the main event!" the booming voice went off again, an enchantment allowing the commentator's sonorous voice to rumble above the roar of the crowd.

The girl was uneasy, having never performed before such a large audience. She was used to fighting in the theatres by now, but the packed stadium offered even greater pressure to put on a good show.

"But first, let's meet our champions. Open the gates!"

The iron gates that enclosed the gladiators made a pained grinding sound as they rose and gave entrance to the arena.

"Good luck out there," Guff said to the group. "You all know the stakes. Don't make me look bad."

The girl stepped out along with her fellow gladiators, the crowd going wild at their appearance. She took a closer look at the patrons of the event, mostly noblemen and wealthy individuals. The lightness of their skins revealed just how different they were from her—none of them had toiled in the hot sun day in and day out.

She checked the second iron gate at the far end of the stadium, looking for clues as to what they would encounter.

Empty. The absence of an enemy only served to increase the girl's tension. The cheers of the crowd continued as she took several deep breaths to regain her composure.

"And what will they face today?" the commentator asked.

The crowd cheered in response. Suddenly, the ground below the gladiators shook violently, throwing the girl off balance. She scanned the arena for the source as she recovered, but saw nothing. A second thud shook the ground.

"Ladies and gentlemen, we are pleased to bring you—"

The ground at the far end of the arena collapsed, and the cause of the shaking revealed itself at last. From beneath the ground, a gargantuan white-furred behemoth rose into view, giving off a blood-curdling roar.

The girl's ears rang from the force of the sound as she took stock of the creature in front of her.

"Whitefang the Terrible!"

The crowd threw itself into a frenzy of screams and applause for the beast that now faced the gladiators. The creature resembled a yeti, resting on its hind legs and front knuckles. It had vicious jaws and red eyes that bore into the gladiators with cold fury. It was nearly as tall as the arena walls themselves, its monstrous size only adding to the delight of the onlookers.

"Will our champions prevail? Or will Whitefang rule this day?"

"What do we do?" one of the boys shouted.

Good question.

"Split up," another shouted. "Go for its neck when it charges!"

"Can we even reach the neck?" asked yet another.

The girl backed off and looked around the stadium, examining the situation.

Too big to take on, she thought, *even if we all strike at once.* Her thoughts were interrupted by a scream from the yeti as it slammed the ground and threatened the opposing gladiators.

Visibility was difficult, the blazing stars of torchlight providing only a modicum of vision.

"Begin!"

The yeti charged forward with blinding speed. The group scattered, escaping the creature's range. One unfortunate boy was caught dead centre of the charge and was instantly pinned to a wall. The wood of the arena wall made a splitting noise as the yeti's impact nearly crushed it. The sound of crunching bones erupted from the boy's body, and his corpse dropped limply to the ground. The yeti made a terrible scream, its bloodlust taking hold.

"First casualty! An instant kill!"

The crowd jeered. The yeti swivelled around to a pair of gladiators as it prepared for a second charge.

Damn it, the girl thought, *we don't stand a chance against that thing.* She looked up at Rahab the slave king, his uninterested look on full display. She quivered with rage.

You brought us out here to die.

The yeti rushed at a pair of boys, this time swiping with its powerful arms as it charged. One of the boys was crushed instantly, the other managing to swing out of the way just in time. He made a quick prod with his spear at the yeti's hand, but it simply brushed him aside and flung him to the ground at the far end of the stadium.

"Another one falls!"

The girl considered her options. She looked to an edge near the stadium. When the yeti had broken out of the ground, it had left an opening there, connected to the stadium's sublevel. She could run toward it, but the yeti was fast enough that it could chase her down and trample her if she caught its attention.

As though reading her mind, the yeti turned to face her. It made its signature ground-slam with its hand, and she knew she was next.

Damn it, what do I do? The girl had fought many times before, and while it was true that she had bested all her opponents, she had never faced such overwhelming odds. She backstepped, a rising feeling in her chest as her legs shook. She could feel it now, that terrible emotion—fear.

Suddenly, she heard a familiar voice inside her head that made her heart skip a beat.

"You can't fight it. But you can still survive. Follow my instruction."

You! she thought. She recognized the voice in an instant, that of the man she met in her vision years ago. She focused intently now; the roar of the crowd on one side, the voice of her unusual ally on the other.

"Dodge underneath it, keep your head down."

The yeti charged at the girl, knocking aside another boy in the way. She lowered her frame and prepared to move.

One moment, the yeti was at the far end of the arena, the next, the girl felt the giant rushing overhead. She had dropped down and gone right between its legs during the charge. She narrowly avoided the yeti's tremendous bulk, wind from its charge buffeting her in its wake. Another splintering sound went off behind her as the yeti collided with the wooden wall.

"Kai-Ji's first female gladiator! An incredible dodge!" the commentator screamed.

The crowd went wild, cheering for the girl's miraculous survival.

What now?

"The cracked wall."

The girl looked to the damaged wooden wall, the area the yeti had slammed into earlier when it had crushed one of the boys. She had some idea of the plan now. Though she was unsure it would work, she could not afford to consider the matter further. She rushed to the broken wall and positioned herself in front of it. The giant charged at her again with renewed ferocity.

Her mind went blank. All that remained was the raw, animal instinct that coursed through her as time slowed. Once again, she moved out of harm's way as the yeti rushed past, the wind left behind by the speeding yeti bowling her over. Another ear-splitting crack went off behind her as the wooden wall of the arena was completely dismantled by the yeti, now leaving nothing in between the enraged creature and the crowd of spectators.

The girl's eyes darted to the audience. Their jovial faces had transformed into sheer horror as they realized what came next. The yeti pounced on the crowd, crushing several noblemen underfoot and swinging with its wide arms at several more.

"Whitefang has escaped! Whitefang has escaped the arena!"

The cheering from the audience morphed into screams of terror as the crowd stampeded to the arena exits in panic. Rahab barked orders as his guards surrounded him in defence. The other gladiators fled in various directions, some after the yeti through the broken wooden wall and some back through the iron gate.

"Toward the far side. Quickly now."

The girl sprinted to the other end of the arena to the empty iron gate. Before her was the hole in the ground that the yeti had emerged from, which connected to a stairwell. She paid no heed to the yeti rampaging behind her and silently dropped into the opening.

Dashing down the steps, she arrived at the stairwell landing. She took a few tense moments to collect herself, the sounds from the mayhem above keeping her on alert.

The underground room was twice as large as the armoury on the other side of the stadium. These were the animal pens, where caged creatures were held for upcoming matches. The cages were currently populated with fanghounds and weretigers, vicious animals when left unfed. The ruckus above alerted whoever had been keeping guard of the pens, and they were left completely barren of people.

Sensing an opportunity, the girl scanned the room before spotting what she was looking for—the cage keys. Taking them, she opened the starved animals' cages. The blood scent of the carnage above lured them up through the stairwell and into the arena. In moments, she heard their vicious growls and pounces, mixing with the screams of the attendants.

"*Keep moving,*" the man's voice ordered her.

The girl ascended a second set of stairs, eventually opening to the outside of the arena. She took stock of the mayhem around her. Though it had only been a few moments, the escaped animals were already running loose through the city, massacring slaves and attacking their former captors. The animals were in a frenzy, tipping over boxes of supplies and torches. The people in the city could be heard screaming and running in panic, some of them in the throes of death, the handiwork of the girl's uncaged animals. Her heart was pounding, but now was not the time for rest.

"*Forward,*" said the voice, bidding her to take advantage of the disarray.

The dark of night cloaked Kai-Ji, the only visible light being that of the torches toppled over by the animals. She darted to the side streets and avoided the chaos in the main roads, making progress on her route to the edge of the city. Using the blanket of night as cover, she moved silently, the voice in her head urging her on. She moved to cross a deserted road but halted her progress as a pair of guards and a captain moved onto the scene. The girl pressed her back to the wall of a building and listened in on the conversation.

"How did this happen? How did the animals escape?" the captain barked.

"That woman gladiator, sir, it was probably her—I saw her run into the holding pens," a guard replied.

"You mean to tell me a girl did all this?" the captain shouted, his rage getting the best of him.

"We don't know, sir, but the animals are tearing the city apart," the second guard said.

"Forget the damn animals. Find the girl, and kill her *now*," the captain commanded, "She should still be wearing her armour; they're easy to spot. They have a spiked pauldron on the left shoulder."

The girl caught her breath as the guards split up in search of her. She could hear one of the guards hurrying down the dark street to her current hiding spot.

"Patience. Your opportunity will come."

As the guard rounded the corner, he inspected the opposite side of the road. Taking advantage of the situation, the girl lunged at the man and wrapped her arms around his neck, placing him in a crushing hold. She held on firmly, her unnatural strength allowing her to overtake the man's best efforts. In the struggle, the guard was able to pull a dagger from his belt, and stabbed her, inflicting a gash on her left forearm. A surge of agony radiated through the girl's body, but her manic high was enough to act as a painkiller while she choked out her victim.

Their silent scuffle continued for several moments before the man convulsed, the absence of air finally limiting his energy. With a last shudder, he fell to the ground, incapacitated. The girl took a moment to hide the body behind the building before continuing. The gash on her arm dripped a trail of blood behind her. She had received wounds before, and her fast recovery always followed; this latest injury would be no different.

"Keep moving," the voice implored again.

She obeyed silently.

Traversing the city became an easier job the farther she got from the centre. Far back in the distance, the wooden stadium had caught fire—a blazing pyre of the girl's creation. The sounds behind her also grew distant as she moved away from the action.

Ahead, the girl could spot the metal portcullis that closed off the city of Kai-Ji with the outside world. To each side of the portcullis was the beginning of the wall that enclosed the entire city. It doubly served as defence from invaders and as an impediment to would-be escapees. Fortunately for the girl, the gate was still open. Her only obstacle was a final guard, situated directly in front of the portcullis.

"Who's there?" The guard had spotted movement in the

shadows, but it was difficult for him to make out any shapes in the night. The guard moved closer to the source of the disturbance, a deadly spear in his hands, pointed in her direction.

The girl had to backtrack.

"Behind the cart," said the voice, directing her to a hay cart nearby.

She crouched behind it, taking care not to make any sudden noises. The guard walked forward, his back to the girl. Once again, she was in an advantageous situation, the guard's attention directed to the empty road ahead of him.

Though she would have preferred to incapacitate the second guard like the first, she knew the gash on her left arm had left it too weak to function. Thinking instinctively, she pulled out the dagger Guff had given her and took a deep breath. She snaked out of the cover of the cart and sneaked up on the man. The next moment, she plunged the dagger directly into his neck.

The guard did not have a chance to react before his body gave up on him. He fell to the ground like a rag doll, blood gushing from the wound. He attempted to breathe, but this only made more lifeblood spill out onto the ground, the dirt below soaking it up like a sponge.

The girl was in shock. Though she had killed before, this was different; this time, she had just willingly taken a life.

What have I done? she thought.

"Don't stop now."

She complied with the command; no matter how she felt about it now, she would have to think on it later. She turned away from the dying guard and ran to the portcullis. Without a moment's hesitation, she bolted through the opening and reached the outside of the city. The border was empty now, with all the other guardsmen having gone to combat the flames of the stadium. The area outside of the walls was a stark contrast to Kai-Ji's innards—while the city itself was primarily made up of dusty roads and workshops, the exterior was covered in natural wildlife, farmlands, and a dark forest directly ahead of her.

The girl kept moving. The only desire on her mind was getting as far as possible from the city now. She ran into the forest, hoping the mishmash of trees would help cover her tracks. She ran for what felt like hours, not giving herself time to think. Eventually, her battle-high wore off, and the pain in her arm grew more pronounced. Her eyes burned with exhaustion. The light of the surrounding forest had turned from a deep black to a still grey¾it would be morning soon.

"This is far enough."

The girl shambled to a nearby tree and collapsed in front of it, her aching body having reached its limit.

"What... what *are* you?" She raised her hands to examine them, trembling as they were. Was it all real? Had she…?

"I apologize for all of this. It was not yet time."

The girl breathed heavily, recovering her energy. The last few hours felt like a dream, but she knew better. "Why did you never talk to me?" Tears streamed down her tired face. She recalled the countless times she'd tried to relive that experience in the scroll. "You said I wouldn't be alone."

"I'm sorry, my dear. But you'll never be alone again."

The girl closed her eyes and tilted her head up, the shock of her escape finally setting in.

"What's your name, girl?"

She had thought about this question ever since her first encounter with the man, always unable to come up with an adequate answer. She felt that any name she gave herself would be a betrayal, like running from her past.

She could not forget all the Kai-Jin she was forced to kill, all the torments of her former masters in the name of the city. The girl had decided, however, that she would not run from her past. She would wear it proudly, and all would know what she represented.

"Kai," the young woman said. "My name is Kai."

CHAPTER 11

TANDEM

SEPTIMIAN DYNASTY, YEAR 242
KINGDOM OF NEMEA, NEMEAN CAPITAL

No tale involving the great Sir Tandem would be complete without an introduction of yours truly. Herein I shall inform you, dear reader, of the highlights of this dramatis persona.

Sir Tandem Taeshelon the Younger, born of Doris, was an orator, entertainer, bard, historian, poet, and lover of women, wine, and adventure. Though primarily lauded as the author of several great pieces of eminent literature, he was as notorious for his skill with the quill as he was with the fine damsels of Taerestris.

Fate often chooses to mingle with us on the precipice of life and death, and it is on a similar such occasion that Tandem the Bard would first meet Tyr Lancelt.

SIR TANDEM THE YOUNGER
TALES, VOLUME I

Vandar the Red halted in his tracks, bidding Tyr do the same. Dawn broke over the spires of Nemea, the capital, which the country was named after. Though the city's silhouette had been visible for days, the two had finally arrived at its entry point. The clamour of thousands of individuals journeying in and out of the city filled the air.

The duo was currently near a bridge on the borders of Nemea. At the centre was Holy Bastion, the tallest structure in the country, an impressive display of Nemean architecture and engineering. While a traditional city might defend itself with walls or moats, Nemea's natural defence was comprised of deadly cliffs on every side of the city.

Hundreds of bridges connected Nemea to the outside world. The bridges were teeming with merchants, caravans, politicians, and families. The bridge Tyr and Vandar were situated at featured an expertly detailed archway. Engraved across it were the words:

NEMEA: FIRST AND LAST HOPE OF TAERESTRIS

"Beautiful, isn't it?" the knight asked.

Tyr nodded, awestruck by the sight. From here, the city resembled a wheel on its side with hundreds of spokes connecting to its central hub. Vandar made his way through the crowd, leading Tyr over the bridge and into the city. The packed bridge took some time to traverse, and in the meantime, Tyr appreciated the view. He leaned over a railing and looked down at the cliffs below.

"Watch yourself," Vandar said. "It's quite a drop."

The two eventually reached the other side of the bridge, entering the city proper. Roads crisscrossed from their location leading into a network of streets, throughways, and back alleys. The two broke free from the crowd clogging the bridge entrance and moved to the buildings ahead, allowing Tyr to get his bearings.

"Welcome to Nemea."

The boy gazed at his surroundings, taking in its splendour. The first thing he noticed was the height of the buildings. Countless marble columns and stone towers rose into the sky, piercing it with their tops. The cobblestone roads were immaculate, with gardens and statues lining every street. In the distance, Tyr could see Holy Bastion, the Nemean seat of power, towering over the city. The hum of people going about their daily tasks mixed with the playful cries of children. Beneath him, he could feel the rumbling of thousands of feet shuffling along the city's street network.

Engravings on the side of each building denoted the street and corner. Navigation was made easier by following the crowd, which moved ever inward toward Holy Bastion. Bells rang out in the morning air, playing welcome notes and little jingles. The smells were incredible. Tyr picked up a new scent every few streets: potent alcohol and fruity beers from dozens of distilleries, meats and spices from local shops, and bread from packed bakeries. Street vendors lined the roads, eager to sell their wares. Much of the food was exotic, coming from the Eastern Realms or lands beyond.

Among the street vendors' wares, he recognized: pan-seared norfish, boiled kippary eggs with plum sauce, pepper poppers that exploded in your mouth, pies filled with everlasting ice cream, sour treacle sticks, salmon fillets with lemony drizzle, jams of every variety, baked chicken with Elfire-roasted potatoes, marble pudding, Xeran cheese curds, sugar-glazed tiplings, Galvador delights, and shimmering glass truffles. Vandar, noting Tyr's hungry eyes, stopped at several vendors along the way to have him try some of the food.

Tyr knew from his studies that the sheer magnitude of Nemea made it the largest city in the world, home to over one million inhabitants; its scale was a testament to the craftsmanship and longevity of human dominion over the land. Not even Nexus Calia, the capital city of Xeras, compared to the vastness of Nemea.

"What do you think?" Vandar asked.

"It's amazing. I've never seen anything like it."

Vandar smiled. As the two walked, passersby stopped in their tracks to wave and bow at Sir Vandar, Tyr feeling the looks of envious young boys and girls upon him.

"Don't worry, you get used to it," Vandar said.

The two continued through the city. The knight took the boy on a tour of the more famous locations, the most impressive of which were the various cathedrals, towering structures that could easily fit thousands within their walls. Glass treated with multi-coloured dyes shone brilliantly in the sun, depicting the Eternal Dragons of legend on the sides of the structures. Rounded domes and miniature lions sat on the tops and corners of public build-ings. Statues of Nemean royalty stood in courtyards and gardens along with busts of ancient Kingsguard knights. Beautiful foun-tains with sparkling white water and ancient trees decorated the common areas, symbols of the country's power and status.

"Tell me, Tyr, have you heard of The Vault of Kings?"

"I've only read about it. The vault contains the royal arms of the old kings of Nemea. It's situated beneath Holy Bastion."

"Just so. Normally, we don't let visitors inside. But I can take you there now if you'd—" Vandar turned away.

Sounds of a riled crowd could be heard several streets over, the citizens nearby running to the cause of the commotion. Vandar instinctively brandished his sword and shield as he beckoned Tyr to join him. As the two closed in on the source of the trouble, the voices of the crowd became clearer.

"Hang the bastard!" said a voice from afar.

"Fight, fight, fight!" chanted another.

The knight and the boy crossed a final street toward a plaza. There they found a throng of people gathered around a raised plat-form with wooden gallows. The platform was tall enough that all in the plaza could see the events unfolding. Vandar and Tyr spotted two people standing upon it. To one side of the platform was a man in noble's clothing, pointing his silver rapier at his opponent. The man at the other end wore a green leather tunic, sported a feathered cap, and held a wooden lute in his hands as a shield.

"It is true!" said the man with the rapier, waving it wildly in the air.

"This heathen has besmirched the name of my clan! Imagine Ophelia, my darling sister, Ophelia. You sneak into her home like a thief in the night and sully her honour!"

The crowd gasped in shock. The man with the feathered cap turned to the crowd.

"No, my friends! It's not what you think! Imagine a woman in plight… the loss of her dearest pet hound sending her into sheer despair! Imagine the hysterics! The fits! I merely gave a woman in need the comfort she required!"

"By lying with her?" the nobleman responded. "Vermin, my dearest sister has told me everything! She wants nothing more than to see her honour restored… and it shall be done!"

"She must have been lying!" the man in green shouted. "I know she would not want this to be the end of me… Of her saviour!"

The crowd booed at the man with the lute, his explanation having little effect on their disposition towards him.

The nobleman pointed at the gallows between them. "I have given you a choice, criminal, which is far more than you deserve. The gallows will mete out justice for my dearest Ophelia! That is, if you cannot handle matters yourself!"

"With all due respect, sir, your sister seemed quite satisfied with my handling!"

The crowd laughed at the nobleman, who was all but enraged now. He moved his rapier and prepared for a lunge when Vandar's voice boomed above the noise of the mob.

"That's enough!" he shouted, pushing the horde of people aside as he moved to the platform. "What have you got yourself into?" he asked the man in green.

Hushed whispers rattled through the plaza. Tyr heard them

perfectly: "That's Vandar the Red! The Kingsguard is here!"

The nobleman paused, looking nervously at Vandar.

The man in green looked incredulous as the knight stomped toward the platform. "Vandar!" he shouted. "H-he's my champion! He will duel you!"

"There will be no duels today," Vandar said. "Please move along, folks."

The crowd quickly dispersed, obeying the knight's commands without a second thought.

"But my family's honour!" the nobleman cried out.

"Your honour is intact," Vandar stated. "I'll make sure Greeny here makes amends with your sister and pays your family a hefty sum as an apology."

"But—!"

Vandar flicked the red blade in his hand, cutting off the nobleman and making him go red in the face.

"Thank you for the cooperation," Vandar said.

"V-very well, sir," he said. "I look forward to his apology."

"Don't worry, he will," Vandar said.

The nobleman took a short bow and scampered off the platform, leaving the knight and the man in green.

Vandar put away his weapon and gave a sigh of relief, crossing his arms. "You really are a piece of work, aren't you?"

"Thanks, Van, you saved my hide there. I swear, if I had an argent for every time some insane woman has played me the fool, I'd be the richest man in all Taerestris," he shouted, putting away his lute.

"Argh, you know I hate when you call me that," Vandar said.

The two walked back to Tyr.

The stranger gave a dignified huff. "It's because you're a dear friend that I use it, Van. It means that I care."

"...And it's only because you're a dear friend that I let you keep using that embarrassing nickname." The knight stopped in front of Tyr and motioned toward him. "This is Tyr; he's in my charge. Tyr, I'd like you to meet—"

"Oh please, I'll have none of your boring introductions." The man knelt before Tyr. He put on a flowery voice. "From parts unknown, a newcomer is introduced. His determination unbending, his suave demeanour, unending. A friend of the great Sir Vandar through and through. A bard, historian, and lover! Sir Tandem, the noble and the brave at your service."

"Pleased to meet you... sir," Tyr said. He held back a laugh.

Vandar chuckled at Tandem's ridiculous introduction and slapped him on the back. "You didn't seem so brave a few moments ago."

Tandem stood once more. "Well, believe me, *Sir* Vandar, I had a plan that was both brilliant and cunning that would have allowed me to quell the crowd... and that absolute madman."

"Or perhaps you got lucky like you always do," Vandar said, shrugging.

"Well, luck is indeed a skill, as you know," said the bard, turning to the boy. "In any case, you seem a decent fellow, Tyr. It's my very good honour to meet you." The bard spotted the boy's golden sword and gave a surprised look. "That's a fine weapon you have there. Let me guess. Magical sword? Shoots fireballs or lightning bolts or some such?"

Tyr nodded. *I think so. Just don't ask me for a demonstration.*

"Marvelous," Tandem said. He turned to Vandar, "Mind if I accompany you for a bit? I fear if I'm alone out here that the brute's family might try to pull a fast one on your *dear* friend, Tandem."

Vandar's brow furrowed in displeasure. "Fine, but only because you—" The knight was cut off by a faint ringing sound from above.

Tyr looked up, trying to find the source of the noise—it sounded like a little bell going off directly above their heads.

"Sir Vandar!" said a tiny voice, "Sir Vandar!" it repeated.

Suddenly, glowing dust materialized above their heads as Tyr located the source of the noise. It was an extremely small woman, no larger than the boy's hand, with purple butterfly wings. The wings flickered and left behind the glowing dust as she moved through the air. She had long, blond hair and a yellow dress covered her tiny body. Her skin was snow white, and two purple stars glowed on each of her cheeks. The fairy hovered in between the three as she spoke.

"Sir Vandar!" she said a third time, ringing her little bell. "There is an urgent meeting at Holy Bastion! Your presence is required! All active Kingsguard are attending!"

CHAPTER 12

PROVIDENCE

SEPTIMIAN DYNASTY, YEAR 242
KINGDOM OF NEMEA, NEMEAN CAPITAL

The king rarely held an audience with the full might of his Kingsguard present. Each acting knight of the guard acted independently, and it was only during the most calamitous of occasions that he assembled his holy court.

SIR TANDEM THE YOUNGER
TALES, VOLUME II

Cecilia Scarlet traversed the threshold of the royal meeting hall of Holy Bastion. Before her was an oval table of wrought iron, placed in the centre of the hall. Light from stained-glass windows streamed their rays onto the surface of the table, highlighting its contents. Covering the length of the table was a map of the known world. It depicted the peaks and oceans of Taerestris, its surface strewn with wooden pieces that denoted the political allies and enemies of the crown.

"Apologies," Cecilia said, finding her seat. "I have only just received the summons, My King."

"No matter," said the old man at the head of the table.

His white hair flowed to his metallic shoulder guards, the silver of his armour complementing his form. His stern face had a focused gaze, the experience of a hundred battles hidden behind his eyes. There could be no doubt about how the position of royalty suited King Remus.

"We were just getting started," he said.

Seated along the table were Cecilia's colleagues—Waine, Vandar, Lorithas, and Stella. Leaning on one wall was the half-giant Wulf.

Wulf wore white armour with golden accents, bits of leather connecting the various plates together; a heavy, two-handed blade was strapped to his back. He was twice as tall as Cecilia and towered over the other knights.

On the other wall was Cecilia's combat partner, the Daylight Assassin, Baou, scanning around the room, as usual. Altogether, the coterie comprised the royal Kingsguard.

"Before we begin," Remus started, "thank you for coming. It has been several years since our last meeting. I'd also like to remind you of the secrecy to which you have all sworn. Today, we will delve into matters that the Nemean citizens need not concern themselves with. Do I make this clear?" The knights nodded. "Good. First, I'd like to review the facts of the situation thus far. Sir Baou?"

"Very well," Baou said. He cleared his throat. "As you already know, trouble has manifested itself in our kingdom of late. Strange happenings in the south, magical artefacts appearing out of thin air, and the recent… revelation that the seraphs remain extant."

Baou turned his gaze to Stella, the winged woman in blue armour. If not for Wulf, she would have been the tallest knight present.

"It is only recently that Stella has joined our ranks," began the king, "Though some of you may have heard her story privately, it's important the rest of you are brought up to speed. Stella?" Remus looked to the seraph.

She stood, her voice resonating throughout the hall. "Thank you, Your Majesty. One year ago, High Priestess Alystra of Skyfall tasked me and my colleague, Mordrin, with a secret mission: Retrieve certain magical relics, the Soulblades, and bring them to her. At the time, I was one of her Isthalin, an elite warrior sworn to carry out the will of the High Priestess. Along with my ex-colleague Mordrin, we served as commanders."

Stella unfurled her wings, putting them on full display. She showed their feathery white colours. The white was interrupted by small black lines that grew outward from her back.

"Our people are sick. They have been for a long time. seraphs have a unique reaction to prolonged exposure to Soul Magic, and it progresses over time." She pointed to the tattoo on her neck. "It is called the Spellseal. Every seraph has one. Eventually, the Spellseal progresses and makes us vulnerable even to Arcane Magic. For a long time, we've hidden in the skies, away from the common folk. That has only recently changed."

The man sitting next to Vandar, the mage Lorithas, raised his hand. He wore a dark hood, obscuring his face. His robe was a deep blue, and the sleeves trailed off and flowed like a cape. Markings and symbols were littered on the surface of his pale skin. A glowing orb the size of an aurum raced around his body, tracing out intricate paths and leaving ghosts of itself in its wake.

"Pardon me," he said. "We haven't met yet, but that is astonishing. You mean to tell me you can't utilize magic at all?"

Stella shook her head. "We can, but using magic harms us and makes it worse. Eventually, it kills the host."

"That's preposterous. Magic is the very fibre of Taerestris. It's like saying you're allergic to water," Lorithas said.

"Yet, it is the case," Stella replied.

Baou spoke up. "I have my theories as to what could be causing the degeneration of seraph organic matter when exposed to magical energy, but so far, my findings are inconclusive. Make no mistake, Lorithas, this is a very real problem for their people."

The Mindweaver brought his hand to his chin, eager to learn more. "Please continue."

"The situation in Skyfall is… deteriorating, to put it lightly," Stella said. "Right now, there is a class war between the seraphs who are affected by the disease and those who aren't. It is causing civil strife and division among our people, a division we have never witnessed. Our people are separating themselves as black-wings or whitewings, depending if we show the marks. We black-wings were the ones tasked with finding the Soulblades."

"Which led to your eventual defection," Lorithas said.

Stella nodded. "That's correct. I retrieved a Soulblade from a Nemean site and delivered it to the High Priestess. She has grown erratic as of late, and hides things from her commanders. Her order was to find all the weapons so they could be locked away."

"Seems as good a reason as any," Baou said. "Cecilia and I visited Magister Francis regarding the blades. They've given us a similar attitude, and practically declared war on us over the damned things."

"But why defect?" Lorithas asked. "It seems you are working counter to your people's interests."

"It is difficult to explain," Stella said. "But I believe these artefacts are to be used for what's coming. If we destroy them or seal them away, we don't stand a chance."

"And what exactly is coming?" asked Lorithas.

"This is why I have assembled a meeting," Remus said. "The situation has changed."

Stella returned to her seat, her briefing over.

Remus spoke again. "The Eastern Realms see it as nothing but a story. Historians say there is little evidence. Skeptics call it a falsification. But with everything that has happened, it is clear to me that the mystics and priests of Nemea have more than religious prattle to offer.

"It may be premature to say, but given all of the recent evidence, I have a strong belief that the ancient myths were much more than children's bedtime stories. I believe that the War of Three in the famous Nemean poem was not a fanciful tale, but a real event that took place in our ancient past."

The knights shifted uncomfortably in their seats at this, recognizing what that would mean.

"With all due respect, I remain unconvinced," Lorithas said. "I have done more studying of the occult than even Sir Baou, I'd wager, and I have never come across conclusive evidence that the Eternal Dragons ever existed, nor that a war between us ever happened."

"It is a common belief in Skyfall that a war did happen," replied Stella, "though the details are kept minimal. What we know is that one was fought with humans long ago. Does that not contradict your skepticism?"

"It all ultimately comes down to faith, eh?" Baou said, pacing back and forth. "True that things have begun happening that uphold the stories. The appearance of the blades is only a part of the puzzle. The knowledge that seraphs still exist adds another point of confidence." Baou opened a pouch on his toolbelt and procured a wooden piece—a miniature seraph. He moved to the iron table and placed the piece on the map, next to Holy Bastion.

Stella spoke again, "Even in Skyfall, dragons are a forgotten tale. We who live in the skies have never seen nor heard of one. But still…"

"Still there remains doubt," Remus said. "Doubt that must be dissolved if we are to respond to new threats properly. Tell me, Vandar," the king looked toward the red-caped knight, "how goes your search?"

Vandar the Red stood now, the room's full attention on him. "I've visited several sites now, all of them empty."

"All of them save for one," said Lorithas.

Vandar nodded. Lorithas had eyes and ears everywhere, and it didn't surprise Vandar that the magus already knew of his discovery. "Aye," he said. "I found a treasure-hunting boy in an old cathedral; he had retrieved a blade and was running from a colossal when I arrived on the scene. He was looking to support his mother in Silico with the reward."

"Where is this boy now?" Remus asked.

"With Tandem in the city," Vandar said. "Though he had originally planned on turning the blade in, I believe he can be of more use to Your Highness with it."

Remus gave Vandar a strange look. "A mere boy? With a Soulblade? What gives you such confidence?"

"I've tried communing with the blade myself," Vandar said. "Every time, nothing. But he speaks to it without a problem. I wager the blade has chosen the boy, and we would be fools to ignore that fact. I expect he will attune it shortly."

"Are you sure?" Remus said. "You know what those blades are capable of."

"Aye," Vandar nodded again. "But I see promise in him. And—"

Remus raised his eyebrow.

"I witnessed that boy getting hit head-on by a colossal. Any normal person would have died from the blow, much less a boy. Not only that, but he walked it off like it was nothing. I have reason to believe he had an instant connection with the blade, and that he somehow used its power to protect himself, though I have not informed him of this."

Remus mulled over Vandar's story before he spoke. "Very well. I leave the boy in your care. As for his mother, I'll have our bank pay out the proper reward. Do be careful."

Vandar thanked the king and sat down.

"Waine?"

Waine stood. He had bronze armour, which covered him head to toe, along with a brown ponytail. He had a sporting green cape matching his surcoat, complete with hanging tassels. He appeared to be slightly younger than King Remus and had a pure white sword sheathed on his belt.

"Your Majesty," he began, his stilted accent emphasizing his words. "Wulf and I have spent the last several months touring the southern front in search of the weapons. We've a few things to report. First"—he unsheathed his white blade and raised it in the air for the other knights to examine—"we located one of the blades just as it appeared in an abandoned holy site. It was a good end to our unlucky streak."

"Well done," Remus said. "Have you attuned the blade?"

"Not yet. Still coaxing it. A stubborn one she is, but I'll suss it out in due course." Waine reseated the relic in its scabbard.

Wulf spoke now, his voice shaking the wooden pieces on the iron table's map. "There's something else, Your Majesty. A catastrophe struck Kai-Ji some days ago. What began as a gladiator match became a disaster. We only just heard as we were returning to Holy Bastion, but a fire appears to have burned down half the city. Kai-Ji is one of the largest Nemean food suppliers. You understand what that means."

King Remus' expression turned from curiosity to concern. The room was silent for several moments before he spoke again. "Very well. I'll review our food situation shortly. Do you have any idea how it happened?"

Waine spoke again. "Apparently, it was one of their gladiators who started it. From what I hear, it was a young girl."

"Always a problem, those slave cities," Lorithas said. "If it were up to me, we would have gone the way of the realms and replaced them with more reliable means by now."

Remus smiled. "You know better than anyone that Nemea would rather their slaves than resort to magic." Remus turned to Waine. "Thank you for the report, and good job finding the blade."

"There is one more thing, Your Excellency. The same time we heard news of the fire, we saw something strange in the night sky. A mysterious light at the top of Dragon's Peak, visible as far as the eye could see."

"Dragon's Peak," Remus muttered.

Waine nodded. "It's safe to say that whatever is going on up there should be investigated, but given the deadly history of that place we felt it prudent to leave the matter for the time."

"Most troubling that is, most troubling," Remus said. After a time, the king stood and addressed the room. "I think that is everything for now. We all know the stakes of this conflict, and the dangers of what could happen should we fail to act. Enemies from the east prepare to seek out the same treasures we do. Moreover, we now have the seraphs acting in similar interest. Bearing this in mind, I now give you new orders. I will be leaving the keep to journey north beyond the Great Divide."

The room grew tense. The king rarely left the seat of power, and it always represented danger when he did, much less to unexplored land like the Great Divide. The look on the king's face had enough conviction to remind his guard that he was certain of this next bold move.

"If there is even a trace of doubt that the legends aren't true, we must lay them to rest." Remus eyed Lorithas. "I believe I know what we will need as proper proof of what is to come."

"There is one problem, Your Majesty," Stella said.

The room focused their attention back at her.

"It concerns a deceased magus of ours. Her name was Reina. Before she died, she created a living map of the location of the blades in Skyfall. If that spell is still active, they will surely know if you leave."

"That is a problem," the king said. "But still… Skyfall has not attacked us yet. I have no reason to believe that should change. As for me…" Remus looked to the red-caped knight. "Vandar, you will accompany me, along with this boy. I am eager to learn what is so special about that one."

Vandar nodded his head, accepting his new orders.

"Wulf, Stella, and Waine shall remain in the city while we are gone. We will need some presence to keep morale in Nemea. As far as the peasantry and our potential enemies are concerned, I remain in the keep. Lorithas, I want you to set to work on the affliction that's affecting the seraphs. Please use Sir Baou's notes. Finally—" Remus looked to Cecilia.

"Apologies my king," she said. "In the east… I know I failed you."

"Nonsense. What happened there was expected of our enemies. Come back to Holy Bastion later tonight. I'll prepare horses and give you your next task."

Cecilia nodded, and the meeting was adjourned. The Kingsguard filed out of the room one by one, before finally, the only two who remained were Cecilia and Vandar. He looked to her and raised his brow.

"So," he started, "what *did* happen in the East?"

"The usual," she answered, sitting down in front of him. "Lying politicians, thinly veiled threats, and a disregard for peacetime laws. What's new in the Great Nations?"

"You also left me alone," he said jokingly.

"I also left you alone. Are we forgetting anything?"

"I missed you. It's been months since I've seen you."

Cecilia smiled, a jovial side that she showed only to Vandar. She brought her hand out and placed it on his knee. The two sat in silence.

"So, you've taken on a charge. Who's the kid?"

"His name is Tyr. His father fought in the Nemean military. Died some eight years ago."

"And now he's following in his footsteps. Like father, like son. Are you sure you want a boy that young running around with a weapon that dangerous?"

"I'll train him," Vandar said, leaning back in his chair. "He has a lot more potential than I ever did as a fighter."

"Oh, please. That bard Tandem has more potential as a fighter than you do."

Vandar laughed, his long, blond hair bouncing with each chuckle. "You're not wrong, Cecil. So."

"So." Cecilia took a deep breath and leaned back against her chair.

"Off on another mission. Any idea what?" he asked, crossing his arms.

"No clue. Can't be too unrelated to the current situation, though."

"Aye. Take Baou with you if you can. I trust he can keep you safe."

"We're not kids anymore. No need to think of me as your delicate sister."

"You know I don't see you that way. You're more important than that."

Cecilia's cheeks flushed. She looked away. *Bastard.* "You know we can't. We're brother and sister."

"Not by blood. And to hell with whatever the church wants anyway. Someday, that throne will be mine. And I'll choose my queen. I'll choose you."

The woman smirked. It was her turn to tease him. "Are you sure you want to go through with that decision? I'm old, after all. There are plenty of younger women you can have." Cecilia brought her hands out and took hold of Vandar's. She felt his warmth. It eased her, as it always did.

"But they are not you. I have eyes only for one."

"Then you'd better fix your eyes."

It was a phrase from their childhood—when the two were young and Vandar would make a mistake, like misplacing his things or an error in sword practice, "Fix your eyes!" she would say. "You're a prince!"

The two gazed at each other for a moment.

Cecilia's left eyebrow went up. "What's that?"

"What's what?"

Cecilia brought a hand to the man's face and plucked a hair from his head.

"Ouch!"

"Take a look at this," she said, presenting him with his stolen strand of hair.

"It's hair. What of it?"

"The colour. You've never had a silver hair like this in your head."

"Hm. What do we make of it?"

"I think you know. The weapons are draining our lifeforce the more we use them. How often have you been using that shield?"

"Erm, well…"

Cecilia frowned.

"You're overdoing it. At this rate, you'll grow old and die before Father does."

Vandar looked away. Cecilia reprimanded him further. "Just don't overdo it again, all right? If a situation arises, just let your little sister handle it."

"I can't promise that. We have a duty to the crown."

"Are you going to make me worry, then?" Cecilia looked at Vandar with a grave look.

After several tense moments, Vandar relented. "All right. I won't overdo it, then."

"Promise?"

"Promise."

PATH OF THE DRAGON

SEPTIMIAN DYNASTY, YEAR 242
KINGDOM OF NEMEA, ABANDONED TOWN

*Dragon's Peak was famous as the tallest mountain in
Taerestris. Over the centuries, hundreds of brave adventurers
and foolhardy explorers had set foot on its mystical spires,
risking life and limb in a bid for the top.*

*None had ever attempted the challenge and lived
to tell the tale.*

SIR TANDEM THE YOUNGER
HISTORIA TAERESTRIA

K ai crossed the entrance to the abandoned village. She had been travelling for days now, with little in the way of sustenance or a good night's sleep. Despite her heavy armour and lack of rest, she marched with ease. Though her parched tongue and grovelling stomach gnawed at her body, they were nothing compared to the corpses of the people she had slain that gnawed at her mind.

Ahead of her were several wooden buildings, constructions of a bygone era. The village was small, made only more eerie by the fact that it was completely disconnected from civilization. No roads in or out of the town were present. The sound of the wind was her only companion, that and the voice in her head.

"We've arrived."

Kai continued wordlessly, reaching the centre of the small town, the dirt intersection beneath her claiming the sweat it was due. She looked up now, protecting her eyes from the radiant sun. Just beyond the village was her objective, the thing she had been seeking for days—the entrance to Dragon's Peak. The mountain had given off a strange light from its distant apex on the same night of her escape. Kai knew it was no coincidence. The psychic had said as much, after all.

As for Kai herself, she had no elaborate plans for her newfound freedom. Heroics and purpose did not guide her steps, but rather a cold vengeance that had to be exacted upon Lord Rahab and her former slave masters. Such a task for just one woman would be difficult, of course; to achieve her aims, she needed power.

"Well?"

"Now begins the true test. Please, sit down."

Kai sat silently, crossing her legs. She took deep breaths, steadying her mind. A drop of sweat trickled from the tip of her nose to the dirt below. Suddenly, the ground beneath the young woman glowed, an ethereal circle with infinitely complex designs, recursive shapes, and odd patterns filling its contents. Kai recognized this as magic; she had seen as much in her days as a gladiator. The circle stretched out from underneath her, enveloping the village in moments. As the circle disappeared, wraithlike figures faded in from the air, ghostly men and women that surrounded Kai. The figures stared at her intently, as if dispensing judgment.

To her front was one such figure, a man in adventuring gear with a sword to his side. Kai stood.

"Welcome," the spectral man addressed her. "Welcome to the path." The figure took a low bow. "You seek the treasure of the mountain?"

Kai nodded.

"Very well. I am Veris. I am bound to this place by dragon's spell. As are the others." Veris motioned to the other figures, all crowding around the young woman now.

Veris continued, his hollow voice carrying oddly in the air. "We were once like you. Bold adventurers who thought we could ascend the mountain's heights and achieve the power of kings. Yet all of us have failed. Now we are damned to guide new doomed souls to its cursed treasure, knowing no eternal rest."

"You have all have tried?" Kai asked.

She examined the other figures. Many of the souls were still in their travelling gear—some of the figures were large, others small, yet they all wore the same sombre look on their faces: regret.

Veris nodded. "It is the magic of this place that keeps us chained here. We await a worthy champion to scale the mountain and achieve the summit. Only then can we be free."

"The mountain. Tell me more about it."

"Several trials await you on the mountain. Each will test you for traits worthy of the peak. Only those of pure heart may fully ascend. But, be warned, you will also find forbidden knowledge. Knowledge that has been kept sacred for aeons. What lies beyond only you can see. Such is your fate."

Kai mulled over the man's words. Her gaze drifted down to the scar on her left hand, the sword that had been emblazoned there since youth. Though she had cursed it for the years of hell it inflicted upon her, she could not deny that the experience had made her strong. Strong enough to fight for what mattered. Strong enough to scale a mountain.

"I'll do it. I accept the challenge."

Veris nodded gravely. He raised his hand, another ethereal circle appearing below the woman's feet. Kai felt herself burning slightly, a sense of vertigo making her lightheaded.

"This contract is sealed," he said. "You are now bound to the mountain. Only two options are afforded to you now: Achieve the summit or remain trapped here, forever.

"There is a wagon at the foot of the mountain, just beyond here. It will provide you with food, rest, and water. Take what you need from it and no more. You'll have no need of weapons. The mountain shall provide everything you require along the journey. Good luck."

Kai nodded. The spirits dissipated, leaving her alone once more. She walked forward and out of the eerie village. Before long, she reached the wagon, where she stopped to rest. Though there was enough food in the wagon for a family, the young woman ate little, in keeping with the spirit's words. She inspected the bloodied dagger Guff had given her, the weapon she had recently used to end a life during her daring escape. Taking one last solemn look at it, she dropped it in the wagon and pushed on to the foot of the mountain.

At the base was an inconspicuous dirt road that led to the mountain's path. Kai began her ascent with a step.

"So," she said aloud, "what is *your* name?"

"*That I do not know. I cannot remember. Every time I try, it feels as though my mind draws a blank.*"

"Well, I'll call you Specter, then."

"*Specter. A name I could get used to.*"

"Do you know much about this mountain?"

"*I am… familiar with this place. I know much of this peak, but many more memories are locked to me now. I cannot access them.*"

"What do you know?"

"Of the trials you will face. They are like none other in the world. Together we may overcome them."

"Tell me more."

"Each trial will test your mind, body, and spirit in different ways. Only by proving your worth in all three will you advance. As to their exact nature, my telling you would not help in preparation. You are either ready for them, or you are not."

Kai walked the path, the sound of her footsteps breaking the silence. The way forward was easy for now, a simple trail up the mountain. Shrubs and wild vegetation decorated the scene, rocky outcroppings littering the path.

"Tell me, Specter, why do you want to reach the top?"

"A part of me feels a connection to this place. Like I have lost something here. I'd like to find out exactly what."

"I suppose that means we both have something to gain from this."

"Another part of me knows of the storm. My thoughts are but fragments now, but we must prepare."

"What do you mean with that?"

"It is not yet revealed to me. But I know the answer lies at the summit."

Their conversation returned to silence once more as Kai focused on her task, the day's sun eventually giving way to the moon. Crickets and fireflies sang their songs, and Kai's thoughts wandered. The path thus far was easy, though she suspected that would soon change.

After a time, she heard what sounded like a waterfall. The rushing sound excited her, eager for a chance to break the monotony of the path. She soon arrived at a cave opening, the rushing sound coming from within.

"I know this place. Your first trial lies ahead. Look there, above the opening."

Kai looked up, peering at the flat slab of rock that hung over the entrance. She could see engraved text on its face.

"What does it say?"

"*The righteous path is narrow.*"

Suddenly, the blue scroll on her belt shook. From it, ghostly energy spilled out before her—the same energy of Veris and his fellow adventurers. Kai looked on, surprised at the figure that took form. It was the old man she'd met those many years ago, only his body now resembled translucent smoke. His lower half was missing, the upper half suspended in the air. The image of the man brought a ghostly hand to its face and examined it, equally as surprised. He spoke. His voice had the same hollow quality of the trapped travellers back in the village.

"I sense it now… the magic of this place. It feels like an old friend."

Kai examined Specter, taking a hand and pushing it through his chest.

"Have you always been able to do that?"

"Never. This is the first time."

Kai looked to the entrance of the cave again, the sound of rushing water teasing her ears. She looked back at her only friend and smiled. "It's good to meet you again, Specter."

The man returned her smile. "Very well. Let's continue."

Kai nodded, and the two moved forward, stepping into the pitch-black recesses of the cave. The rushing sound got louder and louder, and soon the dark cave gave way to its source.

"Stop!" Specter shouted.

Kai halted, catching herself from an unexpected drop ahead. The bizarre scene ahead of her confounded her completely.

The cave had led to a wide cavity inside of the mountain. On the edges of the cavity were thousands of steps that wrapped around the walls, leading farther up the vertical hollow, though Kai could not make out its end. Just beneath her was the source of the noise; in the middle of the gargantuan hollow was a whirlpool of azure energy. The pool shifted and churned with violent force. The young woman heard the screams of men and women escaping the maelstrom.

"What is this?" she shouted, taking another step back.

"The first trial. Look there." Specter pointed to the whirlpool.

Kai could spot the horrified faces of adventurers emerging and vanishing within it, contorted looks aimed directly at her.

"Help me!" one would cry.

"Save me! Save me, please!" screamed another.

Specter's voice filled the room, his voice ringing through the hollow. "This is the fate of those who fail the first trial. Those who fall into the vortex of souls are claimed by its host, forever tormented in the whirlpool."

Kai furrowed her brow. "Is there anything we can do?"

"It is the same as the village. Only by reaching the summit may we free these unfortunate souls."

Kai felt the tension rising in her chest. She had not expected this. She took several breaths to steady herself. "All right. What is this first trial?"

"It is simple. There are thirty thousand steps in this chamber. You must climb them all within the time limit to pass. There are three platforms along the way where you may rest as you need. The third platform will lead you to the next trial."

"What's the time limit?" she asked, trying to ignore the screaming souls just beneath her feet.

"That will become apparent once you begin. Only one with inhuman strength and endurance to match can proceed. Few survive."

"If it's been done before, then I can do it, too."

"Very well. I shall return to the scroll. You do not need my form distracting you." Specter faded away, pouring his energy back into the blue scroll on Kai's belt.

Kai stepped boldly onto the first stair, beginning the challenge. The unsettling sounds of the trapped souls raged below, their ceaseless cries adding to the stress. She could only ignore them for now, though the task proved difficult. The creeping curiosity of how long it had been that those souls existed in sheer torment dominated her thoughts.

Step by step, Kai began her long ascent up the circular stairway. The climb was easy at first, her unnatural strength affording her quick progress. As she moved farther up the steps, the blue whirlpool grew more distant, the sounds of the screams fading into the background. Sometime later, she heard strange noises coming from the bottom of the stairs.

"What is that?" she asked, breathing heavily.

"*Your time limit. As you move up the mountain, the steps below you will fall away, starting from the first. If you are too slow, they will eventually reach you. The steps will collapse beneath your feet, and you'll fall into the vortex below.*"

Kai's heart was pumping. Rather than calm her, Specter's words only served to make her dread worsen. Every few moments, the sound of crumbling rock would reach her ears, the environment having become her inhuman pursuer. Kai hastened her pace, her legs already burning from the climb. To an ordinary woman, the ascent would have already defeated its challenger; but Kai was no ordinary woman.

Pressing on, she continued to rise, slowing her pace when she needed a rest but never stopping. Along the rocky walls of the hollow, small blue gems illuminated the path, providing dim light and urging the mountain's challenger onward.

She had lost track of time at some point. How long had she been climbing? Hours? Days? Weeks? It was impossible to tell now, the only change in her environment being the sound of the steps encroaching on her location.

Specter, she thought, sparing her breath. *Just what exactly are you?*

"*My memories remain… difficult to comprehend. It is like a great fog. I know that I was like you once. I know that I died long ago. How I was sealed into the scroll you have now is a mystery to me.*"

Do you know why you are in the scroll?

"*Only the little I have mentioned. Bits and pieces are returning to me as you progress, however.*"

Eventually, Kai lost the energy to hold even a mental conversation. Despite this, her body continued to move on its own. The sound of crumbling rock grew ever closer, urging her tired legs to keep going. She was drenched in sweat.

"There! Stop here. The first platform."

Kai looked up, consciousness reigniting in her eyes. Farther up was a circular platform that took space in the middle of the hollow. A small bridge connected the platform to the stairway. Though her body felt utterly spent, Kai raced through the last of the steps, eager to finally rest without danger. She reached the middle of the platform before dropping to the ground in complete exhaustion. She lay there for a time, listening to the collapsing stairs as they neared her location. The final stair broke away and fell to the darkness below, leaving Kai in silence.

Specter grew out of the young woman's scroll again, pride on his face.

"I recall the purpose of these platforms. While you rest, we may begin."

Kai looked quizzically at Specter, eyeing him as she sat upright. The stone platform abruptly lit up with the familiar blue circle of magic, transparent shapes filling the room.

"What is this?" she asked.

"The engine of the universe."

Blue orbs connected by spellbound threads rose in the dank air, crumbling to sapphire dust and reigniting the next instant. Stars and planets aligned, new galaxies formed, and the platform lit up with the million lights of the night sky.

"You've made it this far," Specter said, "I will tell you what I recall."

Kai looked on in awe, her tired eyes in intense focus.

"Our world is but one of billions. Long before you or I experienced this meagre existence, there were worlds in other places, in other times. Many were devoid of life, the light of souls being exceedingly rare."

As the young woman gazed out into the infinite, the planets and stars rushed past her, an inconceivable distance zooming through view as one verdant sphere revealed itself, larger than the others.

"This is Taerestris. Our little home in the Great Beyond. In a sea of limitless probability, the spark of life has been gifted to this humble rock."

"It's beautiful," she whispered, taking in the grandiosity of the image before her.

"Of all the worlds we know, we shine alone in the darkness. Taerestris stands today as the last of these flickering worlds, the light of souls extinguished in all others. What do you make of that?"

Kai thought for a few moments, viewing the network of the universe, its grand design playing out before her.

"Are we really alone?"

The thought of that scared her. She'd been alone all her life, and the knowledge of that loneliness on such a grand scale made her uneasy, hollow.

"As far as we can know it."

Kai mulled over his words. Such thoughts were not the sort she was used to entertaining, though in quiet moments she did oft consider the greater game at play. "Maybe there is something special about us. Something that keeps us alive."

"Perhaps. Or perhaps it is merely mathematical probability. It is difficult to know; such enigmatic truths are beyond our ken. Consider it the greatest open matter in the universe."

As Kai contemplated the images before her, she felt her smallness, her unimaginable irrelevance in the sea of lights that constituted the Great Beyond. The light of Taerestris blinked like a beacon in the night, a dazzling star in the emptiness of the void. It was difficult for her to understand, but she felt something stir within her at that moment.

"Maybe it's not important." She felt her mind finally grasping at some inspiration. "Maybe the important thing is what we do with that probability. Even if our world is the only one left, it's important not to let that world die."

Specter's pallid face gave a smile. "Perhaps it is."

A second azure planet grew in the distance, another thread of light connecting it with Taerestris. "Another existed long ago. This second world was home to a familiar race, known to us as the seraphs. Their world was doomed, however. Perhaps it was their own doing, or perhaps it was through unfortunate coincidence. To escape, the seraphs mastered a powerful version of magic, evading their end and travelling here, to Taerestris."

The thread of light grew into a powerful beam, energy moving from the ultramarine orb to the verdant green one. The seraph home planet then crumbled away into a fine, translucent dust. The young woman felt sadness for the lost world.

The billions of lights instantly flickered out, the two bathed once again in only the dim glow of the gemstones near the walls.

"The story does not end here," Specter said. "But we must travel to the next viewing platform to unlock more of my memories." He returned to the scroll.

"Rest as much as you need. The second distance will be much like the first."

Kai pushed thoughts of what she had just learned from her mind—there would be time to consider it later. As she leaned back to the ground to sleep, her head hit a solid object. She turned around to find a basket of bread and a small jug of water. She didn't realize it until now, but she was ravenously hungry. She ate the modest meal before her as she thought of Veris: *The mountain provides.*

After a time, Kai stood. With renewed vigour, she looked to the opposite side of the platform. Attached was another bridge, connecting to a second set of stairs that continued upward. She made quick work of the second set, having now become acclimatised to the climb.

Once again, her legs burned and her heart was set aflame, but her previous success and her curiosity of what was to come drove her onward. She moved rapidly now, the sole sounds those of the collapsing stairs and the ever-distant vortex at the bottom. Visibility was low, given the dim lights around her, but they sufficed. The sepulchral darkness that enveloped her was no obstacle to her goal.

An eternity later, Kai had arrived at the second platform, its design much like the first. She dropped to the ground; her body now taxed to its absolute limit. She had not slept on the last platform, and she felt a dizziness in her head that demanded rest.

She closed her tired eyes and finally slept, the warmth of the mountain hollow providing comfort in the darkness. Hours later, she awoke to another barebones meal, which she promptly devoured.

"Ready?"

Kai nodded.

Specter manifested himself from her scroll, and again the platform lit up with its geometric symbols. This time, the image she saw was Taerestris itself, the peaks and valleys flooding the hollow.

"This world we inhabit was once the land of the Eternal Dragons," Specter began.

Kai looked out at the land and saw flying creatures soaring over its mountaintops.

"They ruled it alone, and alone they would remain until the seraphs arrived from the Great Beyond."

A winged figure in the shape of a man appeared next to the flying dragons. It was much smaller than the dragons, but Kai could see its detail with perfect clarity.

"The Eternal Dragons possessed a powerful energy, one that allowed them to transcend death itself and live forever. The seraphs were not as fortunate, and so they came to revere their draconic allies as masters.

"The two races set about shaping the world in their image. However, the intrigues of life only provided base amusement to an increasingly uninspired court. To entertain themselves, the Eternal Dragons set their magic to creating the common folk, low creatures that had neither the divinity of the dragons nor the wings of the seraphs."

A dragon in front of Kai transformed, becoming that of a human.

"Humans, elves, dwarves, all manner of life sprouted from this simple act of boredom."

The world's races revealed themselves to Kai, both ones she recognized, and forgotten ones that no longer existed. "There are so many. What happened to all of them?"

"War," Specter said. "Before the common folk, there was no such thing. But we were jealous, hateful creatures, and the worst of us stole and slayed and tortured our fellows."

"But, why?"

She had never felt the need for violence; she had just been thrust into it unwillingly. To see the perfect world that the dragons and the seraphs had created torn apart by violence was like drinking poison.

"Perhaps war happens due to our imperfections. The farther we fall from its light, the more hatred seeps into our veins. When you covet what another has, when balance is not maintained, that is where war reveals its ugly self."

The image before Kai turned into a terrible scene; millions of spears flying at the dragons and seraphs of the skies, followed by dark, bloody battlefields and mass graves. One by one, the multitude of races would disappear, leaving but a fraction left.

"What happened to the dragons?"

"They are gone, as far as we know. They have never been seen since those ancient days. Perhaps they are well and truly dead. Perhaps we are all that's left."

Kai's heart filled with a profound sadness, the image burning into her mind. "Isn't there another way? Can we make it better?"

"That is another puzzle lost to us. We have made the world imperfect. In our imperfect world, it is impossible to make things right by words alone."

"But we should try."

"Then let me ask you this. Could you have escaped your captivity without violence? Are you not here on this day because of your skill, your talent for violence, your unique gift that makes you human? In this world of our design, might makes right."

Kai considered Specter's words. He certainly had a point; her great escape was made possible in no small part to her skill in hurting others. Regardless, she could not accept such a notion; it would only justify the deaths of those she had slain. "If the world is imperfect, then we should seek to change that. Maybe we can someday create a world where violence isn't needed."

"And what then? Will people simply put down their arms, cast aside their vengeance, and repudiate their anger? Will the blood of the fallen not demand justice? Will we simply accept love and dissolve our hate?"

"I don't know the answer to that. But I still think we should try. I don't know if I can ever forgive people like Rahab, or Guff, or any of the other ones who did such terrible things. But... I can try."

Though Kai wanted nothing more than to complete her vendetta against Rahab and the slave masters, seeing the world and its history on such a grand scope was more powerfully persuasive than words could ever be. She had learned to kill, and she was good at it, but how could she vindicate that bloody tradition in light of what she had just seen?

The platform burned brightly once more, then sputtered out. The two were cloaked in black again.

"You are a strange one. I am curious to see what forgiveness you'll find in your heart when the ones who wronged you are at the end of your blade. But... your answer is impressive."

With that, he flowed back into the woman's scroll.

"*No more history. The last platform will lead us out. You're almost there.*"

Kai stood and faced the third bridge. She felt nothing in the darkness but guilt now. New thoughts flitted through her mind, questions she did not know the answers to.

Did I really need to kill? And, if not, how many died because of me for nothing?

She moved listlessly up through the last set of steps. Her thoughts made her feel much heavier, as though she were made of lead. The remorse that filled her was more taxing than a thousand of the circular stairways. As she moved, the crumbling steps sounded off again, marking the time that remained. She stayed ahead of the sound, keeping focus. The vortex of souls was out of sight now, the way being lit by a source of natural light that loomed overhead.

She felt a coldness coming from above as she got closer to the top. Drops of snow fell on the steps, making the way more treacherous. Kai could see her breath form a fine mist as she exhaled, her movements keeping her warm. Before long, light from the morning sun streamed in from above, marking the end of the first trial. Kai had found the third platform, feeling the rush of her victory over the steps. As the last step crumbled behind her, she made her way into the landing and looked out.

The third platform had a bridge that led outside of the mountain, a hole in the wall that streamed bright white light into the hollow. Snow covered the exit ground, and a fierce blizzard howled outside. The young woman rested a third time, recovering her strength for what was to come. Her eyes adjusted to the light as she prepared herself.

Kai steeled her resolve, and with a step, left the hollow.

THE SHOOTING STAR

SEPTIMIAN DYNASTY, YEAR 242
KINGDOM OF NEMEA, NORTHERN BORDER

Lands near the Great Divide had piqued the curiosity of both scholar and adventurer for ages, tantalizing them with unknown mysteries and unexplored riches.

Little was recorded about what lay beyond, the only shreds of information being the legendary tales of the half-giant Wulf and the hastily scrawled reports of frightened explorers.

SIR TANDEM THE YOUNGER
HISTORIA TAERESTRIA

Tyr Lancelt sat at the wooden table of the shoddy inn. The port town did not often receive guests, and his party of strangers had caught all the attention. Tandem the Bard sat to his left, scribbling notes on parchment. To the boy's right was Vandar the Red, as well as King Remus, who was now wearing a set of heavy robes and a hood to cover his face. It had been important that the group travel without alerting others to the king's presence, and so far, the disguise had worked.

A fearsome wind ran through the night, with torrential rains mounting an assault against the windowpanes of the inn. The walls creaked and groaned as a sign of their desperate struggle against the storm.

A gruff man wearing plain brown attire and bandages that covered his right eye sat across the table from the party.

"Cross the strait again? Not on me life," he said. "I've sailed 'cross it many times before, but something has changed in the waters, of late."

"Just what exactly did you see out there, good ferryman?" the bard asked, putting down his quill.

The party was looking for passage across the Strait of Sorrow, a body of water that connected Inner Taerestris from the Outlands.

"There's some things that better go unsaid. Things that can change a man."

"We've been travelling for a fortnight now," Vandar explained. "We must take the shortest route north. The voyage should only be a few hours to the other side."

"No means no. Ye might be a Kingsguard, but 'round here that's worth about as much as a ship with a leaky hull," said the ferryman. "Ye haven't seen the mist that has started appearin'. How it chills ye to the bone, and then there's the screams."

"You said you've made the trip many times," Tandem said. "What makes you want to stay away? Surely a few noises and some mist aren't enough to scare a big, brave man such as yourself."

The ferryman thought for a moment, hesitant to reveal what

he knew. A lightning bolt struck in the distance, rolling thunder passing through the building. "It happened the last time I went out. I was transporting some *frontiersmen,* they called themselves. Probably treasure hunters, though, judgin' from their talk. Not that I care about who's who, long as I get my cut. Halfway through the journey, the strangest thing started happenin'. Mist appearin' around us, the kind of thing that freezes ye to the bone. Few moments later, we started hearin' the screaming."

Tyr listened intently to the ferryman's tale. He took a sideways glance at King Remus, who said nothing.

"Have you gone mad? You actually expect us to believe that story?" Tandem asked.

"It be the truth, it be,"

"What happened next?" Vandar prompted him.

"Few moments after that, I passed out. Woke up back on this side of the shore, a sack of coin in me hands and my charges missing. Ain't gone out since."

"And the frontiersmen?" Tyr asked.

"Dunnae. There's a boat on the other side that they could have taken back, but I haven't seen or heard of them. Been weeks now. Gives me the creeps, I tell ye."

Vandar spoke next. "I've never heard of such a strange occurrence. Old man, you've travelled much." He turned to the disguised Remus. "What do you think?"

"Difficult to tell. If we are to believe his story, it could be anything. A mere coincidence, a magical charm, or even ghosts," Remus said.

"A ghost? In the sea?" Vandar asked.

"Ghosts can swim, too, you know," Tandem said.

"The green one might be right," the ferryman said, drawing attention back to him. "I didn't see anything 'fore it all started. What else could creep up on a boat in the middle of water without being seen? Not like there's anywhere to hide, and the sea was clear as day 'fore the mist came."

"Ghosts or not, we must still travel north," Vandar said. "You're the only person with a boat around here. Why?"

"All the others packed up and left to go farther down the coast. Guess they got scared off after what happened. Don't really blame 'em."

Vandar frowned. "Name your price, and I'll double it."

The ferryman hastily responded. "I told ye, I don't care for coin. No amount is worth riskin' me skin again."

Vandar reached into a pouch on his belt and procured a mass of coins of varying sizes and colours. He placed the clinking coins onto the table.

"What's that…?" the man asked, staring hungrily at the money.

"One hundred platums, fifty aurums, and twenty argents," Vandar said. "More than enough to pay for the passage. Actually, that is enough to last you several years without work. You're currently short on clients, correct? If this business is stopping new passengers, I'd say you'd do well to accept our coin."

King Remus went into the folds of his robes and added another stack of platums to the pile, doubling the total.

"I'll even include one of my famous poems, autographed by yours truly. It's worth a fortune," Tandem said as he placed the piece of furled parchment he was scribbling on over the coins.

"…And the boy?" the ferryman asked, his greed having now gotten the better of him.

"In payment for passage, the boy will defend us," the bard said, giving a quick wink to the puzzled Tyr. "He's a seasoned ghost-hunter, and he's exorcized several demons in his short tenure on Taerestris. Trust that you are in experienced hands, my good sir."

The man took a few moments to consider the offer, his eyes jetting back and forth between Vandar, the coins, and the rest of the party before he answered.

"Nae, I won't do it. I promised meself that no coin would sway me."

Before Vandar could reply, the bard quickly stood and scooped up the money on the table.

"Well, then, I suppose we'll just be holding on to this. Shame, too. It would have been so nice to get rid of all this money for once. Guess we'll just keep it."

The ferryman stared at Tandem for several moments before putting his hand up in defeat. "Wait. Fine. Damn it; I'll do it."

"Excellent," Tandem said. "Looks like we're back in business, then."

"How many people can fit on the boat?" Tyr asked. The early morning air stung his face.

"Oh, quite a few, this certainly isn't the biggest cargo I've carried," the ferryman responded. "Even with all yer armour, she'll fly straight and true."

The group stood together on the frigid coastline, awaiting instruction from the ferryman. The sea was calm, a rarity for the tumultuous northern waters near the strait.

A wooden boat rested on the beach, the vehicle of choice for the ferryman. The boat was long and spacious, allowing for plenty of room to manoeuvre on it. Two weathered oars were situated at the back. The man pushed the boat into the water and turned back to the party.

"All right then, get in," he said.

The group loaded into the boat, with the ferryman bringing up the rear. Once everyone was situated, he gave a quick summary of the job. "Here be the deal, sirs. I'll be ferrying ye 'cross the Strait of Sorrow from edge to edge; should be a quick trip. It'll take a few hours to get to the other side, but we should make it 'round early afternoon. Hope ye brought a snack."

With that short briefing, the ferryman began the journey. His oar work was efficient and precise, his limber body and experience lending well to the task.

The rest of the party relaxed themselves, easing into conversation.

"So, ye ever been to sea?" the ferryman asked, the question aimed at nobody in particular.

"Several times," Vandar answered. "I've been on some larger ships as part of diplomatic journeys."

Tandem spoke next. "Myself, I've travelled all the coasts of Taerestris. I'm certainly not one to miss a good story, and my passions involve chasing the comings and goings of the realm." The bard looked toward Tyr. "How about yourself, ever sailed on the open—uh, hey, buddy?"

Tyr was doubled over, his hand over his mouth. The rocking boat was causing turmoil in his stomach, and the boy was focused on not losing last night's meal.

I didn't know sailing was going to be like... "I'm not used to... this..." Tyr covered his mouth again.

The ferryman reached into his pocket and produced a ball of chocolate, handing it to the boy. "Try this. It's black market magic, but it comes in useful in my line o' work. Lotta folk I carry get the same issue. Hope yer Kings*guard* don't send me to prison for it."

Tyr hesitantly took the chocolate, a minty taste hitting his tongue as he popped it in his mouth. He felt the effects of the medicine instantly, the chocolate working its magic and settling his seasickness. He thanked the ferryman and sat upright again, grateful for the man's foresight.

"Sir," Tyr said, looking at Tandem, "you mentioned before about stories in Taerestris. What is it that you do for work?"

"Ah, well, I am a bard, as you know. I often write poetry and musical pieces, performing them for fans and patrons. But, aside from art and women, I have another ambition." Tandem brought out his lute and plucked the strings lightly, adding drama to his words. "It is the role of the heroic writer to stand at the bar of history and record truth, is it not? It is a solemnity that he ought to bear witness. You see, I believe that the world needs writers, historians, men of noble cause, to put quill to parchment and record the deeds of other great men. It is through this exercise that one can preserve the spirit of the generation." Tandem's notes filled the air around them, a beautiful sonata that accompanied his speech. "My biggest dream is the one I've been pursuing all my life. To seek out the biggest story I can, capture its essence on the page, and give it immortality through the power of words."

Tyr nodded, enjoying the bard's dulcet tones.

The bard continued. "I must admit, it's no easy task. Many a time your hero Tandem has found himself a hair's breadth from the jaws of death. But we are all born for something, dear boy, and I feel most at home with my Soul Lute, Guinevere, in hand, battling the enemies of chaos!"

"Soul Lute?" Tyr asked, "I've never heard of that." *Like a Soulblade?* he wondered.

"Why, yes, good Tyr; one expertly plucked note of my lute here, and I daresay I could blast a hole in the ocean wide enough for us to *walk* across!"

Vandar and Remus laughed heartily.

"It was a good speech," Remus said. "Before you ruined it with that ridiculous tall tale."

Tandem played a few distressed notes in response. "In any case, my work involves recording history. I'm working on several books and an encyclopaedia right now. Your good friend, Vandar, is wise and helpful enough to assist me in its creation."

"Tandem is a great writer," Vandar said, "provided he doesn't drone on forever about himself. I've read some of his work; it wouldn't surprise me if his readers knew the colour of his underwear."

"Oh, pish-posh, Van, my works are lovely. You're just envious. And they're purple."

"Tyr," Remus beckoned.

Tyr looked to the disguised king. When he was told that they would be accompanying King Remus, he had felt like it was some fantastical daydream. Travelling with the Nemean king himself had been a surreal experience, but apart from his regal look and demeanour, Remus seemed just like a regular person.

"I understand you have lived alone with your mother since a young age. Tell me about her."

"My mother, well, she lives in Silico. She's lived there most of her life. She met Father while he was touring the country as part of the Nemean army, and I was born a bit after that. After Father passed, she…" The boy fell silent.

"Hm?"

"It's… well… she has a condition. At times, she thinks my father is still alive. Talks to him."

"Ah. Delusion of the mind… Terrible. What do the physicians say?"

"They've tried their medicines, but there's not much they can do."

"That's horrible," Tandem said. "I've seen similar cases in my travels. His death likely turned her world upside down. She must have truly loved your father."

"After that," Tyr said. "All the finances fell to us. I was too young to work, so we had to sell most of our possessions. When… the king… declared the search for the Soulblades, I thought it would be a way to support my mother. By the way," he said, his eyes lighting up, "I wanted to thank you, and uh, and"—he looked to Remus—"and the king, for sending the reward home. Mother will be happy to know I succeeded."

"Happy, indeed, but less because of the reward and more because she will know you are all right. Tell me, how long have you been journeying now? How long have you been away?"

"I left home a little over a year ago now. I wasn't sure how long I would be gone, but Mother is probably worried by now."

"I wouldn't think too much on it, lad," said the ferryman. "A good parent always knows how their little ones fare, even when yer halfway 'cross the world. I'm sure she's patiently waiting for ye to return."

Still, I hope she's all right. It's been a long time.

The party sat in silence for a time before Remus spoke once more. "That shield you carry. It bears your family crest on it. Was it your father's?"

"Yes," Tyr said. "He was a smith before he became a soldier, like Sir Vandar. He specialized in shields."

"Sounds like we would get along well," the knight said with a smile.

"Symbolism in Silico is quite popular." Tyr brought out his red shield as he spoke. "My family name is Lancelt. The symbol here is a wolf."

"A wolf? What for?" Tandem asked, eyeing Tyr's shield.

"It's the family crest. Silico uses wolves to symbolize good—"

"Quiet," the ferryman hissed, drawing all the attention to him. The party looked at the grizzled man as they saw him pointing a shaking finger to the front of the boat.

"What is that, exactly?" Tandem asked, covering his brow with his hand to focus on the distant object. A blob of translucent white appeared on the horizon, quickly approaching the boat.

"It be the mist," the ferryman said. "We're turning 'round." The ferryman stopped and reversed his rowing, moving the boat backwards as fast as he could.

"No, hold for a moment," Vandar said, gesturing to the ferryman.

"Not on me life, lad, we're not letting that... that *thing* catch up to us," he said, panicked. As he spoke, the mist approached the party, faster than the wind could carry it.

That's not a natural mist. It's headed right for us.

"This isn't going to work," Tandem said. "We can't outrun it. Save your energy."

"No, no, no, no, no," the ferryman shouted. "It's come for me!

It's going to take me this time!"

"Calm yourself, damn it," Vandar ordered, as he stood and brought out his red blade. "Everyone, to arms."

Tandem pulled a dagger from his belt. Tyr unsheathed his Soulblade.

Hey, he thought, picturing the girl in the sword. *If you can hear me, wake up. I might need your help.*

The fog blanketed the party and enveloped the whole of the boat, obscuring their vision. Along with the fog came a chill in the air, as though they were on the top of a snowy mountain, their breaths forming vapours in front of their faces. The fog blocked out the sun entirely, plunging the party into near darkness.

"Oh, have mercy," the mumblings of the ferryman continued as he shrank up close to the side of the boat, fear having gotten the better of him.

For a time, the group stood in silent vigilance, pondering what would happen next.

"Tandem, watch behind us," Vandar instructed. "Tyr, and you, sir, keep to the sides."

A few seconds passed, and then they heard it. Unnatural screams rang out from around the boat.

"What is that noise?"

The screams pierced through the fog, assaulting their ears. Tyr's head ached from the pounding noise. It was no ordinary scream, its pitch carrying oddly through the air.

"Lords help us," Tandem cried, clutching his dagger.

"It's been so long since you sent me an offering," a woman's voice called from within the mist. The sound came from all sides, the blanket of fog serving as an amplifier for the voice.

"You came back. Foolish man. This time you will not leave with your life."

"Who are you?" Vandar asked.

"My name is Naoba," the inhuman voice told them. It had an

odd allure, taunting and tempting at the same time.

"What do you want?" the knight asked, scanning back and forth as he reached for Rime. He heaved up the diamond shield and faced it at the front of the boat.

"Food," the voice said. "I need to feed, and you will do just fine."

Moments later, several deadly shards of ice rocketed toward Vandar out of the mist. He blocked the shards with his shield, the boat shuddering backwards in response.

"What could it be?" Tyr asked.

"Hard to say," Remus answered. "It's certainly no mortal creature. This fog is clearly magic."

"A magical fog... likely a river spirit," Vandar said. "We must discover where she's hiding."

The crew kept their guard up as they scanned around the deadly mist to find the voice's point of origin, but to no avail. Another scream went off around them.

A few moments later, a second salvo of ice shards shot out from within the mist, this time aimed at Tyr's head. The boy quickly held his red shield up out of instinct and managed to block the attack, but his body was knocked off balance from the force, almost throwing him overboard.

"Those shields won't save you forever," the river spirit said. New ice shards materialized around the mist, suspended in the air and aimed directly at the boat from every direction.

"We're going to need a bigger shield," Tandem said.

A moment later, the shards all rocketed toward the boat at breakneck speeds.

"Rime!" Vandar shouted, invoking his shield. From the front of his shield, a magical white barrier took form around the boat in a perfect circle, providing complete protection to the party within. The ice shards broke and splintered on the surface of the barrier.

I didn't know he could do that.

The spirit wailed again, followed by dozens of more shards breaking on the knight's barrier.

"Argh," Vandar shouted, "I cannot hold this forever. We must deal with this creature!"

What do we do? Tyr thought, his mind racing. *How do you beat a river spirit?*

The voice in the mist echoed out again, taking on a much more sinister tone. "Your magic is impressive," she wailed. "But a cold death is all that awaits you!"

The mist turned a deadly blue as it rapidly cooled. The cool mist caused ice to form on the water's surface.

"This is bad," Remus said.

"We're going to freeze if we stay in here for too long," warned Tandem, his teeth already chattering.

"You can have a swift death," she promised. "Why choose a frozen torture?"

"Damn it," the knight said. "That fog is definitely magic. If only Cecilia were here—"

Again, the river spirit cried, her savage song disorienting the party. Tyr dropped his shield as he brought a hand to his head to block the sound. He could feel warm blood trickling from his ear. Though the noise was almost overbearing, he could hear an inner voice suddenly speaking to him.

"*Tyr.*" He recognized the voice of the girl. It put him instantly at ease, and he could focus again.

It's you. What do we do?

"*Listen closely, Tyr. You need to destroy that mist.*"

How do we do that?

"*You need to use me.*"

Then you'll tell me…?

"*My name is…*"

Your name is…?

"Lumina!" Tyr yelled, brandishing his blade to the sky, invoking its power for the first time. His body heated up as his weapon enveloped him in a golden glow from head to toe. The energy and temperature coursing through him now were such that he felt he could explode at any moment.

Vandar lowered his magical shield and turned to watch in amazement.

The boy took the blade and swung out at the mist, each slice leaving behind a swath of yellow light that soared outward and cut everything in its path, breaking up the formation of fog and ice around them.

The group looked on in awe as Tyr slashed through the air all around them. The river spirit cried in agony as her mist was torn asunder by the golden rays.

Tumultuous waves crashed around the boat, which nearly capsized from the recoil of Tyr's slashes. The sun above pierced through the fog now, dissipating what remained of it in moments. The golden swaths of energy from Tyr's sword careened out as far as the eye could see, a whistling sound marking their immense speed.

"No! How can you do that! Stop!" Naoba cried, her voice becoming smaller and smaller until there was no more mist left, no disorienting fog to halt the group's advance.

Vandar the Red quickly scanned the water's surface for any signs of their assailant, raising his hand to Tyr. "Hold a moment," he said. Heat and life returned to the group as they looked for their enemy, eventually spotting her.

A girl stood ahead of the boat and over the water, staring at them. She seemed human, save for her seaweed attire and pale blue skin. She looked at the party with dead blue eyes, her body unmoving.

Vandar raised his red blade and trained it on her. The river spirit stayed motionless as her cold eyes turned to Tyr. Before anyone could react, the river spirit jolted quickly past Vandar and rushed at Tyr, ready to make a final desperate attack on his life. She screamed, the fearsome wail of an enraged creature.

Though Tyr was ill-prepared, she never connected with her target. Her body turned into water before reaching him, drenching everyone on the boat. Only a dagger remained where the spirit's body had been just moments before, held aloft by Tandem.

"Damn shame," he said, his face gaunt. "You were a real beauty, too."

CHAPTER 15

PURSUIT

Teleportation is an extremely rare and occult technique in Taerestris. Even Xeran magi have yet to create a safe method of the effect without resorting to the use of Soul Magic.

The immense cost of teleportation methods has led to its being outlawed in most countries.

LORITHAS THE MINDWEAVER
A BASIC GUIDE TO MAGIC

"Just what do you expect we'll find up there?"

Cecilia Scarlet spoke confidently. The sound of her clinking armour was accompanied by her horse's hooves on the old cobblestone street. Her scarlet hair bobbed along with her mount's gait, the colour shining in the brilliant light of the setting sun. She was presently several days away from the capital in the old district of a sleepy Nemean town. The area was deserted, the citizens having relocated to the newer quarters across town. Across from her was her colleague, the Daylight Assassin, atop his own mount.

"Hard to tell. We don't have much to go on when it comes to Dragon's Peak. Much less about that light at the summit."

"Do you think the mountain is really protected by Dragon Magic? It seems farfetched, to say the least." *I doubt all these recent events are disconnected.* The voice of King Remus went off in her head. *If there truly is another artefact in our midst, we must deal with it promptly.*

Cecilia had been tasked with ascending the peak; a feat that had never been accomplished in history. Naturally, she accepted the task without hesitation, confident in her and Sir Baou's abilities; no mountain would deny the will of her king and adopted father.

The knight in black spoke again. "You know my general position with respect to the existence of the dragons. Though all we have is circumstantial evidence, I see it as the simplest explanation for all of this. The alternative is that someone used Soul Magic to spellbind an entire mountain."

"I suppose we'll have to reach the top to know one way or another."

"Seems like it's our only option for now. I will tell you one thing, though."

The Iron Wall looked at her companion and raised her brow in curiosity.

"I've practised enough Soul Magic to know the relative cost

of enchanting environments. The price of such a spell would be enormous, far outstripping the power that sacrificing even a hundred years of a magus' life can grant him. Not even my own… *methods*… could muster that kind of power. If it's not a dragon, then whoever placed that spell must have been an extremely powerful sorcerer. I doubt someone like that could even exist."

A frigid wind blew between the knights. There was a long pause in their conversation.

"In any case, the little we know is better than going in blind," Cecilia said, lightening the mood. "Your magical knowledge continues to impress me."

"Is that a compliment from the great Cecilia Scarlet, or have I already gone senile?"

"That's the only one you'll get today."

At that moment, a whistling sound went off behind them. An enormous blue javelin flew past the two and crashed into the ground just ahead of Sir Baou. His horse stopped in its tracks and stood on its rear legs, protecting itself from the impact. Bits of cobble and rock hit the pair of knights, the force of the javelin's slam nearly enough to knock the duo from their mounts.

"What the hell was that?" Cecilia shouted, swivelling her horse, scanning the environment behind them.

Baou was already scouting the rear, pointing far off in the distance. "There." He identified a pair of dark silhouettes in the sky, the backdrop of the setting sun making them easy to spot. "Two unknowns… winged… they're well-armed."

Behind the knights, Cecilia noticed the javelin was dissipating into blue particles, the weapon fading into the air. "They're magic users." She unsheathed Nemoris.

"Wait. Let's see what they want first." Sir Baou dismounted his horse, stepping forward and placing a hand within his coat. The handle of a gleaming gladius stuck out near where he placed his hand.

The silhouettes grew larger as the winged creatures caught

up to the knights, a flurry of wind in their wake. The two landed elegantly on the street a short distance from the knights. Their wings remained fully outstretched in a dominant pose.

Cecilia steadied her horse as she examined their pursuers. One was a seraph, much like Stella; her wings were a solid white, though spotted with dark markings, signifying the disease. She held a silver glaive at them. The glaive was longer than Cecilia was tall, and it was sharpened to a deadly sheen.

The second seraph was far stranger-looking. Tattered black wings and glowing red eyes made up his appearance. He wore more decorative armour and carried a glaive of similar style and length to his compatriot. Floating in an arc above the black-winged seraph were various weapons in a deadly fanned display. The weapons twirled in midair as though held aloft by invisible threads.

"Well, this is a surprise," Baou said. "Does Skyfall send more of her subjects to join our cause?"

The black-winged seraph smiled. He spoke with a weighty tone befitting his frightening image. "The others mentioned powerful knights that represented a great threat to our people. I'm beginning to doubt their assessments."

"Who are you?" Cecilia asked, pointing her blade at him.

"Mordrin. Skyfall Isthalin."

Isthalin? Like Stella?

"Taela, Skyfall Isthalin. We had a few questions for you."

Cecilia clenched her teeth. For now, they were a captive audience.

"What are you planning to do with the Soulblades?" Mordrin asked, cutting straight to the heart of the matter.

"Self-defence," Baou said. "Returning the blades to Nemea is the crown's top priority."

"And what then?" Mordrin asked. "Might one enquire what your Nemea would do with such a magnificent power?"

"Keep the peace," Baou answered. "Our agenda is the same as yours."

As Baou spoke, he tapped his foot on the ground. The taps were easy for the unobservant to miss, but not Cecilia. The two had designed a clever method of communication using nonverbal cues, after all. She had received the message—Baou was stalling for time.

"What about you?" Baou asked. "My blade recognizes the magic that you're using. From what Stella tells us, magic is toxic to your bodies. Is your mangled form the result?"

"You'll watch your tongue when addressing him," Taela threatened. "How much has that traitor Stella told you?"

Mordrin raised a hand. "It's all true. We're a cursed people. But we all have our parts to play. Mine was doing what our High Priestess could not—to use the great power housed in these weapons. Whatever damage my body may endure is irrelevant."

"But why?" asked Cecilia. "Is your race not a peaceful one?"

Taela responded. "If Stella has revealed all she knows, then you should be aware that Alystra wants the weapons currently in your possession. With them, you humans pose a threat to Skyfall."

"And what kind of threat is that?" Cecilia asked, "Nemea is not a conquering nation. Our realm is an established one. Moreover, we were not even aware of the existence of Skyfall until your colleague decided to join us."

"Do you take us for fools?" Taela asked. "Are you claiming innocence while you are on your way to collect more of the blades?" Taela raised her silver glaive at Cecilia, its sharpened point glinting in the sunset.

"Spare us the power politics, human," Mordrin said. "Tell me, where is Stella now?"

"In the capital city," Cecilia answered. "Along with the rest of the Kingsguard. Believe me, you will not reach her alive if you try."

Mordrin laughed at her threat, a cold cackle that dripped with malice. "The rest of the Kingsguard, eh? The use of magic is a dangerous proposition for seraphs, indeed. But one which has granted us great insight." Mordrin flicked his hand, and his fan of weapons was instantly pointing at Cecilia. "How did you think we found you? Some of you are not in Nemea. You're divided."

Damn it, Cecilia thought, *that map Stella spoke of is still tracking the blades, then. This is bad.*

"You're out of options. Hand us the blades," Taela said.

Cecilia looked at Baou. Sweat dampened her temple as she gripped her horse's reins. She recalled a lesson in magic she had learned long ago. A magus normally requires verbal incantations to cast spells. However, if one was skilled enough, they could *Mindweave*, casting magic wordlessly. Lorithas was the creator of Mindweaving; Sir Baou was also a practitioner.

"Now!" Baou said. Instantly, a flash of light encompassed the street, blinding the seraphs. The knight remounted his horse during the flash, and the two were immediately barrelling down the empty road, away from the scene.

In the moment of confusion, Mordrin had launched his artillery of weapons in Cecilia's direction—the woman's horse was just fast enough to move out of harm's way, however. Several old buildings ahead of Cecilia were hit instead, the force of impact toppling them to the ground with a crash.

"Thanks for the distraction," Baou said, their horses galloping forward. "I could only weave a localized blind in such short notice."

"Save the thanks for later. Those two are still after us."

Behind the knights, the seraphs had quickly recovered from the blinding spell and had taken to the skies. Ahead of the knights was a dilapidated fountain marking the centre of a four-way intersection.

"Which way?" Cecilia asked.

Mordrin launched another spear at her as her horse veered out of its path.

"Split up; I'll take the right," Baou said, looking back at their fast-approaching enemies. "Circle around, meet back at that fountain; get back here quickly. I only need a moment to single one of them out."

"Got it. Don't die on me, Baou," Cecilia commanded as the two split paths. Cecilia didn't look back, focusing all her attention on escape. Overhead, she heard Mordrin giving orders.

"Take the male! I'll handle the other!"

Cecilia smiled, thanking her luck. *Wrong choice, bastard.*

Mordrin shot toward Cecilia while her horse gave everything it had to keep away from their pursuer. The black-winged seraph launched a salvo of ethereal weapons at Cecilia, faster and more numerous than before. Cecilia quickly rotated her body to meet the barrage.

"Nemoris!" she shouted, invoking the neutralizing power of her blade. She swung her sword at the missiles, the dispelling arc of its magic dissipating the oncoming attack.

Cecilia rounded to the right as the road ended, swerving out of the way of a second barrage. Her horse continued its gallop, while its rider dispelled the magical attacks the seraph made against her.

The woman charged down the street, taking backward looks to check on her pursuer. She rounded another right as Mordrin faced her, preparing hundreds of blades now. With a flick of his hand, the hail of arms bolted toward her.

Cecilia invoked Nemoris once more, dissolving the magic of the blades. As she finished her slash, a red glaive flew in through the magical salvo, cleaving through her silver armour and plunging through the top of her left shoulder. The speed of the impact pushed the glaive clean through, leaving Cecilia with a gaping wound in her shoulder. The force of the blow nearly knocked her off her horse. Instantly, she had lost all strength in her left arm; she grabbed the horse's reins with her sword hand.

He snuck in his real weapon in that last attack.

Her vision turned dark as she attempted to stabilize herself.

A wound this large meant she could no longer pose a significant threat against Mordrin; her death would likely follow soon after. Her body shook and shivered as she struggled to maintain consciousness, the life pouring out of her in a torrent of red.

Running out of options, Cecilia turned another right and raced back toward the fountain, praying for the best. She would not be able to move much in her current state, and fighting was an impossibility now—but perhaps she didn't need to. Baou had only asked for a moment of time after all.

I hope that was enough.

Mordrin materialized a final set of phantom blades, ready to finish off his prey. Cecilia kept moving, waiting for the final attack. She did not look back at Mordrin to check on his enemy—such a feat was impossible in her state, now. Though she heard the blades readied moments prior, she did not hear their approach. She tilted her head slightly, looking ahead and spotting the white fountain, the meeting point. Next to the fountain were two figures, one lying on the ground surrounded by a pool of red. Standing over it was another, calmly waiting.

"Sister!" Cecilia heard overhead, as her horse careened to a stop at the fountain.

Taela was on the ground; the Daylight Assassin had his gladius pointed at her throat. It was a black weapon with spikes protruding out of the crossguard. The most unnerving feature, however, was a blood-red eye affixed to the base of the blade. The eye swivelled maddeningly in its socket.

Cecilia used the last of her strength to sit upright and watch the scene unfold, Mordrin's storm of blades now aimed at Baou.

"I'd be careful if I were you," the knight said. "Your sister, is it? She's quite hurt."

"Don't you dare," Mordrin yelled, his blades now turning back to Cecilia as a threat.

"You have me misunderstood," Baou said. "I have no intention of killing anyone today."

Cecilia gazed at Taela's unconscious body, a gash across her chest that Baou had no doubt caused.

Baou spoke again. "I've put a triage spell on her. But it won't last forever, especially with that seal of hers. She needs medical attention, fast."

Mordrin's summoned blades disappeared into the ether as he approached his sister. He had lost the battle.

Baou stepped aside as he let the blackwing lift his sister in his arms. "Damn you," Mordrin said, his red eyes gleaming with anger. "This won't go unpunished."

"Take her," Baou said.

Without a word, Mordrin took hold of his sister and flew up with astonishing speed. He spent no further time on the knights, their presence having now become insignificant in light of his hurt sister. He carried her away, their silhouette disappearing into the sunset in seconds.

The fight over, the knights took a moment to recover.

"Sorry," Cecilia said, panting heavily. "…Got hit by his glaive."

"Don't worry. I can heal a wound like this. Lie here."

Cecilia followed his instruction, dismounting and collapsing against the marble of the white fountain. She felt her body going cold from the amount of blood she had lost, and her chest was now completely numb. The knight weaved a complicated spell, and the numbness began to disperse.

"The Daylight Assassin, healing the injured… Poetic." She chuckled, her laugh cut short as she coughed up blood.

"Spare me the jokes. This healing spell will work quickly, but the less you move, the better."

Cecilia tilted her head back and closed her eyes, the warmth of Baou's spell coursing through her body. She had lost a fair amount of blood, but Baou's magic would be enough to restore her vitality.

Sir Baou let out a raspy cough as he continued the spell, clutching his chest and panting heavily. He winced in pain.

"Don't overdo it, Baou. You know the price of using that magic."

"It's fine. I still have enough strength… for now. More importantly… They know some of us are absent from the city. And that blackwing one is definitely trouble."

Cecilia coughed again. Her eyes drooped down in exhaustion, but she forced out a few more words.

"Mordrin is his name… Stella told me about him. Never mentioned he was so disfigured. It seems he's acquired a Soulblade of his own."

Maybe it's that glaive? The details were difficult for Cecilia to piece together in her current state, but she did not recall Mordrin invoking a name when he used his powerful magic. Whatever Mordrin was doing with his Soulblade was certainly unique.

"This conflict is getting out of hand. Skyfall is obviously hostile now."

"…And you've already devised a plan, haven't you?"

"As Remus said, the situation has changed. We'll have to deal with the mountain later. If their map shows Soulblade locations, it is safe to say that they can't access whatever is up there, or they would have gone there already."

"There's no way we can contact the king quickly enough to warn him about this."

"Right. That's why this next part is a bit tricky. I managed to place a tracking enchantment on the female before you showed up."

"Ever planning ahead, aren't you?" Cecilia smiled.

Baou completed his healing spell. "I'll prepare a teleport for both of us. Now that we know where Skyfall is, we need to negotiate terms. You should be fine in a few days. Once you're healed up, we can go."

"A direct confrontation in enemy territory. Are you sure about that?"

"It's the best path forward," Baou said. "Though the two

seraphs here had no qualms with killing us. We will need to have some form of leverage."

"And that leverage is?"

"Nemoris."

Cecilia nodded, realizing what Baou had in mind. She felt her consciousness fading now. Her vision turned dark. "But one thing—If that bluff doesn't work, what then?"

"I haven't figured that part out yet."

SEEKING SHADOWS

SEPTIMIAN DYNASTY, YEAR 242
KINGDOM OF NEMEA, DRAGON'S PEAK

At the edge of the world, legendary shadows faded.

Old champions bound by the shackles upon them.
A battle no one would witness, for a cause long forgotten.
One last time the fading legends would do battle at the edge
of the world.

SIR TANDEM THE YOUNGER
TALES, VOLUME II

Kai felt the steady falling snow burn at her hands as she pulled herself upward, a million tiny stabs of frost that plummeted from the skies.

Had her body not gone numb to the chill wind days ago, perhaps she would have surrendered to the little bites. Surrounded by the wintry weather, Kai traversed an unstable ledge, taking care not to fall. The task was made no easier by the slippery footing and her heavy armour.

"Why not remove your pauldron?" Specter would ask.

You know why, she would answer.

To the young woman, leaving her Kai-Jin armour behind would be death, like forgetting all those she had slain. Keeping the armour on was a lighter load.

Kai moved up the mountain, scaling its side with obsessive determination. The young woman used her hands to climb a steep wall of frozen rock. Though the wall was painfully cold, her body moved nonetheless, eager to complete the task. Kai reached the top of the frozen wall and vaulted over, finding herself standing on a snowy plateau. The plateau was wide, large enough to fit a farm. The only things that separated the plateau and the abyss below were sparse rocks and small hills interspersed throughout the area.

So, she thought, *have any of your memories come back?*

"Nothing since the last time. But we are close."

Kai trudged along the plateau, content with the stability it offered. As she progressed, the icy winds died down and snow transformed to water. It was not long before the melting snow gave way to a wide, stone path. Embers and orange sparks drifted in the wind, their brilliant glow lighting the scene unnaturally.

"What is this?" she asked, noting strange figures along the path.

"I... remember this."

Lying on the ground were the remains of dead soldiers. They seemed to come out of a scene from centuries past, outfitted in rusting ancient armour. Some had arrows jutting out of their bodies, others impaled with swords or spears. The image looked like a great battle had taken place, a graveyard of metal and blackened flesh as its legacy.

"These soldiers… they are familiar."

How so?

"I remember the armour."

Specter manifested from Kai's scroll, inspecting the bodies. There was barely anything left of them now. Time had reduced their forms to little more than ashen bones.

"Specter," Kai said, "I think it's important I tell you this now." The pale shade looked back. "Some time ago, I met a woman. A psychic. She told me a great many things. If not for her, I wouldn't have come to this mountain." Kai walked along the path, surveying the mass graves. Specter followed. "She knew about you, and the day we first met. I haven't pieced it all together, but—"

"But?"

"She called you a king. It's starting to make sense to me now. Specter, did you know?"

The shade contemplated for a few moments. "Nothing about being a king. My memories are still incomplete, but I do recognize these men."

"I don't understand it yet, but I think these might be *your* soldiers."

Specter furrowed his brow.

The two continued on the path, more armoured corpses littering the way. Eventually, the path concluded into a circular area. Just ahead was an unexpected sight.

Directly in the centre of the circle was a massive knight, kneeling on the ground, unmoving and lifeless. On its back was a tattered red cape, a faded lion emblazoned on the fabric. The ancient armour was corroded like that of the other soldiers. Its helmet faced the ground. In its right hand was a great, black blade, more akin to a butcher's cleaver than a sword.

The circle resembled an arena. More lifeless knights lined the edges, all kneeling and facing the centre. Behind them were dilapidated stone pillars that marked the cliffs beyond. As Kai stepped into the circle, she felt the ground tremble.

Behind her, Specter spoke. "Could it be…? Gothric?"

The ground stopped trembling. The great knight suddenly shifted, centuries of dust falling through the cracks in its old armour. Though the eroded metal revealed little, Kai could see the dark figure within the crevices, the shrivelled black skin of a dead body.

"Who is Gothric?" she asked.

"Gothric, Gothric… what happened to you?" Specter looked at Kai. "I remember now. You're right—I was a king. Was." Specter held a hand to his head. "A king of Nemea. Many years ago. How long I do not know. I recall the castle, my soldiers, and… my Kingsguard. How could I have forgotten?

"Gothric was my greatest knight. I entrusted all my secrets to him, and he lent me his extraordinary strength to defend the realm. Yes… their names are all flooding back to me now. Ceal, Gothric, Bolverk. So many others."

"Why is he here? What about the soldiers?"

"I cannot remember! But why?" He looked to his former Kingsguard. He closed his hands into fists.

He did not speak, but Kai knew what he felt at that moment. Longing. Remorse. Guilt.

The old knight shifted again, like a statue coming to life. He stood slowly, rising to meet the two facing him.

"We must learn more," Specter said. "But you must pass Gothric first. This will be your second trial."

Gothric stood fully now, towering over the young woman. His face was hidden almost entirely by his helmet; there was only darkness between the slits. Gothric raised his giant sword, pointing it at Specter.

"Gothric," the shade said, "I am sorry, old friend. All this time and yet you continue on. You still do not know peace."

The old knight's sword trembled in the air. No sound escaped his helmet. He lowered his sword again and raised his left arm, placing a fist over his chest in a military salute.

Specter did the same. "I know not who did this, but this is wrong. Gothric did die, but not here. Not on this mountain. He couldn't have."

Specter returned to the scroll again, his voice permeating her mind. *"You must defeat Gothric. You will have three days. If you cannot defeat him within that time, you will die here. Look there, behind him."*

The young woman moved her eyes behind the pillars of the arena, taking note of a small hill that led on up the mountain.

"That is the path forward, should you succeed."

Kai nodded. She approached a corpse lying nearby. A sword was lodged in its midsection. She pulled it free and tested its weight as she turned back to Gothric. She felt the rising feeling in her chest again.

"His strength has faded. Nonetheless, Gothric will not be easy to defeat. He was always my best."

Not anymore.

With a small flourish of her newfound blade, Kai began the second trial. Without hesitation, she approached the ancient knight and attacked. The combat was gruelling. The knight was much faster than she had anticipated, and each powerful swing would leave winds that buffeted her body. She fought Gothric with all her might, using the skills she had acquired from her training as a gladiator, but to no avail; she could not land a hit. Gothric's silent assault kept her on the defensive.

The two fought with the strength of titans; the clash of their blades filled the air.

It is said that two great warriors who fight on the battlefield will sometimes peer into each other's mind. The blade reveals the truth of one's experience, and in combat, the truth can never truly hide. With each mighty swing, Gothric told Kai his story. With the force of his slashes, she saw eternal dedication to his king. With his unrelenting aggression, she learned of Gothric's pride and Nemean honour. Finally, with the noble movements and gestures of his body, she learned of the tragic tale of his end—slain in battle defending his family.

She fought Gothric for a full day. Though the old Kingsguard's assault was uncompromising, neither he nor Kai could make a successful strike on the other. Day turned to night, and Kai eventually tossed aside the old sword, ending her first attempt. Gothric knelt once more, resettling his blade on the ground and assuming his statue-like demeanour, accepting Kai's temporary truce.

That night, Kai rested uneasily, mulling over what she had learned. She sat in the darkness, staring at the brilliant sky. Beyond the clouds was that shining light at the top of the mountain, looming ever closer, taunting her with the power she sought. Despite her past successes, she still felt there were so many things to know, so many mysteries and puzzles waiting to be solved.

"Specter," she asked, "what is Nemea like? Please tell me."

The voice filled her mind. *I still have but pieces of the full picture. But this I can tell you. I remember the city. It was small then.*

"What was the city like? The people?"

A burgeoning empire, if you could call it that. I remember the faces of the people, faces with not a care in the world. Then... something happened.

"What was it?"

I still don't know. All I remember is the aftermath—mass graves. Countless families wiped out. A city in ashes. Tears.

Kai thought hard on Specter's words. A thought was beginning to emerge. There was more to Specter's past than he was letting on. It couldn't all be disconnected from the story he had told her during the first trial. Though she didn't want to consider it, she was no longer certain about his intentions. For the time being, she pushed the thoughts out of her head. As Kai drifted to sleep, her mind wandered to Gothric, what he fought to defend in his time and what she was fighting for now.

We're not so different, you and I.

On the second day, Kai adapted her strategy. Procuring a spear from another body, she challenged Gothric once more. With a spear, she would have the ranged advantage against her foe, allowing her to be more aggressive. She fought restlessly, using the spear's range to land her first blows on the knight. Though she found more success with the spear, her attacks merely grazed Gothric's armour, the old knight's speed proving to be too much.

Through their combat, more emotions came flooding in from Gothric's blade. Perhaps this was his first true match as a shade, or perhaps she was the first to ever get this far up the mountain; it didn't matter. There was joy in their deadly dance, one fighting to maintain past glories, the other fighting to create her own. Gothric was weakened now, a shell of his former self, but the raging spirit of the warrior continued to burn brightly within him. His zeal for battle impressed her. She had always fought out of her forced bondage or for survival, but she had never fought for the thrill of combat itself.

His attacks were more powerful on the second day, his black blade bearing down on his opponent. Though she had the ranged advantage, it seemed that the old knight was getting stronger, the excitement of battle rousing him from his ancient stupor. He telegraphed a certain bloodlust, the kind that can only be awakened by an equally powerful opponent. It took everything Kai had within her to dodge the knight's strikes and avoid his blows; if only a single strike connected, it would surely mean the end of the trial, and her life.

Again, day turned to night, and Kai retreated once more, having failed a second time.

"He's too strong," she said to Specter. The midnight moon shone on the two warriors. "I can't land a hit."

Gothric knelt in front of her again, unmoving. The young woman rested on the ground, inches away from the old knight, her head to the night sky. The stars twinkled, brilliant figures in the black sea above. In that dark, Kai contemplated her trial and what was to become of her the next day.

"*Only one day remains.*"

"I know. But I don't know what to do."

She felt anxious again, the fear of what a loss would mean like a hand on her throat. Her eyes grew heavy, her mind desperately searching for a solution. Though her anxiety made it difficult to do so, eventually, her exhausted body surrendered to sleep.

Only those of pure heart may fully ascend.

Kai awoke with a start, Veris' voice echoing in her head. Above her, the dawn's sun cast its pale light onto the arena. Kai stood promptly, moving to a skewered knight. Gothric stood in response, readying his battle stance for the third time.

"I know what to do now," she said. "I know how to win."

The young woman pulled out a pair of swords from the skewered knight as she examined them.

"*What have you arrived at?*"

"It's just an idea, but…"

Back at the base of the mountain, Veris had said that the tests would be trials of purity. This isn't a test of strength at all. It isn't *about* fighting."

She flourished the two swords and trained them on Gothric. One of them was slightly shorter than the other, allowing perfect movement in combat. She knew exactly what was being asked of her now, in this second trial. She could do it. She would.

"I've been too afraid of getting hurt," she said. "I think… I've been afraid of that all this time. It's holding me back."

Kai steadied herself as she stared down her opponent. During her previous combats with Gothric, she recognized how the old knight would swing this way or that, betraying his real feelings, the pain of his loss, the heaviness in his heart, and even the joy of fighting. Despite his heroic strength, Gothric exposed himself to Kai completely in this way. He was showing her how a true warrior fought.

If she wanted to win, she had to let go of her emotions, the ones she wanted to hide. Although she had impressive strength, her fears and worries would often grip her like a vice. It had happened in Kai-Ji, and it had happened during her ascent. This was what she needed to confront—her real enemy was not Gothric, but herself.

"The only reason I am still here is that I've been lucky and had help. On my own, I am just scared. I won't hold back anymore."

With that, Kai leapt to Gothric, mounting a full assault. She took no time to guard herself, leaving her body open to counters from the knight. As if by magic, her blows suddenly began landing. She attacked recklessly without a care for herself, smothering the fear that had gripped her the previous two days.

If you're not prepared to get hurt, you can't achieve anything. She repeated in her mind. Her blades found their target, crushing blows finally being dealt to the old Kingsguard. Her movements were like a whirlwind, her swords a vortex of steel.

Gothric's attacks were also at their peak. His metal pierced her; a thousand cuts covered her body. It didn't matter. She didn't feel them. They weren't real. Though the black blade sliced through her body, it dealt little damage. Kai had realized the secret of the trial. She had no fear.

Kai kept her attacks focused on the old knight's arms, weakening his strength, crumbling his offence. The fight became simple now, victory the only thing on her mind. She pushed aside all her thoughts, all her worries and distractions. Only the moment mattered.

She pummelled Gothric with blow after blow, and eventually landed a direct stab in the knight's chest. Gothric made his first sound, a low roar as he let fall his black blade. Kai dropped her weapons as well, her trembling hands unable to maintain their grip. Blood dripped from her wounds to the ground.

I did it.

With the last of his strength, Gothric knelt before Kai, his head tilting down as he acknowledged her success.

Specter manifested himself again, placing an ethereal hand on Gothric's shoulder. "Goodbye, old friend."

The knight made a final low roar in response as he collapsed to the ground, his long service finally over.

The young woman dropped alongside him, drained from the performance. There was silence for a time. Kai had defeated her enemy—but her enemy was not Gothric. It was her fears that the mountain had asked her to conquer.

"Specter," Kai said, "Do you think it… he… was alive?"

"Perhaps. It's more probable that he was like me—a shadow of my former self. You've brought him peace. I should thank you."

Kai nodded, and the ground trembled once more.

This time, it seemed as though the entire mountain shuddered beneath her. After several moments, the tremors stopped.

"What was that?" she asked.

"It means you are almost ready. You've rid yourself of your weaknesses. The mountain quakes as it purifies its challengers. There is but one more trial awaiting you."

Specter motioned behind the arena before returning to the scroll.

"Right," Kai said, as she lay next to Gothric's body. She placed a hand on his armour and felt a sombre connection to a worthy opponent. "But let's rest for a moment. The mountain can wait."

DRAGONCALLER

SEPTIMIAN DYNASTY, YEAR 242 – OUTLANDS, GREAT DIVIDE

A user can speak with their Soulblade directly. This is known as Communion.

When a Soulblade accepts a new owner and enters into a contract with them, it is known as Attunement.

Finally, the use of a Soulblade's effect in the field requires calling out the name of the blade and is known as Invoking.

SIR TANDEM THE YOUNGER
HISTORIA TAERESTRIA

Tyr struggled to keep up with the rest of the party. The group trekked through the snowy tundra of the Outlands, freezing temperatures keeping the four in constant shivers. Vandar led the group, his diamond shield acting as protection from the frigid gusts that would occasionally bear down upon them.

"Tyr," Lumina would say, *"it's so beautiful."*

Easy for you to say. You're not the one who has to deal with this cold.

Tyr had to admit, however, that the Outlands were truly a sight to behold. He had experienced the snowy cliffs, frozen lakes, and frosted evergreens that populated the strange land. The hostile days were one thing, but the serene nights were another. Their silent evenings often left time for contemplation, the group huddling together around a fire with only the sound of the wind to lull them to sleep. Here there were no people, no expectations, no worries.

Tyr had taken the time to commune with Lumina and get to know her better, feeling their connection grow stronger since the day she had given him her name. For Tyr, however, that wasn't the pivotal moment—he replayed a different memory in his mind, a conversation he had with her prior to invoking her power.

In the white world on her regal chair, he had told her: *"The king said that you're in good hands—and you are. I want to learn more about you, though; I've decided to keep you."*

He recalled her smile, how she'd quivered at the idea. *"Tyr, thank you."*

The group stopped in their tracks. Tyr's mind snapped to the present.

"There," Remus pointed. "We've arrived."

Tyr looked ahead of the party into the distance. An immense translucent wall of light had appeared, a wispy blend of brilliant greens and whites. It had no concrete borders or edges, its light merely fading like vapours into the air. The smoky colours of the wall danced with themselves, shifting and morphing like a mixture of liquids. The wall stretched out as far as the eye could see.

"The Great Divide," Tandem said. "I've heard of magic walls, but this…"

"Come," Remus said. "We'll be the rare few who dare cross it."

"Hopefully we'll be the rarer few to cross it back," the bard replied.

The group made their way to the wall before coming to a stop. Its height was impressive from afar, but up close it stretched seemingly to the heavens themselves.

"Tyr," Remus said, "what do you know about the wall?"

"Only what I've read about it, Your Majesty." Tyr recited what he studied on the subject. "The Great Divide is a magical phenomenon that surrounds most of Inner Taerestris. Lands beyond are deemed inhospitable by common folk, so it's mostly unexplored territory. I read in a book once that what lies behind it is a complete mystery."

"Very good," Remus said. "Now watch."

The king brought a hand from within his robes and grazed the wall. Waves rippled out from the point of contact along the wall's surface like a drop of water hitting a lake. Remus stepped forward into the thin layer of the wall and phased through it, the barrier granting him passage. He motioned for the rest of the group to join him.

Tyr went through it, surprised by its warmth as it let him pass.

"That's one way to warm you on a cold winter's night," Tandem said.

"Welcome to the Outlands," Remus said. "We're in unknown territory now."

Their surroundings were not vastly different from before, yet an odd, unwelcome feeling permeated Tyr's mind. It didn't help that Lumina shared the same opinion.

"I don't like it here, Tyr."

Hopefully, we won't be long.

The group marched for a short time before stopping once again, the magical wall still visible behind them.

"This should be far enough," Remus said. "Stand back, everyone."

Remus pulled his cowl off, freeing his silver hair. The king knelt to the ground, grabbing a lump of snow and examining it. Just under the snow was a blue surface, frozen water that was now exposed. The king stood once more and unsheathed his sword.

Tyr craned his neck to get a closer look at the king's weapon for the first time. It was a pale white sword with various symbols carved upon the blade. The sword seemed to dazzle brilliantly in the dull light of the tundra, glowing particles emanating from the metal. The crossguard featured dragon wings as part of the design.

"We found this one only recently," Remus said. "And more recently still have I acquired its name—and its unique power."

Remus took a deep breath as he held the blade in both hands, pointing it down at the icy surface. With great force, he plunged the blade into the frozen water, invoking the power of the weapon. "Avenir!"

A wave of wind rippled out from the point of impact, blowing the snow away. Tyr looked down for a moment—the group was standing on a frozen lake, previously hidden underneath the snow. He struggled to maintain his footing as he watched the magic of the sword in action.

The blade shone a bright red as the frozen lake cracked and buckled under its power. The roar of a dragon escaped from the centre of the blade, echoing out and travelling through the snowy tundra. The sound was like rolling thunder, a magical cry of immeasurable might.

Then, they waited. A few moments passed, and Tandem spoke up. "...Was that it? What did you do?"

"Wait," the king commanded.

I have a bad feeling about this.

Time passed. The only thing that filled the silence was the sound of the icy wind. Then, it happened.

"Look there," Vandar said, pointing at the horizon.

Tyr saw it now—a dark shadow looming in the skies. Shapes grew from each side of its silhouette as the shadow grew larger. It was only when it gave a now-familiar roar that Tyr confirmed what it was.

"With all due respect, Your Majesty, you better be damn sure about this," Tandem said.

A dragon.

Its cry reached them in moments, shaking the ice they stood upon. Tyr reached for his blade instinctively, but King Remus held his hand up, bidding him to stand by.

Soon the dragon was over them, its gargantuan wings causing little tempests to form beneath it. It landed over them with another roar, crashing on a frozen peak as bits of icy rock crumbled to the frozen lake below. The dragon's mouth was wide enough to fit the four of them. Golden scales made up its skin, which featured white spikes. Its eyes shone brightly, dazzling blue flames burning in each iris. A bright blue tether between the king's sword, Avenir, and the dragon's neck appeared, giving the appearance of a leash. The dragon gave a snarl as it examined the four below them.

"Well, this is interesting," it said. "Very interesting."

The dragon's imposing mouth made no movements as it spoke, its resonant voice reaching the party's ears through other-worldly means.

Have you ever seen a dragon?

"Never."

Remus stepped forth, addressing the serpentine creature. "I am Remus Septimius, King of Nemea. It was I who bound you to my blade."

The dragon's pupils grew smaller, focusing on Remus. "Tiny humans. You should not be here."

"We have a few questions, Mr Dragon, and—"Tandem said.

"Drake," it interrupted Tandem. "I am a drake." The drake brought a scaled hand to the tether formed by Avenir, testing its flexile strength. "Powerful magic."

"We mean you no harm, great drake," Remus said. "We are merely seeking information."

The drake snarled at Remus again. "By binding an eternal dragon to your will?"

"Drake,"Tandem said.

The drake snorted at Tandem, flecks of fire escaping its nostrils. The bard took a cautious backstep.

"White-haired one. It takes much energy for you to use this binding. You have nothing to fear. We young drakes are not like the elders."

Remus nodded. He stumbled forward, grabbing the handle of his blade for support as he let out a hacking cough. Blood spilled out of his mouth and onto the cold ice.

"My king," Vandar exclaimed.

With effort, King Remus reseated the blade in the folds of his robe, the blue tether now broken. "It is fine." He breathed heavily. "That magic does tax me so. I'm afraid I am not as spry as I used to be."

"Thank you," the drake said, flexing its nostrils in gratitude. "My name is Mynax."

"Well, Mynax, if a historian may ask, just how old are you?" Tandem said, an eyebrow raised at the scaled creature.

"I have lived for three thousand years."

"Young, indeed,"Tandem replied.

The drake moved its snout closer to the bard again. It took several deep breaths with its nose, inspecting the man.

"Wait a moment," Tyr said. "If you're a drake, how big are dragons?"

The drake turned to the boy as it engaged in the same ritual, acquiring his scent. "Hmmm. Perhaps two or three times my size. Some are even larger."

"Do dragons really live forever?" Tyr asked.

"That I do not know. Perhaps someday we will die. The elders have been here since the beginning of time."

"How long is that? So far?" Vandar asked.

The drake once again performed its sniffing ritual on the knight before answering.

"Five hundred thousand years," it said, sending a shock through the party.

"Five hundred thousand?" Tandem said. "That's unimaginable."

"Perhaps. But we dragons have a different perspective of time." Mynax looked toward Remus, sniffing him out as it did the others. "You humans are carrying dangerous weapons. Weapons of magic. Powerful magic."

"The world is dangerous," King Remus stated. "It pays to come prepared." The king pointed back at the vapoury wall in the distance. "It appears this land is under the effect of its own powerful magic. Might it be Dragon Magic?"

"Yes," Mynax said. "It is the spell of a dragon, crafted long ago."

"Could you tell me exactly why this barrier was put in place, and by whom?" Remus asked.

The drake shook some snow off its body and responded. "This I do not know. The elders choose not to talk about it. It was put in place to prevent our kind from mingling with yours."

"Are you telling me the ancient stories are true?" the king asked. "The War of Three is not merely a myth?"

"This I also do not know. But this barrier has kept us inside for a very long time. Its strength is finally waning."

"What will happen once it dissolves completely?"

"Hmmm," Mynax said, deep in thought. "The elders are different. Different from the young drakes. They want to escape this barrier. I see only hatred in their eyes."

"Well, I don't see a problem with that, I would feel a bird in a cage if I had been locked up in this dreary place for thousands of years," Tandem said, drawing the drake's attention. "N-not that it isn't nice, of course."

"What do your elders have planned?" Remus asked.

"This I do not know," Mynax said. "They are restless. I see them go to strange places near the border, perhaps having meetings. They keep much information from the younger drakes. We do not desire war. The elders are a different story."

"This is all so confusing," Tandem said. "But it is apparent to me now that there is an overabundance of evidence that purports to this War of Three being more than myth. We have a real dragon in our midst."

"Drake," Mynax said.

Far off in the snowcapped mountains, a thunderous roar bellowed out and reverberated throughout the area, startling the group. Snow fell from rocky hills like small avalanches.

The drake turned its head back to the source. "You must leave. I cannot guarantee your safety here."

It's another dragon.

A second roar went off, this one much louder and closer.

"It is an elder. They will not want to see this."

"But we still have more questions," the boy blurted out. "What about—"

"The information is useless if we're all dead. Now move!" Remus shouted, his forceful tone commanding action.

The group started running. Tyr took a last look at Mynax, burning the image of the drake in his mind. He wasn't sure if he would ever see something so magnificent ever again—he would be sure not to forget.

Behind it, the shadow of the elder dragon approached the party with shocking speed. The group moved as quickly as they could on the frozen surface, but it was no match for the speed of their winged pursuer—a black-scaled menace with imposing horns and a spiked tail.

"The wall!" Remus said, pointing ahead to the protective barrier.

Behind them, the elder dragon shot off huge fireballs in their direction, a hellstorm of heat that destroyed the land around them. Hills collapsed and the snow melted. The frozen lake underneath them cracked and buckled, making their escape more perilous. Huge chunks of ice sank, and the water below gushed out violently.

Tyr jumped from one such piece of ice and onto solid ground. The dragon was above them now, casting its wide shadow overhead. It breathed in for a few moments before firing off another ball of flame, this time directly at the group.

"Rime!" Vandar shouted, the magical barrier manifesting and shielding the group.

The fireball hit the shield, its flames dispersing along its surface and then onto their surroundings. The group raced through a hellish landscape, moments away from reaching the Great Divide.

The dragon knew where the group was headed—in response, it cast a powerful spell, raising a wall of ice just ahead of the group to block off their escape. Miniature quakes shook the ground as the icy wall rose and morphed into place.

"You're up, Tyr," Vandar shouted, lowering his shield for a split second.

"Lumina!" Tyr shouted, invoking the power of his blade, feeling its glowing energy coursing through him again. He wasted no time in delivering several slashes of his blade at the icy blockade. The magic of his Soulblade made easy work of it, the ice crashing down and revealing a small path forward.

The dragon was a hair's distance away now, breathing in a third time and shooting a stream of fire from its nostrils. The four had just made it through the magical barrier and onto the other side when the fire hit. Tyr pivoted around to see the magic of the vapoury barrier at work, keeping the dragon's flames at bay. The flames spread out and covered the wall, blocking the view to the other side.

The boy looked around to check his allies. The party was drenched with sweat from the heat of the dragon's flames, but they were safe and accounted for. The fires on the other side of the wall dissipated.

The dragon behind the wall crashed to the ground and looked to the party, flashing red jewels for eyes. For several tense moments, it stayed there, growling low.

King Remus moved back to the edge of the wall, staring the dragon directly in the eyes. The dragon stared back fearlessly.

"Well," Tandem said, catching his breath, "is it going to say anything?"

The elder dragon's pupils flicked to the bard, its nostrils flaring at him imposingly. Tandem jumped back.

The dragon turned around, ever so slowly, making sure the four could see the full might of its hulking stature before spreading its wings wide and flying away.

Tyr scanned the destroyed backdrop left behind by the elder dragon, but there was no sign of Mynax. The drake was gone. The boy sheathed his sword, Remus already trudging away from the scene.

"My king?" Vandar asked.

But the king gave no response.

CHAPTER 18

CECILIA'S GAMBIT

SEPTIMIAN DYNASTY, YEAR 242
KINGDOM OF NEMEA, INN

Seraph society has only recently been rediscovered along with the advent of the Soulblades.

Under the rule of the church, the seraphs lived prosperously, their lifespans lasting hundreds of years.

SIR TANDEM THE YOUNGER
NOTES FROM STELLA THE MIRACLE

"Y**ou've done this before, right?" Cecilia asked.

"Once," Baou replied.

The two stood in a quaint, wooden room on the upper floor of an inn. Cecilia had fully recovered from her wounds, thanks to Sir Baou's healing spell, and they were now ready to make their move. The room was cleared, the furniture pushed to the walls, and space was made in the middle.

Sir Baou moved to the centre and muttered his incantations. "From what Stella has told me, I have a basic mental map of the city's layout. We'll only have one chance to make our entrance. Hopefully, my placement is correct, and we don't have to improvise."

"And if the portal placement is wrong?"

"We might have to fight our way through."

Cecilia nodded, placing a hand on the pommel of her blade. She looked to Baou, noting the beads of sweat rolling down his temple. Sparks of energy traced out in the form of a circle on the ground.

The tax of using that magic must be enormous. "A suicide mission, then."

"Only if we fail."

Sir Baou finished his spell, manifesting a whirlpool of blue energy in the room's centre. The portal churned as it drew the surrounding furniture to it with its gravity. Sparks continued to fly off the portal, ricocheting off the walls.

"It's done," he said. "It's not exactly stable, so stay alert."

"Stable?"

"Well, you'll see what I mean. Just don't get lost down there. See you on the other side."

Without hesitation, Sir Baou unsheathed his gladius and leapt into the portal, his body melting into the swirling, blue energy and vanishing from sight. Cecilia followed suit, brandishing Nemoris. She took a deep breath to steady herself and jumped into the unknown. As she phased into its depths, she was enveloped into the darkness that followed.

For the next few moments, she plummeted through blackness. The only thing that signified her movement was the feeling of falling and the sound of things rushing past her. Twinkling lights formed nearby. The lights grew closer as Cecilia shot past them. As they grew, the flashing points opened up around her and she could see through them.

Other portals.

Through one, she saw green farmlands. Through another, she saw the misty top of a mountain. The portals multiplied in number until she was surrounded by hundreds of them, all with diverse destinations, many to places she had never seen nor heard of in her travels.

Cecilia looked down and spotted a portal growing directly beneath her feet. She recognized the top of Sir Baou's dark hair in the image. He stood on a marble floor. She saw the image quickly grow and fill her field of vision before she dropped through, completing the teleportation. Her metal boots hit the marble with a clatter as she landed next to Baou. The portal above her head faded away.

"What is the meaning of this?" a regal voice above her asked.

Baou, you bastard, you did it, she thought.

Cecilia looked up to find herself in a cavernous room resembling an auditorium, she and Baou at its centre. The marble floor had intricate red designs featuring winged creatures. The sides of the tall room were covered in frescoes, and black columns rose up to support the glass ceiling. Surrounding them on the edges of the room were legions of seraphs, a thousand of their deadly glaives trained directly on them.

No doubt about it, Cecilia thought, *Skyfall's seat of power.*

Sir Baou pointed his gladius upward at the voice. "High Priestess Alystra. A pleasure to finally meet."

Cecilia's eyes followed the tip of Baou's gladius to its target. High above them, situated on the far wall, was an ornate stand with the High Priestess in the very centre. Cecilia noted her silky white vestments, replete with jewels and golden trim. Her hair was a pale white, flowing seemingly without end. Cecilia was not surprised by the image of royalty, but by the unique number of wings on her back.

Six instead of two. At least it makes finding her easy.

Around the wall were various other stands with more seraphs, likely the High Priestess' advisors.

"You!" said a familiar voice. A demented-looking blackwing landed a distance in front of the knights. He pointed a clawed hand at them.

"Mordrin," the High Priestess called, "you know these two?"

"Yes. They are the ones who nearly killed my sister. I'll have your heads!"

"You will do no such thing," Alystra said. "You have disobeyed my orders once, and now you seemingly lead the enemy right to us. Do not make this your third mistake." She turned to the two Kingsguard. "Why have you come here? Speak plainly, or you will be skewered."

Baou nodded toward Cecilia and the two sheathed their weapons.

"Right," Cecilia said. "I understand given our recent… scuffle with one of your subjects, this may seem contradictory. But we're here to negotiate peace terms."

"Continue," Alystra said.

"We have some idea," Cecilia said, "of the struggle the seraphs have experienced due to the toxic effects of the Spellseal. Stella has—"

"You dare throw her name in our faces?" one of the advisors shouted. "The one we *knew* as Stella is dead and gone. All that remains of her is a traitorous creature, unfit to lay claim to our divine heritage."

"Contain yourself," Alystra said, raising a hand at her advisor. "What has she told you of us?"

"Nothing distasteful. She loves her nation," Baou said.

"Though you may not agree with her methods, she has Skyfall's best interests at heart. She is still on your side."

"Ah, more of this," the High Priestess said. "Stella is deranged. The curse grips her mind and speaks lies to her, claiming the greater good. Even you humans should be able to see that. She came to me with a proposal to hand the blades over to you humans, to fight against make-believe enemies. A traitor and a liar, that is all Stella is."

"There's the crux of the problem," Cecilia said. "We have reason to believe everything she said is true."

Hushed whispers circulated the room. Alystra's eyes narrowed.

"End this foolishness," said a voice from the walls. "Enough lies," said another.

The High Priestess spoke again. "Stella made bold claims before her exile. Claims regarding the blades and their purpose. What proof do you have?"

"Isn't it obvious?" Baou said. "Strange lights coming from mountains. Swords of legend revealing themselves. A magical wall surrounding the land, getting weaker by the day. Does any of this not even pique your curiosity?"

"What magical wall?" Mordrin asked. He looked at the High Priestess.

"You didn't know?" Cecilia said. "About what lies north. Beyond the barrier. It's only rumours, but with everything that's happening, I find it more than likely that dragons—"

"You will cease your fantastical prattle," the High Priestess commanded.

"There is no such thing in the north!" a clergyman shouted.

Mordrin narrowed his eyes. He realized now that this was the full extent of the secret the High Priestess was hiding. He looked to the clergy, their stone faces revealing their complicity in the act. Not only had the High Priestess withheld information about the humans cursing them with the Spellseal, but she also knew about these dragons. He had not told the High Priestess about Bolverk's revelation regarding the war, and he would keep it that way. For now, he would continue the charade.

"Dragons?" he asked. "Like the old stories? You must think us credulous to suffer these lies. They have never existed, a species with little ground in reality."

Mordrin needed more information, but he had to be careful about it. He had to know about these dragons.

"And we thought the same about seraphs until one of your commanders showed up on our doorstep," Baou retorted. "How much proof do you need before you realize the gravity of the situation?"

So they believe the dragons to be real. Perhaps before Stella's exile, he would have thought otherwise, but now, he was inclined to believe it. After Bolverk had confirmed the seraphs had lost to the humans in their ancient war, anything the High Priestess claimed as the truth could no longer be trusted. Mordrin had pieced it together, at last. The puzzle that connected everything, a web of deceit that he had finally broken through—and Bolverk was the key that unlocked it. The seraphs and humans had a war, that was known. The seraphs lost and were cursed with the Spellseal for that transgression. This was the key point that the clergy had hidden from the denizens of Skyfall. He had heard enough.

"I know their kind," Mordrin said. "They come here to ask for peace, to have us sit idly by while they collect the weapons. The blades belong to us. We must use them for our own protection!"

"Unhinged," the High Priestess said. "You are all unhinged. Lowborn blackwings and foolish humans believing maddening whispers and playing politics. The blades must be locked away, never to be used by anyone."

Mordrin winced. It hurt to hear the High Priestess say such a thing about him, but after his transformation, how could she not? His mutilated body was the direct result of his defying her orders.

"Let me ask you a question, then," Cecilia said. "I understand Skyfall is capable of moving anywhere in the world. Have you ever attempted to cross the divide between Inner Taerestris and what lies beyond?"

"No," Alystra said. "We do not meddle in such affairs. It simply does not interest us."

Cecilia bit her lip.

"Let us be clear," Baou said. "What we're proposing is a truce, however temporary. Some of my colleagues are dispatched now, beyond the barrier, gathering proof of the Eternal Dragons. I propose that we call a halt in searching for the artefacts while we find real evidence of the mythical dragons."

"And what do we have to gain from such a truce? Your colleagues are already out there, in the north. Who can say if you are not right now seeking more of the weapons?"

Another falsehood, Mordrin thought. His desire to learn more got the better of him, and he spoke out of turn. "The map in the scrying chamber shows several of them in the north. There are no blades there, aside from the ones they carry with them. That, at least, is true."

"The Blackwing lies!" an advisor shouted. "We cannot believe one whose mind has been completely muddled by human magic!"

The tension in the room rose along with the zealous accusations. Chaos would ensue in very short order if matters were not resolved immediately.

"Damn it," Baou whispered to Cecilia, "this isn't going as planned."

"Then we'll have to improvise."

"A touching story," the High Priestess said. "The humans are selfless, promising peace and false truces while they storm in here using the very magic we abhor."

"What about your race then?" Baou asked. "Are you content staying here idly, while your trapped subjects degenerate from a curse they cannot cure?"

"They disrespect our divinity!" someone screamed.

"I will not have you speak of our people as if they are prisoners," Alystra said.

"Yet prisoners they are, good priestess," Baou said. "The world is in peril. The legends of old have risen again, and all sides are poised on the brink of war. The only hope for both of our races is to work together against our common threat."

The seraphs surrounding the knights grew restless, their glaives looming ever closer.

Alystra's eyes narrowed. "Thus far all I have heard are the supplications of a madman and the fabrications of an enemy that nearly killed one of my subjects. The curse is real. The blades you possess are real. Your dragons are not. Your barrier is not… Yet, still, I *might* consider your truce. In exchange, you must give us the weapons you two currently possess. It's the only way to confirm your sincerity." Baou shook his head.

"With all due respect, you know we can't do that."

Alystra's eyes narrowed again as she considered Sir Baou's words. She waved a hand. "Enough of this. Slay them."

The guards charged toward the two knights, halted by Sir Baou, who quickly erected an impassable magical shield in response, walling the knights off from their aggressors.

"Soul Magic!" said one of the guards. "Stay away!"

Baou incanted again, muttering phrases and preparing a second teleport spell. "Cecilia, take over. We need to leave, now!"

Cecilia brandished her blade and pointed it directly at the High Priestess. "Let us go, or I'll use my blade. I can use it to negate magic wherever I wish."

"Magic?" Alystra snarled. "And what advantage will that be to you here? We have no use for magic."

Realization dawned across Mordrin's face. Whatever happened, he had to prevent Cecilia from using that blade. "You wouldn't dare!"

Cecilia flipped Nemoris and faced it toward the marble floor. "You may not use magic, but Skyfall does. Before I die, I'll make sure this beautiful city you've built comes crashing to the ground."

Whispers ran around the room.

"She's not serious!"

"I don't believe it!"

"It's no bluff; I've seen her blade in action," Mordrin shouted.

"We have to hurry this up," Cecilia muttered.

"Almost ready," Baou said. Sparks appeared below their feet as Baou progressed with the spell.

High Priestess Alystra was livid. She had taken in the full severity of Cecilia's threat. The seraph shook as she addressed the Iron Wall. "This isn't the end of things, human. We will take those blades. One way or another."

"I'm glad you see it our way."

The next instant, Baou lowered his magical shield and completed the teleport spell, the vortex below their feet dragging the knights through the floor and back into black space.

Cecilia heard a whistling above her as she looked up. Her sight was met with Mordrin's phantom blades chasing her through the darkness. Her falling speed was just enough to avoid the blades rocketing toward her.

Can't use Nemoris here, she thought. *I'll have to deal with this on the other side.*

The woman found the exit once again, this time a portal tied directly to the king's throne room in Nemea. She crashed next to Baou, grabbing him and throwing him aside.

"Move!"

As she heaved him out of the way, Mordrin's phantom blades emerged out of the portal and struck the ground where the two had been standing. The impact of the blades destroyed the stone floor and sent rubble flying in every direction. Dust and soot filled the room.

Baou gave out a loud cough, letting Cecilia know he was still alive.

"Baou? Cecilia?" a stilted voice said nearby.

Cecilia rose and recognized an older knight in bronze armour, his sword at the ready and a confused look in his eyes.

"Waine," she said. "We have a problem."

DISTANT HAVEN

SEPTIMIAN DYNASTY, YEAR 242
KINGDOM OF NEMEA, DRAGON'S PEAK

Little was known of the eponymous Kai before her legendary escape from the slave city.

Familial records were not kept for slaves, which made her unnatural strength a complete enigma.

By all accounts, she was a full-blooded human and displayed no magical talent; if that was true, then where did her great strength come from?

SIR TANDEM THE YOUNGER
TALES, VOLUME II

"How long do you think we've been on this mountain?"

"Difficult to say. I rarely keep track of time anymore."

The trials of the mountain weren't the only difficulties involved in its ascension. Though some parts were simple to traverse, other sections of the mountainside could only be climbed by hand. Kai was presently scaling one such section, eager to reach level ground.

"How long have you been in the scroll then?"

"Centuries, at least. Much of it was in slumber. Things only changed when the slaves of Kai-Ji found me."

"They must have thought you were only an enchanted scroll."

"I thought the same, for a time. People have memories. I did not. Only a mission."

"Do you ever feel trapped?"

Kai cleared another ledge.

"Never. The task is all that matters."

"After learning you were a Nemean king? And after seeing your Kingsguard? What if it's a curse?"

Specter did not respond. Kai clambered over a final rock connected to a platform. Ahead of her was a set of stone stairs. She squinted her eyes to get a good view. The task was made more difficult by the light fog that enveloped the area. The low hush of the mountain was unnerving, like the creaky notes of a home in the dead of night. Faint rumblings of some faraway creature mixed with the distant rustlings of rare plants. Vegetation was scarce this high up, and the sound of passing gusts would occasionally reach her ears.

Kai ascended the stone steps, noting the thinness of the air.

We're close.

A novel sound now interrupted the hush of the mountain. It resembled the roll of thunder, reverberating through the light fog. It faded in and out in time like a pendulum. The colour of the fog changed as Kai continued, shifting from its dull grey to hues of blue and orange.

Kai hurried along the mossy steps, her skin wet with condensation.

As she climbed, the fog gave way, and a new scene unfolded.

Around her were the clouds that she had previously mistaken for fog, leading into the nothingness below. Up ahead was a stone platform with moss interspersed on its surface. On the edges of the platform were broken pillars and supporting columns that arched into a shattered dome at the top. Walls would have existed between the pillars, but now they were half missing, time and the elements having reduced the structure to near rubble.

"*This is it,*" Specter said, manifesting his body. "This is the peak."

The two climbed to the top of the steps and reached the entrance of the ruined structure. She could now see what was causing the noise and colouring the fog. At the far end of the open building, beyond an iron doorway, was a metal pedestal.

Fixed to the pedestal was a set of two blades in a crossed pattern. The taller sword had a silver hilt, with a blue line of light running down the length of the blade and disappearing into the pedestal. The shorter blade had a darker handle with an orange streak down its centre. The pair of blades pulsed, sending their energy to the heavens like a beacon. The dazzling display overpowered the light of the sun.

"The power of kings," Specter said. "Just rewards for ascending the mountain."

Kai walked briskly to the weapons.

"What do—"

The iron doors between her and the blades slammed shut, blocking off access to her prize with a loud thud.

Something's not right.

She scanned the doors for a clue. Behind the wall, she could still see the pulsing energy of the blades rushing to the skies.

"Seems like you've covered quite some ground."

Who—?

Kai wheeled around to face the voice greeting her but found nothing. The voice spoke again, this time near the doors.

"Well, at least you're attentive. But that alone does not a worthy champion make."

Kai spun around again, finding the source of the noise: A young boy about half her height, pale-faced and white-skinned, stood in front of the doors. He sported curly orange hair and wore a grey tunic. He had a bronze sleeve that travelled from his right shoulder to his fingertips. On his back was a metallic wing of the same bronze colour. Half of his face was covered with a similarly metallic mask, the bare side revealing a bright blue iris.

"Who are you?" Kai asked.

The young boy chuckled. He bowed deeply. "I have no real name. But you may call me the Archon."

The boy spoke with a measured pace, expressing himself with a deep tone that did not belong on such a young child.

"I see you have brought a friend along on your trip. I daresay we can't have that." With a flick of the Archon's hand, Specter turned to dust in the wind and disappeared.

Specter?

Specter?!

"Don't, worry," the Archon said. "I'll return Numator once we are finished with our deliberations."

"Numator?"

"Ah, yes, he does have that little *problem* with his memory, doesn't he? Yes, his name is Numator, Ancient King of Nemea. He has done something dreadful, you see. Something very dreadful, indeed." The Archon motioned to the doors. "The king saw fit to split his soul in two. Three, if you count the sliver of his essence that resides in that blue scroll of yours. Yes, Numator is the first—his body is in that long sword behind the doors. Venator is the second—his mind. It's in the short one. The rest of his spirit is in the scroll."

"Then that must mean," Kai thought out loud, "he wasn't cursed?"

"Oh, don't be so naïve," the Archon said. "What would you do for eternal life? What would anyone? He speaks of vague motives, but his intent is crystal clear. You need only read between the lines. But he's not all bad; he really does have a task. A mission, if you will." The Archon paced around the young woman. His footsteps made no sound. "There are forces in this world, Kai, that seek power. Some of that power proves to be too much in the wrong hands. It is why you are here. And so am I."

"What do you mean?"

"You've already learned much of this world's history, far more than perhaps should be shown to such a youth. War is again returning to the peaceful sands of our cosmic shores. And each time it returns, the stakes are higher than the last. Victory costs, Kai. The dragons, eternal as they are, do not forget past grievances. Even now, they plot and conspire as the barrier protecting your kind from theirs weakens."

Kai was surprised by the revelation. Though the boy before her spoke of war, she could not help but feel some joy in knowing the fate of the dragons was not the total extinction that she had previously thought.

"The dragons, then, are still alive?"

"Well, they wouldn't be very eternal if they weren't."

"How do you know all of this? Who are you?"

"Haven't you asked that already? I believe the more apt question is, *what* am I? Well... I am the last of my kind." The boy raised his metallic hand in the air, ethereal runes fading in and out of existence.

He's casting a spell.

"It is my duty to seek out those who would obtain power, and measure their worth. Whether here, or on otherworldly vistas, I continue my celestial dance."

The Archon finished his spell, the sun above Kai giving way to the moon in moments. Day turned to night as she blinked, and by the time the Archon lowered his hands, the stars of the night sky twinkled above.

"Sit," he said. "I'm sure you're tired."

"I'll stand, thank you."

"Of course." The Archon motioned to the night sky. "Those dragons, the progenitors of magic, threaten your world with fire and brimstone. Would you see them turn everything to ash?"

Above her, a constellation of a dragon appeared, burning all the stars in a small portion of the sky. The portion was pitch-black now.

"Magic. Wherever it appears, leads to ruin—destruction, damnation. Of the few worlds containing life that once existed in the Great Beyond, all have succumbed to magic. This is a secret that we Archons are privy to."

The constellation of the dragons disappeared, and now the stars blinked in shades of reds, purples, and greens, as if on fire. Slowly, they too faded to nothingness.

"Magic corrupts. That's what I believe Numator was trying to say when he… well, did what he did."

"What was that?"

"You'll find out soon enough. For now, do sit down."

Kai obeyed the boy this time. He moved his metallic hand to cast another spell.

"The only hope for your people now is to entrust these weapons to the right hands, and so it is that I offer you an audience." The Archon pointed to Kai, and a magical circle appeared beneath her. "This is your third and final trial. I'm going to ask you several questions. If you are not honest, it will activate my enchantment."

This won't be easy.

"I've spellbound you to the river of time. Unsatisfactory responses will increase its flow tenfold. Tarry too long and you'll have nothing to return to in the world below. You'll meet with a desolate land of ruin. You'll have been too late to change anything. Too many unsatisfactory answers and you'll find yourself at the very end of time itself. Do be careful."

Kai nodded, readying herself for whatever questions he would have for her.

The Archon sat directly in front of the doors, staring at her. "Tell me, when you lived as a slave, did you ever find it strange how your wounds healed? How you were stronger than the others? Don't you find it strange how you've managed to make it this far?"

"…Yes, I do find it strange. But I'm the strongest person I know. I knew I wouldn't fail this mountain."

"You're quite lucky, knowing you can't fail, you know. What *would* you know of failure? Of trying so hard to reach something and missing the mark?"

Kai grit her teeth. "I'm not *lucky*. It was hard. It still is."

"That is where you're wrong."

The circle beneath the young woman lit up, increasing the flow of time.

The boy continued. "You'll never experience pain like others. You'll never experience an injury that ruins you for life, that prevents you from reaching your goals. To you, everything is possible. Every problem can be dealt with. Imagine for a moment that you were blind."

The Archon snapped his fingers. Kai's vision went dark. She couldn't see a thing.

"Now imagine that you were deaf."

The sounds of the mountain disappeared.

The Archon's voice invaded her mind. *What if you could not taste? Could not smell? Could not feel? Could not think?*

As her senses failed, her world turned to nothingness, and her mind shattered. All she could sense was the overpowering darkness that enveloped her. The will to breathe, to escape, were the only things she recognized. She felt herself suffocate, with no ability to take in air. Only when her torturous experience turned to pure despair did her senses return.

Kai coughed loudly, grabbing at her throat as she gasped for air. The light that entered her eyes blinded her as she adjusted to the view. She was back at the top of the mountain with the boy.

"*That* is what helplessness feels like," said the Archon, "There are some in this world who are damned to that experience as their only reality. Or worse. Never forget it."

"I… I understand. I'm sorry."

"Never apologize either. If you want to help, you must make things better. That way, we can reduce the suffering in this world. You are strong—and it is because you are strong that you are lucky. Keep it in mind."

"Why? Why is my body like this? Why am I different?"

The Archon smiled. "Powerful though I may be, I am not all-knowing. I am merely a custodian, after all. There are some things which even I cannot explain. Though I have my guesses."

Kai nodded, knowing he would not entertain the subject further. She looked up at the sky. The moon was moving faster than usual. The Archon's time spell was working to great effect.

"Next question. Why are you here?"

"Power. I need power to make a change."

"What kind of change?"

"I thought about it since the day I escaped. First, I want to free all of the slaves who were like me, trapped to live a life they never chose. After that… I don't know."

"Don't be so simple," the Archon scoffed. The circle lit up again, increasing time once more. Kai looked to the horizon and saw the moon give way to the sun, dawn breaking on the mountaintop.

"Even if you were to free all of them, some of them know no other way but the path that has been given to them. Would you rip them out of the lives they are accustomed to into one fraught with danger and the unknown? One that they did not choose? Again, you must think of more than just yourself, or your desires."

"I can't accept that. It's wrong. Whatever happens has to be better than… what they have now."

"Then you would take sole responsibility for what happens

next. If you make this choice for them, they will only turn to blame you when things go wrong. And if there is one truth I have gathered from my experience, it is that things always go wrong."

"Let them. They'll find a way. A lot of things went wrong for me, but… I made it here."

The Archon smiled. "You are wise beyond your years. Good. Moving on. The power you seek is uniquely attuned to violence. Tell me, do you really think you can rid the world's evils with that? Will a flick of the blade solve all your problems?"

Kai recalled the conversation she had had with Numator. She needed time to think on it then, but she was sure of it now.

"No. Violence isn't the only answer. Sometimes you need to talk about a problem, or work with others."

The Archon shook his head. The circle lit once more, time increasing pace by a factor of ten. Every second that passed the sun sped across the sky.

Not good.

"You don't truly believe that, do you? You talk about improving the world, but I can sense it—you have a taste for blood. For a cruel vendetta. That is not what your great power should be used for."

Kai looked down as the sun set. Time was moving quickly, but she could not rush her thinking. She searched her feelings, and she knew the Archon spoke the truth.

"You're right. I do want revenge. I'm not perfect. But I still want to make things better, that is what's important."

The Archon tilted his head.

"And violence is to be used… rarely. I think… hurting and killing won't fix all of my problems."

The sun had now set, and the moon began to rise. One day had passed.

"Acceptable. Think on this more. You are on the right track." The Archon leaned back, his eyes piercing the young woman. "You are very young. Have you ever lost a friend?"

"No."

"Were you afraid of the dark when you were little?"

"No."

"Have you ever held the hand of someone you love?"

"No."

"Have you ever felt half of a whole?"

"No."

"Do you want a place for secrets?"

"No."

"Have you ever felt alone?"

I...

"Have you ever felt alone?"

"...Yes."

The circle lit up a fourth time, causing time to speed up once more. Day turned to night and back quickly, making it difficult for Kai to keep track of the time.

Two days. Three.

"Difficult, difficult, difficult," said the Archon. "How can you hope to have an opinion on life if you have not yet experienced it? How can you make such important decisions for others if you have not seen their struggle through your own eyes?"

I've seen enough, Kai thought, but she knew it would not be a satisfactory answer. She thought hard about his question, searching for the gem of truth she knew he wanted.

Four days. Five. Six.

"If I lack wisdom, then I hope to acquire it... and learn from others who have it."

"Very good," said the Archon, smiling, "Always remember that with age and experience comes that wisdom. Do not be afraid to make mistakes on your journey. It is a part of being young."

"Final question. As I see it now, you have a choice. As you can see, I have some measure of power myself. With a flick of my hand, I can make everything go away. Your past. Your struggles. Your pain and your hardships, gone.

"Or... you can have the power of kings; you may challenge fate for a better throw against destiny. If you accept things as they are now, you may seek to change this corrupt and failing world. The people will hate you. There will be times where there is no right path forward. Given this, through all your struggles, you may learn that you could not change a single thing in the end. What will you choose?"

Seven. Eight. Nine.

Kai smiled. This was the easiest question he had given her so far. She did not truly know if there was such a thing as destiny, but she knew she was given a special chance that others did not have. It was a chance she would not spoil.

"Do any of us have a choice?"

Ten.

The Archon nodded. The circle below Kai disappeared, and she saw the sun stand still directly overhead. The metal doors behind him rumbled. Kai turned her head back, and the Archon was gone. His final disembodied message carried in the wind.

"We are very lucky to have you. You may pass."

HISTORY REPEATING

SEPTIMIAN DYNASTY, YEAR 242
KINGDOM OF NEMEA, NEMEAN CAPITAL

Although Nemea was historically a war-based nation, the capital city itself had a relatively small standing army.

Nemea was surrounded by cliffs on all sides, preventing would-be invaders from breaching the city.

SIR TANDEM THE YOUNGER
HISTORIA TAERESTRIA

Cecilia Scarlet kept her hand steady on Nemoris' pommel. Standing beside her was her colleague in his bronze armour, keeping his usual dignified gait. His green surcoat and tassels drifted along in the wind.

"Tell me, Waine, what has the mood been in the city?"

"Normal as can be, Your Excellency. The king shall soon return from his voyage, and the citizens will be none the wiser."

The two patrolled the neat path toward the Levi Fountain, the marble masterpiece at the centre of the People's Square of Nemea. The open area could fit an audience of one hundred thousand, and it was the official spot for King Remus' speeches. It was a regular day, and the square was full of people bustling to and fro. Behind the square were the grandiose porcelain steps that led to Holy Bastion.

"Though I am still unsure of the purpose of these patrols. What makes Baou so convinced those seraphs are plotting something?"

"They know the king is missing," Cecilia said. "Seems like the perfect time to try and retrieve the blades, when we're divided like this. And..."

"Yes?"

"Back at Skyfall, Baou cast a tracking beacon on the city before we left. The city has been moving in our direction ever since. They're close now."

A cold wind blew through the square.

"They are close?" Waine asked. "Why not rally the armies, then?"

"Not enough time. And, as you know, rallies are left to the king to declare. We're on our own until he returns."

"And these patrols are our best option?"

"For now, yes."

"If those winged heathens are after these relics"—Waine motioned to his sword—"we should take them far away from here. Staying here only endangers the people of the city."

"That's the problem. If we leave, His Highness will return, and we won't be here to protect him. It's a difficult situation, but the king's safety is our top priority. He's due to return any time now."

"I don't like this. I don't like this at all."

You and me both, Cecilia thought.

The pair arrived at the fountain. A ragged ball darted in from the side and hit Cecilia on the leg, clattering against her armour.

"Sorry, Princess Scarlet!" said a voice.

Two young boys rushed to the knights and bowed deeply, giving Cecilia time to retrieve the ball and hand it back to the blond one.

"It's busy here, you know," she said, giving him a smile, "You should be more careful, or you might hit an angry grandma."

The boys chuckled, as the blond one took the ball. "You're right, Princess Scarlet, I apologize. We'll find somewhere else to play."

Cecilia patted the boy on the head as the brown-haired one brought attention to himself. "Hey," he said. He pointed his hand at a cloud above. "What is that?"

Behind a cloud was a dark shadow, monolithic in size and familiar in shape. It crept along with incredible speed. It did not take long before Cecilia recognized the mass.

Damn it. "Hey," she said. "It really is quite busy here. Why don't you two go back home?"

The two boys looked at her and nodded, eager to follow orders.

"Yes, Princess Scarlet," they chanted, running from the scene.

"Is that really...?" Waine asked.

The shadow peeked out from the cloud and revealed itself. The lower half was made of rocks shaped like icicles. The upper half was a brilliant collection of white towers and spires with a marble statue in the centre. There could be no doubt about it.

Skyfall.

"Weapons at the ready," Cecilia said, unsheathing her blade and raising it to the sky.

"Citizens! Please go back to your homes," she yelled.

Waine unsheathed his own blade. "Your king commands it," Waine shouted. "We cannot guarantee your safety should you remain here!"

The people of the square froze in place, looking up and spotting the floating structure approaching the city.

"What is that?" one asked.

"A city in the sky?" asked another.

"Are we in danger?"

"Please remain calm!" Waine shouted. "Go to your homes! That's an order!"

Some spoke in hushed tones; others yelled out for answers.

"They're coming," Cecilia said. *Baou, wherever you are, I hope you're seeing this.*

The floating city approached. Thousands of smaller shadows erupted from its depths. The multitude of shadows covered a wide swath of air space and blocked out the sun. They cast their darkness over the People's Square, a looming threat that grew ever closer.

The citizens grew restless as they saw the shadows morph into the shapes of winged creatures. It wasn't long before they noticed the glaives held in their arms. In response, the people ran in panic, flooding out of the square.

"Where are the others right now?" Cecilia asked.

"Patrolling other parts of the city. With this many enemies, they are sure to attack other areas."

Looks like it's just us two, then, Cecilia thought.

A small cadre of Nemean guards poured out of the entrance to Holy Bastion. The blazing red dyes of their armour shone brightly against the backdrop of the castle.

"Sirs," one of them called. "What is the danger?"

"Skyfall seraphs," Cecilia said. "On your guard, now."

The thousands of winged creatures filled the sky, flying quickly toward the city. Their postures took on a deadly slant, their long glaives and javelins pointed down in a dive. Church bells across the city went off, ringing through the streets and alerting the citizens that danger approached. Cecilia heard the screams of frightened citizens.

"Look there," Waine said. "Enemies incoming."

Above the square was a group of seraphs encircling the area, weapons at the ready. The seraphs launched their long glaives, hitting the cobblestone surrounding the general area and blocking off all exits. The glaives stuck out from the ground, forming a makeshift metal cage around the square. The two knights and the palace guards were trapped inside, along with hundreds of citizens.

Cecilia recognized a menacing figure among the mass of seraphs. "Mordrin," she called out to him, "where's the High Priestess?"

Mordrin landed directly in front of Waine and Cecilia. Above him was the familiar fan of menacing blades, ready to be launched at his enemies.

"The High Priestess has no need to sully her hands with such an insignificant task. We are merely here for the blades. Comply, and no harm will come to your people."

"Too late for that," Waine said. "Those who march on Nemea will find themselves at war. That is our code."

"Then we'll turn this city to rubble before your very eyes," Mordrin said. He motioned to his fellow seraphs. "Kill them!"

Instantly, the winged enemies lunged at the knights with glaives outstretched.

Cecilia rolled out of the way of their attacks, taking stock of the scenario. *Twenty seraphs, including Mordrin. Ten of us, counting myself. And all the citizens...*

Cecilia's eyes darted to one side and noticed a group of entrapped Nemeans attempting to flee the scene. Mordrin had already sent off a hail of phantom blades at them, eager to make good on his threat. The group was situated too far away for Cecilia to arrive in time—she would use her Soulblade to close the gap.

"Nemoris!" Cecilia invoked her blade and swung. She increased the potency of her invocation, covering the entire square with its nullifying power, quickly dematerializing the phantom blades before they could reach their target.

Though Nemoris was an efficient weapon, she could not disenchant such a space repetitively. Negating magic was cheaper than casting it, but it still required vast amounts of soul energy to do so over such a wide area. She already felt her body weaken with a single use of the blade's nullifying effect.

Damn it. This is bad.

Mordrin trained his glaive on the nearby guardsmen and rushed toward them. The guards put up a good fight but were skewered in no time. The huge stature and powerful strikes of their enemies meant the guardsmen simply couldn't defend themselves. The average seraph was far larger and more physically powerful than a human, and an elite such as Mordrin could make quick work of entire battalions.

We don't have a chance right now. We need help. "Waine!" Cecilia shouted. "Use it!"

"Very well," Waine answered, flourishing his blade in theatrical fashion. It was the white blade Cecilia had seen him show off during their previous meeting with the king. Though Waine had not yet attuned the blade at the time, he had made progress with the spirit within and was ready to show it off. He flung the sword up in the air over Mordrin, and then invoked his blade for the first time: "Fantasma!" In a flash, Waine's body vanished from sight. A trail of energy traced from where his body vanished and to his sword before the knight reappeared above the seraph. With blinding speed, the knight dropped on top of Mordrin, delivering a crushing blow. Waine had caught the blackwing's right arm in his dive, plunging the sword deep into the muscle.

Mordrin screamed in agony, the surprise attack having worked to great effect. Waine dropped the seraph to the ground, and the two collided against the cobblestones.

Cecilia rushed to the fight, protecting Waine from the other seraphs. The seraphs were far stronger than she was, and to counteract that fact, she had to maintain a defensive style while providing backup to Waine. Getting too close to one of their glaives would likely be lethal, and Cecilia kept her distance. Mordrin pushed the knight off and flapped his powerful wings, taking to the air.

"Not so fast!" Waine threw his blade at the blackwing again, blinking in front of him once more and making a decisive strike with his sword. Another cry went off as Waine scored a second hit, this time creating a gash on the seraph's chest. Mordrin flew further back as blood from his wounds dropped precipitously to the cobblestones below.

There're still too many of them, Cecilia thought, surveying the area. *We need to handle the others.*

Waine, as though reading Cecilia's mind, relented from the chase against Mordrin. Instead, he used his blade to blink around the square, making fast attacks on each of the remaining seraphs before they could react to his movements. Though Mordrin was wounded, he was not neutralized; with a wave of the hand, he launched hails of magic blades at Waine. In response, with each salvo launched, Cecilia nullified the magic.

"Nemoris!"

Cecilia coughed loudly, the magic of the blade heavily taxing her body. The job was made more difficult by the precision timing she had to use. Nemoris worked indiscriminately to disenchant all magic in the area of effect. If one of her swings accidentally overlapped Waine's magic during a blink, it would leave him wide open to attack.

Mordrin continued his assault, shooting wave after wave of blades, this time aimed at Cecilia. The barrage was seemingly endless, and it was apparent that he could keep this up far longer than Cecilia could counter it. Realizing she would lose a battle of attrition, she stopped using the magic of her blade, resorting to manually dodging the seraph's attacks.

"Even you have your limits!" shouted the blackwing as he flew high into the air and prepared a hailstorm of weapons. The other seraphs flew up to avoid the oncoming salvo, leaving the Nemeans to their fate. Hundreds of blades littered the sky, and with a flick of the hand, Mordrin sent them crashing to the ground like torrential rain.

"Cecilia!" Waine shouted.

The woman was out of breath, quickly approaching her limit. *I can keep going,* she thought, preparing her blade.

"Hold," said a familiar deep voice.

As Mordrin's blades rushed down toward their targets, they were diverted away as if a gale wind had blown them off course. Mordrin's blades fell limply to the ground and dissolved. Cecilia collapsed, panting in exhaustion. A robed man popped into existence next to her.

"Lorithas," she gasped.

"No time for pleasantries, I'm afraid. Here comes Wulf now."

The armoured half-giant burst onto the scene from outside of the makeshift cage surrounding the square, a trail of ground beneath his feet, conjured up by the sword in his hands. He broke through the glaives with little effort, then made another wide swing with his gigantic weapon. This time, a wave of terrain traced around the square's perimeter, toppling over the remainder of the glaives, freeing the captives within. Nemean citizens rushed out of in terror.

Wulf landed in front of Cecilia, his weight cracking the stones of the square. "Apologies. Baou and Stella are still busy defending other parts of the city. They are quite numerous."

Cecilia had been focusing on the fighting, but she could now listen to the chaos that was taking place around her. She could hear the clashing of metal beyond the cage, the sound of fires rising in the distance, and the screams of frightened Nemeans filling every street and alley.

Cecilia stood, steeling herself. "We need to end this fast. We need a plan." Above them, she could see the city of Skyfall approaching their location, its dark shadow encompassing the centre of the city. In moments, it would hover right over them. *Could they be...?*

"Lorithas," Waine said from afar, "let's handle them now."

Waine was in the air again in a second, blinking around with his Soulblade. Wulf followed suit, riding a patch of terrain with his own weapon and dealing heavy strikes to the invading seraphs. It was quick work, and Lorithas' fireballs only made it more apparent how much of a gap there was between the winged creatures and the elite Kingsguard.

Despite their larger size and strength, the seraphs had only known peacetime—and they were engaging experienced veterans. Waine's flurry of attacks eventually reached the bleeding Mordrin, who was now fighting defensively and attempting to escape the range of Waine's teleporting blade.

Cecilia looked up again and watched the floating metropolis move over and behind them, eventually settling itself directly over Holy Bastion. *I see, now. Clever bastards.*

Now recognizing his disadvantage, Mordrin called off his attack. With a wave of his hand, his seraphs followed suit, flying back up and away from the scene. The mass of attacking seraphs flew back in the direction of Skyfall, retreating momentarily. Waine blinked back down, rejoining Lorithas and Wulf with a slam of his blade against the concrete.

"Looks like the square is safe for now," Wulf said, "but they number in the tens of thousands. We can't protect the entire city."

"Maybe we don't have to," Cecilia said. "They want the Soulblades. If they're not coming after us, then they're going for Baou."

Lorithas nodded. "Which means we should seek him out."

"That's not the end of it," Cecilia said, pointing at Skyfall. "Look there. Their city is positioned right over the keep. This makes it easy for them to get inside the castle. Whatever happens, we can't lose control of the throne."

Waine spoke next. "So, we must secure the castle, as well as defend the city and find our colleagues. Difficult for so few of us. Additionally, the guardsmen of the city stand no match against such overwhelming odds."

"I have an idea," Cecilia said. "Lorithas, Waine, I want you two to secure the castle. We will have to find Stella, as she can cover the most ground among us—I'll have her try to find the king. He remains our priority. He should be close to us now, with Vandar."

"What will we do?" Wulf asked.

Cecilia turned to the half-giant. She felt lightheaded from using her blade to such an extent in combat. Sweat covered her face.

"I need to rest a while, so I'll wait here, but I want you to use that sword of yours and find the others. Bring Baou back here and tell Stella to find the king."

"And then?"

"If we can't fight them on equal terms, our victory condition has changed. We'll need to do something more drastic."

"Drastic?" Lorithas asked.

Cecilia motioned toward the city hovering over Holy Bastion. "If the enemy force is stronger, then we have to go for the head. We'll strike the High Priestess directly."

STORM OF STEEL

SEPTIMIAN DYNASTY, YEAR 242
KINGDOM OF NEMEA, NEMEAN CAPITAL

Mordrin the Blackwing would become a name both hated and feared by common folk everywhere.

Unlike other seraphs, Mordrin subsumed magic and augmented his power with the Soulblade Bolverk—making him a potent enemy.

SIR TANDEM THE YOUNGER
TALES, VOLUME II

"When did it start?" Vandar asked.

"Not long ago," Stella said. "But the situation is dire."

Tyr held onto the golden knight as he urged the horse to gallop faster. Next to them were Tandem and Remus on their own horses with Stella gliding right above them.

A disaster welcomed them home.

In the distance, Tyr saw rising smoke columns engulfing the Nemean capital. Crimson fire mixed with the grey smoke. The thousands of winged creatures in the air added to the chaos like a frame taken from some old war painting. The massive structure known as Skyfall hovered above Holy Bastion in the centre of Nemea, as if to declare dominion over it. It was the first time Tyr had seen the floating city, but it was impossible to mistake it.

Tyr made a sideways glance at Remus. His eyes shot daggers. Lumina's thoughts filled his mind.

"He is not talking."

Given the circumstances surrounding Nemea, Tyr felt he knew why.

"How many seraphs?" Vandar asked.

"It is difficult to say," Stella said, "We've done all we can, but the city is simply not equipped to deal with an invasion of this scope."

"Tyr. This is going to be dangerous. Are you sure you want to go?"

I'm sure.

"You have my name now if you need my power. But be careful with it."

I will be.

The group raced through the hills and broke into the entrance of the city, one of its many bridges allowing easy access inside. The streets were deserted near the edges, most of the citizens having evacuated or hidden in buildings for safety. It was deathly quiet on the outskirts. As they approached the centre of Nemea, however, the scene transformed. Tyr could spot seraphs causing havoc on the streets. Buildings had toppled. Citizens lay on the ground, unconscious or worse. Some were covered in the distinct red of their lifeblood. Children much younger than Tyr roamed throughout, many crying for their mothers.

"Where is Cecilia?" Vandar asked. Tyr noticed that his voice trembled.

"She is at the People's Square. She is exhausted, but alive."

Tyr saw both Remus and Vandar breathe a sigh of relief; the entire mad dash here they had both wanted to ask for Cecilia, but it seemed they were too afraid to know the answer.

"What of the others?" Tandem asked as they made a sharp turn toward the square.

"Wulf is retrieving Sir Baou," Stella said. "I am not sure of his current status. He was out fighting in the city when last I saw him. That was some time ago. The rest are within Holy Bastion, awaiting the king."

"Watch out!" Tandem shouted, a glaive being launched their way.

Vandar quickly raised his shield and blocked the attack without a word. He continued firing off questions, the surprise glaive only slowing him down for a moment. "What do they want?"

"The relics," Stella said. "That's their only demand."

Tyr bit his lip. *No way I'm giving you up.*

"There's Cecilia now," Tandem said. "Up ahead!" Tandem pointed to the fountain in the centre of the People's Square, a battered, red-haired woman resting against it.

Vandar quickly dismounted and ran to her.

So, this is Princess Cecilia Scarlet, Tyr thought. *She's even more beautiful in person.*

"Cecilia!"

She raised her hand. "I'm all right. I just needed some rest. Your Majesty." She nodded toward Remus, who also dropped off his horse. Tyr followed suit and dismounted, along with Tandem.

The king finally spoke, taking the edge off the party. "I'm glad to see you safe."

The ground shook suddenly, as a faraway building toppled to the ground.

"I can take you to the throne room at the top of the keep," Stella said. "Mordrin is there now. The others are within the castle, awaiting you, King Remus."

"Aye," Vandar said. He looked at Remus and Tandem, then motioned them to the base of the castle. "You two go through the entrance there. Stay with the others. Tyr—"

"I'm going with you." He unsheathed his golden blade. "I can help, if you'll let me."

"Quite the spirit," Cecilia said. "He's picking it up from you, Vandar. And we can use all the help we can get right now."

"Right," Tandem said. "But after the castle is secure, what then?"

"I'm waiting for Baou and Wulf to get back," Cecilia said. "I have a plan."

"I don't like the sound of that," Vandar said. "What kind of plan?"

Cecilia smiled. "Don't worry. Nothing suicidal. Hurry now."

With that, Tandem and Remus went off to the entrance of the castle.

"Take care, Tyr," Tandem said. "We're counting on you and Vandar both."

Stella faced away from the knight and his protégé, spreading her wings wide and revealing her back to them. "Grab on," she said. "I'll fly you up to the throne room. Once it's clear, His Majesty can return to the throne."

"Who is Mordrin?" Tyr asked.

"Stella's former colleague," answered Cecilia. "After the battle here, I saw him fly up to the throne room alone. He's looking for a fight."

"Then he will get one," Vandar said. He gave a final look toward Cecilia. "Don't die."

"Good luck."

Vandar grabbed hold of Stella's back as he waited for Tyr to join him. With a jump, the boy reached up and followed suit. The seraph kicked off the ground with a powerful motion, catching the wind and beginning the ascent up Holy Bastion.

"The rest of the city is in disarray," she said. "I will be more use aiding the citizens. I will drop you near the throne room and return to help where I can below."

"Thank you," Vandar said. "We will take care of it." The knight turned to the boy. "Tyr, there's something you should know about the Soulblades before we reach the top. It will help us greatly."

"What is it?"

"It's about the price of using these weapons."

"Lumina spoke to me about it. She said invoking her power requires part of my soul."

"Aye. What you might not know, is how much more powerful the blades are when someone like you uses them."

More powerful?

Tyr looked below at the city, grimacing at the destruction. Though the seraphs were only after the blades, they had spared no mercy on the denizens of Nemea. Anger welled within him. He did not know what awaited them in the throne room, but he would put a stop to the madness; with Lumina, he could make a difference.

Tyr turned back to Vandar. "I don't understand. I'm not trained like you are."

"It's not about training," Stella's voice reached his ears, "A Soulblade draws its power from the life force of its wielder. The younger you are, the more life force you have. You're the youngest one of us here. You wield much more power than you know."

Tyr recalled the times he had invoked his blade. In both instances, he had created intense blasts of energy, rivalling even those of the eternal dragon they had encountered. While he had seen Remus edge to his limit with a single use of his blade, Avenir, Tyr had not felt any signs of slowing, despite his rather clumsy use of Lumina.

Is that true?

"Yes… *But you must still be careful, Tyr. Nothing lasts forever.*"

Stop me if it's too much, then.

"Keep it in mind, boy. Your strength may turn the tide."

"We have arrived," Stella said. She landed on a balcony overlooking the city. A short distance above them loomed the city of Skyfall. Tyr and Vandar dropped to the balcony.

"Thank you," Vandar said, readying his red blade.

"I'll be back as soon as I can," Stella said. "Please be careful."

"Thank you," Tyr said.

"And pleased to meet you," the seraph did a quick bow toward Tyr before she flew off.

"Let's move," Vandar said.

The two hurried past the balcony and into the inner castle, Vandar the Red leading the way. They moved past overturned tables, destroyed busts, and ruined tapestries as they made their way to the centre of Holy Bastion—the royal throne room. It was eerily quiet as they pressed on. The chaos of the city below had faded to a low murmur. Their steps echoed as they continued through the castle. An ominous feeling took hold of the boy.

The duo pushed onward, tracing through the pathways of the palace before finally arriving at the entrance to the throne room. Tyr looked at the Nemean throne room for the first time.

To each side were twisting pillars adorned with unlit candles. Between each pillar was an entrance that led to other parts of the castle, the throne room serving as the heart of the network. Marble statues depicting ancient Nemean royalty lined the walls that led to the seat of power. The throne itself was beautifully decorated, with glinting jewels and shining metals composing its silvery surface.

Sitting directly on the throne was a seraph with tattered black wings, looking unlike any the boy had seen thus far. Shafts of sunlight shone through the windows on his ragged form, lines of blood streaked throughout his dark skin. It surprised Tyr to see a seraph so different from Stella. The seraph's head rested on one of his clawed hands as he addressed the newcomers.

"So, you've finally made it. I must say, I'm rather disappointed in your progress. I thought you would bring the king sooner."

"Where are the others? Why are you alone here?" Vandar asked, gripping his red blade tightly.

As if to answer, the castle rumbled, pieces of the ceiling tumbling to the ground.

"On their way to your king now," the seraph said, "Once he is slain, the city will be ours." He slowly stood from the throne and made a deep bow. "But I must introduce myself. My name is Mordrin the Blackwing. And you are?"

"Taking back the throne now," Vandar said. "You won't leave here, neither with the blades nor with your life."

Tyr could feel the knight shaking next to him, not out of fear, but with great rage. He was furious.

"Ah, the Soulblades," Mordrin said. "Such a curious set of artefacts." Mordrin walked slowly toward Vandar, a fan of ethereal weapons manifesting themselves above his head. "When I first stole the power of the blades, I could not fathom the true nature of their ancient knowledge. The blade I acquired, Stella's gift to me, has told me much. You see, with its help, I know the truth of things. I have seen the line of cause and effect tracing the history of our races."

The room filled with more of the magical arms, all were pointing directly at the duo. Vandar raised his diamond shield.

"But such furtive knowledge makes us so much more than we once were. You feel it, too, don't you? The blades have secrets, ones they wish to keep safe. What grand plan are they aware of? Each only knows but a fragment of the whole story."

The weapons twirled in the air. Mordrin was ready to attack.

"What story?" Vandar asked.

Tyr readied his sword.

Is that true? Is there something you're not telling me?

"The High Priestess committed an inexcusable sin. The profane church hid something from our people. A clandestine truth they knew all along. At first, I could not understand it. But now I see. I'll tell you what I've learned: That *your* people are the ones who created the Spellseal. The Spellseal that cursed my sister and banished us to our isolationist hell. The curse on us all. I cannot forgive that deed."

With a gesture of the hand, the blades rushed toward the knights, a vicious attack with the intent to kill.

Vandar invoked his shield. "Rime!"

The ground below the two quaked as Mordrin's blades broke upon the barrier.

"Damn he's strong," Vandar said, gritting his teeth. "What do you mean?" the knight asked. "Humans caused it?"

"That's correct," Mordrin said. "The strange circles on our bodies are oddly familiar to the magic runes you humans cast. I had my doubts, but the Soulblade I acquired confirmed my suspicion. It was your people who did it!"

Vandar charged forward with his red blade. He made a quick slash at the seraph, who materialized a weapon to block the attack. With a grunt, Mordrin slashed at the knight with his clawed hand, easily tearing through the lion's head of his chest armour. The blond knight backstepped and steadied his shield in front of him.

"Lumina!"

Behind the two, Tyr had invoked his blade, the now-familiar energy radiating from his body. He made a powerful slash in the air and shot a golden missile at the seraph.

Mordrin's reaction was instant, conjuring up another blade and slicing the missile in half in an impressive display of fearless confidence. The split energy from Tyr's missile damaged the ground and a pillar behind the seraph. He shot off a set of three ethereal spears at Tyr.

"*Swing!*"

Without a moment's hesitation, Tyr mimicked Mordrin's defence, slashing the spears with his blade, a beam of golden light breaking the spears and dissolving them.

Mordrin laughed, the cruel sound bouncing off the walls of the spacious throne room. "For a child, you're quite powerful. Impressive."

"Listen," Vandar said. "I don't know who or what caused the curse upon your people. But we promised Stella that we would find a cure for it. For all seraphs."

The Blackwing laughed again. "Do you know why the High Priestess hid the terrible truth from us? It was her mortal fear. If the people of Skyfall knew about the true cause of the Spellseal, it would doubtlessly ignite a revolt. A war against the humans, one she concluded could not be won. I may have agreed with her justification then, but with this newfound power, things are different."

Mordrin summoned a blade next to him, transforming it into a multitude of different weapons.

"With these, we may change the very course of history."

Vandar had heard enough. With an aggressive roar, he was back on the enemy, pushing him backwards with deft slices of his red blade. He closed the distance and activated his shield once more. "Rime!"

The magic of the shield pushed Mordrin away from its protective bubble, sending him back with great force. Mordrin landed on a wall with his feet, a flap of his wings cushioning his landing.

Tyr swung his sword several times at the seraph, sending more magical missiles at Mordrin.

The seraph quickly moved out of the way as the shots blasted a hole in the back wall of the throne room. The hole led to the outside. Sensing an opportunity, Mordrin kicked off and flew through the wall and out of the castle.

"Much better," he said as he formed dozens more blades and aimed them through the opening.

"Behind me!" Vandar shouted, jumping in front of Tyr. "Rime!" The ethereal weapons bounced off Vandar's shield once more.

Vandar?

The knight let out a cough, blood splattering on the ground. Vandar breathed heavily. "He's strong," he said. "We must end this quickly."

Mordrin continued sending his hailstorm of projectiles at Vandar, the knight powering through with his shield. The two attempted to move out of the seraph's line of sight, but the blades followed them regardless.

"Push forward!" Vandar steeled himself as the two advanced at Mordrin, hundreds of blades turning into thousands that broke upon the knight's barrier. As they got closer, Mordrin's attacks only grew more relentless. The flurry of blades was like a waterfall of clashing energies, battering against Vandar's shield again and again. The knight dropped to one knee.

"Tyr, stop him!"

The boy looked at Vandar, noticing strands of his blond hair turning grey.

"Vandar!"

Tyr experienced the next few moments in slow motion. The knight's barrier sputtered out, exhaustion from overuse of the shield. Sweat rolled down his face. The seraph's assault was simply too much. Tyr tried to shove the knight out of the way, to get him into safety, but it was too late.

By the time the boy looked up again, a glaive was protruding from Vandar the Red's back.

DAYLIGHT ASSASSIN

SEPTIMIAN DYNASTY, YEAR 242
KINGDOM OF NEMEA, NEMEAN CAPITAL

*Sir Baou received top marks from military school and later
won countless battles as Nemea's chief strategist. His tactics
in the war room were trumped only by his prowess
on the field.*

*His ability to Mindweave was second only to Lorithas, but
Baou had another secret—a seemingly infinite reserve of life
energy, a catalyst for his Soul Magic.*

SIR TANDEM THE YOUNGER
TALES, VOLUME II

"Glad you could make it," Cecilia said.

"Apologies," Baou replied. "It's the same everywhere right now."

The two were joined by the half-giant Wulf at the fountain of the now-destroyed People's Square. Baou was covered in minor cuts and bruises. The Iron Wall wobbled in place as she caught her breath.

"You don't look so great," Baou said.

The woman gave a weak smile. "I'm fine. Don't think I have much more left in me, but I'll survive." Cecilia straightened herself and sheathed her blade, taking a few tender steps. "I can still fight. But we need to end this quickly."

"What's the plan?" Baou asked.

Cecilia directed the group to the floating city above the keep. "Simple. We need to get back in there. Find the High Priestess and take her out."

"Not so fast," Wulf said. "Most of the seraphs are still in their city—and likely armed."

"That's why you're here," she said. "Wulf, you have a lot more strength than those seraphs. You can take out scores of them easily." She took a deep breath. "The seraphs are a prideful species. If we cut off the head, they'll certainly retreat. We need to fight our way through the city and into the statue up there. That's where she'll be."

"Worth a try," Baou said. "Anything is better than letting more citizens die."

"Can you teleport us back up there, Baou? That would make our job easier."

Sir Baou sighed. "Afraid not. I'm exhausted as well. Whatever I have left I'll need up there for the fight."

"I can take us up," Wulf said. He flourished his heavy blade. "The terrain will carry us."

"Right," Cecilia said. "Let's go."

"Try to keep your balance," Wulf reminded them.

The two stood next to the half-giant as he invoked his Soulblade. He placed the weapon in his calloused hands and thrust directly at the ground. "Albion!"

The ground under the trio quaked. The stone erupted to form a platform as it pushed upward, reaching for the sky and carrying its human cargo with it. Beneath them, the ground turned into a rising pillar. Cecilia and Baou fell onto the platform as it shook violently, speeding up to Skyfall.

A portal would have been so much easier than this.

In a few moments, the group was over the city and up to the edges of Skyfall, only inches away from the floating city. The knights disembarked from the makeshift platform, hopping over onto more stable ground.

Baou gave a raspy grunt as he collected himself.

"Don't know how we'll get down, but we are *not* riding that thing back, Wulf."

"Save it," Cecilia said. "We need to move."

Before setting out, the three took stock of the situation. Navigation would be simple: There was only one direction the streets could take them from this edge of the city. The statue in the centre also served as a visual aid to orient the group. Cecilia would make small mental notes of the city layout, in case they needed to backtrack later on. No guards were nearby, no enemies to be seen this far from the core of the city.

Cecilia unsheathed her sword and pointed it at the city's centre. Towering above the buildings at the heart of Skyfall was the statue of Sithe, where High Priestess Alystra was likely waiting. "I'm sure we'll encounter resistance on the way in. Wulf, I trust you can deal with them."

The giant nodded as he took a forward position, his human colleagues bringing up the rear. The trio of knights set off through the abandoned streets; it was not long before they encountered enemies. The party rounded a corner and spotted a lone seraph on patrol. Sir Baou quickly cast a sleeping spell on the patrol, making quick work of him before the party continued. The next obstacle was a surprise attack.

Two seraphs charged full-force toward Wulf from a nearby rooftop, glaives at the ready. With one sweeping motion, the half-giant swung his blade in the air and sliced the oncoming attackers in half. The motion was swift and effortless, a tribute to his titanic strength.

Their dash through the city went on for a time, the group occasionally stopping to avoid a passing patrol or to otherwise confront them. Though the city itself was populous, the bulk of the enemy forces were fighting below in Nemea; security was relatively light in the seraph capital. Before long, the knights reached the statue of Lady Sithe. The statue obstructed parts of the setting sun, the rays of light that surrounded her form giving the goddess an even more divine appearance.

"There," Baou said, pointing straight ahead. "That courtyard. Looks like we'll have to fight through."

Beyond the party was a plaza, much like the People's Square below. This one, however, featured a battalion of seraphs armed with deadly weapons. The group of enemies blocked passage into the statue. One of them noticed the unexpected knights nearing the plaza.

"Enemies! Nemean enemies!"

Instantly, the battalion rushed at the humans with their weapons poised. Their speed was great, their powerful wings allowing them great propulsion; Baou would have no time to cast a magical defence.

"Albion!" Wulf invoked the power of his blade, sending gargantuan slabs of terrain at the seraphs, instantly transforming their reckless dive toward the knights into a dangerous collision with hard rock. Wulf's attack killed those who were unfortunate enough to be in the way. He used his huge sword like a club, decimating the enemy seraphs with each cleave. Baou assisted by neutralizing several enemies with great balls of fire.

Thought you were exhausted.

Cecilia remained on the defensive, lacking the range advantage that the other two enjoyed. As they pushed through the hordes of seraphs, she took opportunistic strikes against any enemies that got too close, her sharp blade easily cutting through the ones that got within range.

Cecilia could see the entrance to the statue now, at the end of the plaza. To get there, they would have to fight through more seraph ranks.

"There're too many of them," Baou shouted, waving his hand and transforming a javelin aimed at his head into a fine dust.

"Albion!" Wulf thrust his blade into the ground and caused the plaza itself to undulate with great force, creating waves of terrain that rippled out and grew as high as the half-giant himself. The waves pushed back and toppled the seraphs that could not get away in time.

Wulf invoked his weapon a third time, producing another small platform beneath the three knights and catapulting them forward to the entrance, leaving no time for the surrounding enemies to react. Their mad dash had succeeded; the Kingsguard had at last breached the entrance to the statue. Beyond the entrance was a path that led to a long series of steps.

"Keep moving," Baou said. "They'll be coming."

The knights pushed on. Their daring assault had worked well thus far. The hard part was done—the harder part lay ahead.

This is our only chance. If we fail here, it's over.

As they climbed, Baou and Wulf created walls of rock and magic behind them to close off the path to the pursuing seraphs. The distant clanging of metal against the makeshift walls was confirmation that they were working. Soon enough, the three had arrived at the end of the steps into a familiar room. Once again, Cecilia spotted the hundreds of guards inside, weapons all pointed at the trio. Around the far end was the clergy, white seraphs donning regal outfits. Nearby were the multitude of other officials and advisors to the high priestess.

One of them raised a finger toward the knights. "Glaives!"

"Wait," said the figure who sat in the centre seat, high above them. She spoke with authority. "So, the brave knights return. This time with another one of the blades. Do you see the chaos you have caused in my city? The destruction those weapons are capable of? We could feel the quakes from here."

Baou stepped forward, ever slowly. "You must be joking. Is it not painfully obvious that you alone have started this conflict?"

"High Priestess Alystra," Cecilia said, as she and Wulf marched forward to keep near Baou. She raised her blade and pointed it at the seraph. "We don't have time for games anymore. No more talk. Call back your army or—"

"Or?" Alystra sneered. "Or you use that blade of yours and cause my city to topple? If you do that, you'll let it fall right over your castle. You have no power here."

Cecilia bit her lip. She had guessed before why the floating city was positioned over Holy Bastion, but now it was certain. Crashing the city with Nemoris would be a catastrophic loss for both sides—a loss she couldn't accept.

Damn it.

"Give us the blades or all that will be left of your capital will be rubble. This is non-negotiable."

"Enough of this," Baou said. He flicked his hands and materialized a great ball of fire, sending the missile hurtling toward the High Priestess. Just before it landed, a blue translucent wall manifested itself, taking the full force of the fireball and dispersing it throughout its surface.

Magic? Cecilia spotted the cause above the High Priestess. A familiar blackwing had her arms outstretched, a wince on her face. Bandages covered her chest. Her lips were mouthing incantations. *Taela.*

"Finish them!" Alystra waved her hand, and hundreds of weapons were once again flying in their direction.

Wulf moved in front of the two knights and invoked his blade. "Albion!"

With a wide arc of his sword, more walls of terrain formed to block the deadly barrage. With another flick of his blade, the walls pushed back against the seraphs, encasing them all in cocoons of magical rock. Albion's power prevented their slightest movement, and the knights now had a direct line to the high priestess.

Baou shot off another fireball, this time at Taela, who dodged it with a quick flap of her wings. The seraph's concentration broke, however, and she left her charge unprotected for a split moment.

This was all the time Baou needed. He pulled his gladius from within his coat and pointed it directly at Alystra. Without hesitation, he invoked the weapon. "Catastro!"

In a split moment, a needle-thin beam of light ran from the tip of the gladius and travelled up to Alystra's chest. Once the beam connected, it became taut like a string, pulling the seraph away from her podium and toward the gladius.

The High Priestess was paralyzed by the magic of the blade. Her body then began to glow a brilliant white colour, obscuring her features. The beam continued pulling with immense force, savagely ripping a glowing copy of Alystra from her body.

Cecilia had known how Baou performed his assassinations—but it was another thing to see it in person. Baou's secret technique was the method with which he stole the soul of his target, severing their spirit from their body. Cecilia looked to the High Priestess's corporeal form. It was unmoving. *Dead.*

Alystra's spirit form continued the struggle, however; she tried to fight back against Catastro's pull. "No!" she screamed, a hollow tone in her voice. "Let me go!"

Above them, Taela dove to try and stop the knight, but Wulf rushed between them, blocking her passage. In her bloody and damaged state, the Isthalin was helpless to do anything now.

The clergy around the room gasped in shock at the scene developing before them.

"What is he doing to her?"

"Help the High Priestess!"

The gruesome tearing of body and soul continued as her spirit approached the knights. Slowly, Alystra's spirit form funnelled into Baou's gladius. Parts of her face were now gone, only a fuzzy afterimage remained. The arms went next. As the ghastly spell continued, the white energy that comprised Alystra's divine soul travelled from the gladius and through Baou's hands before enveloping his own body. Soon, Baou himself was humming with the energy he had stolen, and the knight was shaking violently.

Cecilia knew Baou's secret now—how he was able to cast such vast amounts of Soul Magic. It was with the absorbed life energy he stole with Catastro; the difference, this time, was that the life essence of a seraph was far more potent than that of a human. It would be impossible to fully contain a seraph's essence in a human body, much less one as divinely powerful as Alystra's within himself.

He's going to die if I don't stop this. Doing the only thing she could, Cecilia brandished her weapon and pointed it directly at the beam of light between the weapon and Alystra's physical body. "Nemoris!" With a swing, she cut through the thread connecting Baou's gladius and Alystra's soul, interrupting the magic and severing the bond.

"Argh!" Baou dropped to his knees as his body burned with violent energy.

Cecilia looked to the seat of the High Priestess. What remained of her soul was now returning to her lifeless body. As her spirit re-entered its vehicle, her eyes opened.

Taela rushed to her side, bits of blood dripping through her bandages. "High Priestess?"

"Leave her. Baou needs help, now!" Wulf yelled, grabbing the spasming Baou with one arm and motioning Cecilia to follow him.

The Iron Wall looked back one last time to see the result of Baou's magic. The seraph's soul had returned, but her eyes were lifeless and unmoving. The brilliant glow that had emanated from them was gone. Cecilia saw Taela grabbing at Alystra, attempting to get a reaction. She screamed in grief. The room was in an uproar.

Cecilia turned back to follow Wulf.

The last thing she heard was Taela's desperate cry for the husk that was once the High Priestess.

BLACKWING DOWN

SEPTIMIAN DYNASTY, YEAR 242
KINGDOM OF NEMEA, HOLY BASTION

The unique gift which Mordrin had obtained allowed him to utilize a Soulblade's power as if it were his own.

Though the result was grisly, Mordrin proved that the Spellseal could be overcome.

SIR TANDEM THE YOUNGER
TALES, VOLUME II

The knight collapsed to the ground. He let fall his shield with a terrible clang. The boy blinked in shock as he processed the events. Vandar was defeated. Mordrin's overbearing assault had finally broken through his defence. A phantasmal glaive had impaled the knight directly through the chest, slicing through the armour. His red cape darkened as torrents of lifeblood seeped out of the wound.

The glaive dematerialized, leaving nothing but a scarlet chasm in Vandar's chest.

Tyr's hands shook. He moved forward and faced his mentor. The threat posed by the seraph was irrelevant now; without Vandar, the boy knew they could not win.

I...

Mordrin landed next to the throne as he paused to examine his handiwork. The knight's barrier was impressive, no doubt, but when it came to an endurance contest, a human's strength could never match that of a seraph. The man, already old and flagging, could muster but a token defence. Seraphs, with their hundreds of years of life at their disposal, had far greater reserves of vitality in comparison to humans, who lived but mere decades in their prime. The chasm of difference between them was simply too wide to overcome.

The boy, however, is another story, thought the seraph.

The gleaming bolts of energy the young one sent had been a terrible thing to face. Even being caught by just one of those golden missiles would surely destroy Mordrin's body. Though the blackwing could no doubt defeat the boy in an even struggle, his body was nearly exhausted now. Breaking through the blond one's shield had been no easy task; doing it after all of his prior fighting had made it much more difficult.

He felt his right arm throb with pain, a reminder of his fight with the teleporting knight. Mordrin released the thought and focused on the situation. He raised his clawed hand, conjuring more blades. *I will end this now.*

"Boy," he said. "No. Tyr." The knight's eyes fogged over, consciousness fading quickly.

Above them, Tyr could hear the familiar whistle of an approaching magical salvo. They would both die here.

Vandar smiled. He lowered his right hand and grazed the surface of his dazzling shield, speaking its name with pained breath. "…Rime."

Around them, the familiar barrier sprang into life and enveloped the two. The magic weapons launched at them clashed and broke upon Rime's barrier. They were surrounded now by the flurry of magic on magic, as though they stood in the centre of a storm. It was impossible to see beyond the maelstrom of sparks and runes just beyond the barrier. The sound was almost deafening, but the boy did not pay it any heed. His focus was on the man in front of him.

The knight looked up at him and placed a trembling hand on his shoulder. Blood streamed from the sides of his mouth. "Tyr, you… You *must* defeat him. Protect the king."

"I—" The words were stolen from his mouth. A sick feeling grew in the pit of his stomach as he watched Vandar bleed.

"…I can't."

Vandar coughed, tides of crimson flowing from his mouth. "You can. You're here because of your own strength. It's time you understand that. It's time you use your great power."

The blond man raised his head, his blue eyes trained directly on the boy. His intense glare was fearsome, powerful. The dying knight before Tyr looked like a proud beast. He would not accept the boy's hesitation.

"Do you hear that calling? I hear it still. To protect the people.

Here it is." The knight motioned toward Mordrin. "If you don't stop him, who will? Will you let this continue?"

No, I won't let that happen.

Vandar's body shuddered. His time was running out. His hair was almost entirely silver now, his skin like that of a man many years his senior. He resembled Remus himself.

"Tell Cecil... Tell her that I'm sorry."

And with that, his barrier gave out.

Tyr wheeled around before the body dropped. In a flash, his blade was trained on the dark-skinned seraph, rising power energizing his body. There was nothing left to do now but to follow Vandar's final instruction. Tyr couldn't bear the thought of looking at his mentor again. His heart was full of pain. He would take it out on the one who caused it. He would eliminate Mordrin.

With weapon held aloft, Tyr rushed at the enemy, ready for his next attack. He swung his brilliant blade, sending bolts of solar energy at the seraph.

Mordrin produced a fan of blades to block the bolts, diffusing the missiles as they hit the makeshift defence. It mattered little to Tyr, however. If Mordrin had whittled down Vandar's barrier, then Tyr would do the same to the seraph.

"Lumina!"

Tyr unleashed a devastating barrage of golden missiles aimed at the seraph, who could do nothing but block the attacks. Stone crumbled away around the throne, and the wall behind Mordrin opened up completely, revealing more of the open sky outside. The light of the setting sun entered the room and cast it in an orange glow.

Tyr gave his opponent no quarter and pressed the attack. The image of Vandar lying lifeless on the ground filled his mind's eye, and the boy rushed forward with blinding fury. He was angry. He was crushed by Vandar's defeat, and he wanted nothing but to see Mordrin dead.

Mordrin's fan of blades shattered just as Tyr approached him. The seraph was pinned down, with only one way out. He kicked off through the broken wall and leapt into the air; Tyr followed in pursuit. He jumped through the air and was right on him. Before the seraph could do anything, Tyr stabbed him just below the collar. The Blackwing screamed in pain as the two hurtled down to the ground.

They were falling now. Tyr's eyes darted for a moment behind the seraph, spotting a balcony that jutted out beneath them. He approximated the distance and closed his eyes as he prepared for the landing. He did not let go of the blade, twisting it into Mordrin's flesh, maintaining his death-hold. He would end this now. He heard the bloodied seraph flapping his wings to no avail; they were falling too quickly. The next moment, the two slammed against the stone of the landing. Tyr heard the seraph's bones snap from the impact.

The boy opened his eyes as he pulled his blade out of the seraph. To his surprise, Mordrin was somehow still alive; the fall had not finished him. With a sweeping motion, he lifted Tyr as though he were a toy and threw him against the opposite wall.

The boy hit the wall hard enough to shake him out of his rage, pain shooting through every corner of his body. The collision against the wall had crumpled his entire body. He knelt on the ground; his vision became blurry. Though Tyr had done heavy damage to his opponent, it was not enough to subdue him.

He looked up to see Mordrin, now completely covered in his own blood, his spiky hair matted with it. The red streaks covering his black hair and skin gave him an even more horrifying appearance.

"Idiot boy, fighting for a cause you don't even understand."

Tyr gave no response, too winded from his recent hit to give a proper reply. He was dizzy, and he saw double. He blinked several times to gather himself, recognizing the silhouette of the bloodied seraph as he summoned another hail of magical arms.

The boy stood slowly and raised his sword at the seraph.

"Tyr, he's too strong. You can't-"

But Vandar...!

As the boy prepared to invoke the blade once more, he saw Mordrin peer at the sky above Holy Bastion. He dematerialized his phantasmal blades. Tyr followed his eyes and took in the image; thousands of black dots littering the heavens, all gravitating toward the floating city above the castle.

Are they...?

Mordrin had not paid any heed during the fight, but he saw it now. The seraphs who'd been on the offensive were retreating back to Skyfall, toward the great statue of Sithe, right where the High Priestess would be.

Mordrin looked back at the boy. He had put up a good fight but finishing him now would take too long—especially with that magical blade. His duty to Skyfall and the High Priestess were more important than this boy.

Why are they returning to Skyfall? Something was wrong.

"Are they retreating?" Lumina asked.

Tyr locked eyes with Mordrin once more. Before the boy could make another move, the seraph was in the air, blood dripping down to the stone of the balcony.

The Blackwing snarled at the boy with a cold glare. "This isn't over."

Tyr flicked his blade at the blackwing in response.

The next moment, Mordrin had taken off, a blur of black and red, rushing back to the floating city.

AWAKENING

SEPTIMIAN DYNASTY, YEAR 242
KINGDOM OF NEMEA, DRAGON'S PEAK

I have walked its dusty plains and climbed its highest peaks. Taerestris knows me.

KAI

The entrance now lay open. A cool wind danced across her cheek. Behind her, she could feel the returning presence of her spiritual companion. Numator. Specter. She didn't look back.

"Time has passed. What happened?"

"I met a strange creature."

She tried to keep her mind blank. The mood between them had subtly changed.

"We can talk about that later. Shall we?"

"Yes," Specter said. "Our prize is within reach."

Kai looked ahead at the pair of blades fixed to the pedestal. They glimmered in the light, still sending out their pulses of blue and orange toward the sky.

I'm ready.

With a step, she crossed the threshold of the metal doors and neared the pedestal. The blades were now within arm's reach. She squinted as the light of the blades enveloped her. The weapons were fixed to the metal. She reached out with both arms, taking hold of the grips.

Once again, the mountain quaked beneath her. She paid no attention to it as she delicately pulled the blades free of their fixture. The thunderous roar of the energy emanating from the blades was deafening. Kai effortlessly released the blades from the pedestal, freeing them completely.

She could no longer see the mountain, nor Specter. Around her, the colours of blue and orange mixed with each other. The torrent of energy felt like standing in a rushing stream. She was surrounded by the swirling power. Kai looked ahead, staring deeply into the colours. The colours took shape, powerful images coming into focus.

The blades first showed her a familiar face: Specter, Numator. He was not merely a king of Nemea, but the *first* king. She saw his rise to power, a bloody trail that ended with him on a throne of silver.

The colours shifted. She saw the war of Taerestris; one fought between the humans, dragons, and seraphs. The War of Three. At the centre of it all was the white-haired King Numator, sewing chaos, and the seeds of strife that would further fuel his war campaign.

Next, the blades showed the king surrounded by his lieutenants as they imprisoned a dragon. Stealing its fire, the king used it to create his own powerful magic. With this magic, the king laid waste to the dragons.

Swirling in and out of existence, the blades relentlessly showed their secrets—memories from King Numator himself. Kai witnessed the rise and fall of ancient Nemea, the lust for power of its first king, and finally, the magic he cast to divide the three factions from each other. Kai's eyes burned with the truth; her mind inexorably seared with forgotten knowledge.

With one last pulse, the energy surrounding her dissipated.

Kai dropped to her knees, a cold sweat running down her forehead. She caught her breath. The blades were still in her hands.

"Kai," said the voice of Specter behind her. "Thank you." Though his voice was familiar, it was somehow different. Palpable.

She stood and turned to face him. He was a spectre no more. In his place was the physical form of the spirit that had accompanied her on her trip out of Kai-Ji and up the mountain. This was the old man she had met in her vision so many years ago. The long-haired King Numator stood just several steps away from her.

He smiled at her as he spoke. "It appears the rest of my essence was sealed within the blades. I finally feel myself again." The king brought out a hand and closed it into a fist as he inspected his newfound form.

Kai's hands shook. This was the moment of truth. "Specter," she said. "Do you remember your name now?"

The king tilted his head. "I remember much now... but it seems my name is still lost to me."

Kai's anger rose. Her legs trembled. *You... it was always you.*

The king spoke once more. "Worry not, my child. We will recover the rest of my memories, you and I." The king smiled and brought a hand to her.

This isn't right. You're lying. Your name is... "Numator!"

Kai brandished the blue blade and invoked the king's own power for the first time. A wave of energy traced out from the tip of the sword. The invisible wave of magic encapsulated Kai. It then encompassed the ruined cathedral. Then the mountain. As it grew in size, the objects caught within froze in place, save for the blade's wielder. First the plants, then the wind. The faint rumblings of the mountain halted. Even King Numator himself was frozen in time. This was his power—and Kai's opportunity.

She rushed at the king; her mind filled with killer intent. Her job was made easy with the magic of the frozen time. She took the orange blade and pierced the king's chest just as the enchantment wore off. The two were on the ground now, blood spilling from the king's new body.

"What are you doing!"

"It was you!" Kai shouted. "You caused the war with the dragons!"

It had taken her some time to figure it out, but the memories the blades showed her had made it fully clear—this was all the fault of the one before her. She pushed the blade in.

"You gave humans destructive magic!" She twisted it. "You imprisoned your own people within these weapons! You created the mountain and trapped everyone here! You cursed the seraphs so they could never use magic!"

With every accusation, she pushed the sword deeper into Numator's chest. Lines of energy pulsed once more from Kai's blade, draining the life force of the one who had created it—King Numator himself.

"Foolish girl! This was all for the protection of our kind! Of our species! It's all ruined if you strike me down!"

"You lied to me!" Kai shouted, pushing harder on the blade. "This was all your doing!"

Kai's eyes burned with tears. Once more she was killing, though she saw no other way forward. Numator had lied to her. She had seen everything the man was capable of, travelling across time, playing with the souls of his subjects. He had caused the first war and engendered the desire for vengeance that the dragons and seraphs no doubt felt. It was he who had stolen the magic of dragons and spellbound the mountain; it was Numator himself that had trapped the souls of Veris and the others. She had seen enough.

Kai pushed the blade as deeply as she could into King Numator's chest, the sword drinking in its creator's energy.

Numator placed a hand on the blade. His body shook. His eyes turned red as he spoke softly. Tears gathered. "Kai, no. Not here, not now. We can't leave the future of the world to destiny."

The woman's voice trembled. "You're wrong. The world isn't your plaything. If you don't understand that, you don't deserve another second."

With a scream, Kai pressed down once more on the handle, running the king through.

He gave his last words. "You have made… a grave mistake. Not only for yourself, but for the world." The king's eyes closed at last, the orange blade completing its deadly task.

The deed was done. The king was dead.

Kai let go of the weapon as she looked upon the dead king. It was unmoving. "Specter?" she asked, her voice quivering.

No response.

She breathed heavily; her body felt weak.

With great effort, she stood and looked at her surroundings—no Archon, no Numator, no voice in her mind.

She was alone again.

With a heave, she freed the blade from the dead king's chest and let it clatter to the ground next to its twin. Silently, she moved to the end of the ruined cathedral, where the rock gave way to the clouds that hid the cliffs below.

Wordlessly, she placed her hands on the metal cage on her belt and opened it. She brought out the blue scroll, the object that had fascinated her for years. Delicately, she unfurled the scroll and peered into its centre.

It was blank, as it had always been.

The young woman wiped away her tears. She took the blue scroll and released it, letting it drop into the clouds below. She looked back at the king behind her, and the blades next to him.

Slowly, she moved back and picked up the swords, fastening them to her belt. She took one more look at the body of her former friend, King Numator. He had betrayed her, but she would make his mission her own now. She remembered the words he had told her when they first met.

A storm is coming, he had said—that, at least, was no lie. After what she had witnessed on her journey, she could be sure of that. Plans had now been set into motion, and their consequences would be dire. The coming conflict would be more than life and death. It would involve the fate of Taerestris itself. Kai steeled her resolve.

"Whatever comes, I'll deal with it. My way."

VANDAR THE RED

SEPTIMIAN DYNASTY, YEAR 242
KINGDOM OF NEMEA, CASTLE ATRIUM

*A great man once told me he had felt a calling.
I think I understand it now.*

TYR, THE SHOOTING STAR

*I*sn't there something we could have done?

"*Tyr...*"

I feel so powerless.

"*We're not gods, Tyr.*"

Then, what are you?

"*We're... like you.*"

Tyr sat on a stone bench in the courtyard of Holy Bastion, twirling his blade as he spoke to Lumina. The spacious room had an impressive opening at the top to allow plants more sunlight. He was alone now, the distant footsteps of the bustling castle staff reaching his ears.

Can you die?

"*I don't know.*"

Why do you hide so much from us? From me?

"*...It's complicated.*"

The boy's conversation was interrupted by a figure coming from the far entrance. Tyr looked up to see the silver-haired King Remus. He donned a red garb and necklace. The old man gingerly stepped forward as his gaunt face met with Tyr's. The king smiled weakly at the boy.

He sighed before he spoke. "It seems that our friend Tandem has already left the city. Something about needing a vacation after everything that happened."

"How is Sir Baou?"

"Hurt, but alive. He did a very dangerous thing, but it was because of him that we didn't lose everything. It took great resolve to do what he did."

King Remus stepped forward and sat next to Tyr. Birds landed near the rafters and chirped their songs, blissfully unaware of the problems of humans.

"The seraphs," Tyr said. "They're gone, right?"

"The last of them retreated along with the blackwing. Losing their leader demoralized them completely. Though it was not a pretty victory. Now we must rebuild."

Tyr didn't respond.

Remus continued. "I curse myself for not coming to the throne room, instead. I should have been there."

Again, Tyr didn't speak. He swallowed back his feelings.

"Tell me, what was he like? Mordrin?"

After a pause, Tyr replied, "He's strong. I think he could beat any of the Kingsguard."

"But not you. You fought him off bravely until help arrived. Almost destroyed the entire throne room while you were at it." Remus gave a half-hearted chuckled. He sighed. "We failed. The seraphs would have been great allies if only their leadership was not so unwilling to negotiate."

"What will they do now, do you think?"

"For now, nothing. Lorithas is investigating the city for any traces of them, but it seems they have truly retreated back to the skies."

"About Sir Vandar—" Tyr started.

Remus raised his hand, his stern features softening at the name. "His body has been prepared. We will hold a funeral to-morrow. I trust you will join me? I don't want to be too forward, but I think he would have wanted you at his side with me."

Tyr swallowed his emotions. The scene had replayed over and over in his mind since it had happened. The drops of blood on the marble floor. The glaive that had impaled his mentor. The rage he had felt afterwards. The cold look on Mordrin's face as he did it. The look of pure vengeance; a vengeance that he now felt within himself.

"*Tyr…*"

"Yes, I'd like to be there for it. Sir, what will happen to his shield?"

"In Holy Bastion, there is an area known as the Vault of Kings. It is where we keep the royal arms of past nobility, among other treasures. It will be interred there, in his tomb. I doubt the spirit in the shield would attune with anyone but Vandar anyway."

King Remus stood. "There is one other thing you should know," he said.

Tyr looked up at Remus.

"Vandar spoke highly about you. He had faith in you and believed that you had much potential. It's because of him that we decided to let you keep your weapon. I personally did not believe in this potential until I saw you in action in the north. Because of that, it is only right that you know."

"That I know?"

"Yes. About the truth. It was many decades ago, when I was a younger man. As you may know, I had a queen once, Remilia. She was beautiful, intelligent, and caring. The most amazing woman I've ever met. She was wonderful. And one of her wishes was to have a real family, with a son and a daughter. Nemean law prevents the king from having children, but..."

"But?"

"Do you know Vandar's full name?"

"Vandar Julius, right?"

"That's his official name. But Vandar's actual name is Vandar Julius Septimius. He is my son by blood."

"He was your real son? The rumours were true?"

Remus nodded. "Yes. Does it surprise you?"

"I... I suppose not." The likeness between the two was near perfect, after all. "Does anyone else know?"

"Just myself, Cecilia, and now you."

The two sat in silence for what seemed like aeons as Tyr attempted to think of something to say. He settled on a basic question. "But why tell me? Why risk anyone letting your secret out?"

"You've shown yourself to be a trustworthy character. I know Vandar would have wanted you to know. And also, I don't have much left to lose. My wife is gone now. My son, as well. Only my daughter Cecilia remains."

"Your Highness?"

"Yes?"

"What about Cecilia, then? She's an orphan from the Eastern Realms, right?"

"Yes. By the time my wife died, I could not fulfil her wish to have a daughter. Adopting a daughter is rather rare for a Nemean king, but it was the right decision."

"I see," Tyr said, looking down to try to avoid the king's gaze. "I'm sorry to hear that."

"Bah. It's all old news now. I shouldn't get like this in the first place. I'm just glad I have someone to tell."

It was then that the king stood and cleared his throat, changing subjects. "So then, Tyr. This next question is quite important."

The boy looked at King Remus, the sadness gone from his face now, replaced by that regal focus that could only belong to a true ruler.

"After the funeral, my knights will return to service. But, with Vandar's passing, there is one seat at the table that will be empty. The seraphs will most certainly return. The Eastern Realms will want to strike Nemea while it is weak. And after what we have seen in the north, the stakes are even higher. We need all the help we can get."

Tyr gripped his blade tightly. He knew it would be a little longer before he would see his mother again.

"Will you join us at my table?"

EPILOGUE

SEPTIMIAN DYNASTY, YEAR 243
OUTLANDS, NORTHERN FRONT

The skies above the jagged mountain peaks raged violently, carrying murderous intent. Snow fell in an erratic
fashion. The environment was tinted with the ice-cold
blue of eternal twilight, the paragon of a desolate wasteland. The
scene was sparsely populated with shrubbery, plant life that ar-
dently defied nature's design.

All was still in the land of everlasting snow. Then, a disturbance sounded somewhere far off. The ground shook with the
movement of some titanic object in the distance.

The shaking continued, growing in magnitude and frequency,
as the silent vista was broken, a serpentine beast disrupting the

wind and snow. The beast flew on wings of black steel, its gargantuan body clearing the side of a nearby mountain, imposing its stature upon the peak of a singular mountaintop. The peak was irregular, and the serpentine creature climbed with all four of its clawed legs into the centre, through an entrance hidden within.

With a roar, the tailed beast dropped into the mountain, descending into the dark depths below. The creature's flight was perilous, dodging outcroppings of ancient rock and stone, navigating the cavernous deeps of the mountain. The inner workings of the structure seemed much larger than it appeared on the outside, with various tunnels and paths leading to other, more tenebrous destinations. Lighting was plentiful, with vision provided by the molten magma that flowed along the walls.

Before long, the beast had arrived at its goal, a slab of ground shaped to serve as a makeshift floor in the heart of the mountain. The winged creature landed on the ground as it lowered its powerful legs and waited on all fours. With the beast having completed its journey, the caverns were now silent, the only audible sound being the nearby magma flows and the breathing of the hulking creature.

Moments went by before, finally, the room shook with the roar of a second winged creature.

The metallic beast looked toward a small alcove to the opposite end of the room, as a red-scaled creature entered, making its way to the black-scaled one. It landed quickly, taking a few quaking steps before halting. The two gazed at each other before the black one spoke, its mouth unmoving.

"Lyth," he said, addressing the red creature, "where have you been?"

"South. Something has happened to Mynax."

"Mynax? One of the younglings?"

"That's correct. The binding placed on him…"

"What of it?"

"It seems," Lyth said, "The human has called upon him once more."

"What could they want?"

"It is a mystery. Another thing: "While I was south, I saw something in the skies. A flash of colours."

"Farallon, you felt it, too, did you not? The old king. After all these years. His presence is missing."

The black dragon brought his head up and down. "Yes. A chill that I have not felt in millennia. Something has changed."

Lyth shook his head. "It must be the humans."

"We have waited far too long for this, Lyth. We must act now, before those humans learn about what they've done."

"It's still far too strong. As of yet, we cannot traverse the fog."

Farallon flared his nostrils, specks of flame erupting from them. "To think that humans are once again misusing their stolen power. Do the others know?"

"I am not sure. Perhaps we should pay them a visit."

"Yes. There is not much time left before we are free, brother. We will need the assistance of the other tribes."

"They will not agree to help easily. They have become dazed. Calmed to a stupor within this oversized prison. They do not have the motivation that we do, Farallon."

"We are their elders, and they will listen," said the black dragon. "We will rid ourselves of the chains that bind us, one way or another."

"The humans," Lyth said, "they pose a threat, along with the seraphs. They still have the old king's magic."

"With his death, that magic will soon fade." The black dragon spread his wings and roared as he prepared to take off once more.

"Come, Lyth. Our work begins."

www.ingramcontent.com/pod-product-compliance
Lightning Source LLC
Chambersburg PA
CBHW030901060726
47591CB00005B/1371